The
GUIDE to BOOK
PUBLISHERS
1999

*The complete guide to book
publishers in the UK & Ireland*

- 2nd Edition -

© Writers' Bookshop 1999
ISBN 0 9529119 9 X

First published by Writers' Bookshop
Remus House, Coltsfoot Drive,
Woodston, Peterborough PE2 9JX

Edited by Anne Sandys

From the publisher

This is the second edition of this guide to book publishers in the UK and Ireland. The information it contains has been supplied by the publishers and editors themselves, and is current at time of going to press.

We hope to continually improve the book's usefulness to writers and other users, and welcome any comments or suggestions for future editions.

A note from the editor

If you are a writer, this guide is intended to help you target your submissions of work more effectively and increase your chances of getting published.

Writers do need all the help they can get, but it's not entirely a one-way street: compiling this guide, I spoke to publishers who were actively seeking new material, and who welcomed the opportunity to reach writers who might supply it. This is especially true in the non-fiction area, and in more technical fields; I spoke to one editor of a series on financial markets who, the moment he heard I worked on non-fiction titles, blurted out 'How do you find your writers? I'm desperate!'

So, while I wouldn't argue against the conventional wisdom - the writing market *is* fiercely competitive, after all - there are always exceptions to every rule. It is possible to get published while everyone around you is not, and the information in this guide will help you begin to track down your best chances of doing so.

The publishers listed range from small presses to large publishing houses with overseas affiliates and many imprints. Most entries include information on the types of book published - subject areas, readership, etc - the editors responsible, and in some cases, an indication of how to approach them.

Often the entry will indicate the editor's interest - or lack of interest - in unsolicited manuscripts. Do note that this usually means your whole complete manuscript, and, if sending this is discouraged, it does not rule out your sending a brief outline or synopsis with a covering letter.

If you read the entries carefully and adjust your approach accordingly, you will be making the most of what I hope is a useful writer's tool.

Good luck.

Anne Sandys (Editor)

AA Publishing

World travel guides, guides to Britain, walking and cycling guides, road maps of Britain and Europe, road atlases of Britain and Europe, accommodation and tourist guides to Britain and Europe, general travel-related illustrated books.

Editor(s): Michael Buttler, Connie Austen Smith
Address: Fanum House, Basingstoke, Hampshire RG21 4EA
Imprints: AA Publishers
Parent Company: The Automobile Association
Payment Details: Generally, fees are negotiated, rather than royalties.
Unsolicited Manuscripts: No

AAVO

Specialises in books about television. On Camera and Directing On Camera are classic how-to handbooks about tv production and direction, both written by Harris Watts, a former Senior Instructor at the BBC's production training school. In 1999 AAVO will also publish the new edition of The PA's Survival Guide by Cathie Fraser (formerly a BBC training book); and Better Than Working by Richard Hakin, an amusing and often touching account of life in a camera crew.

Editor(s): Harris Watts
Address: 8 Edis Street, London NW1 8LG
Telephone: 0171 722 9243
Fax: As phone
Email: tottatv@aol.com
Unsolicited Manuscripts: Yes, if about television

Abbotsford Publishing

Publishers of quality titles on poetry, children's books and local history. Member of the Independent Publishers' Guild.

Editor(s): K Simmons, H Clayton
Address: 2a Brownsfield Road, Lichfield, Staffs WS13 6BT
Telephone: 01543 255749

ABC-Clio Ltd

ABC-Clio Ltd publishes bibliographies on the countries of the world (The World Bibliographical Series) as well as general A-Z style reference works on high-interest topics including: world history, American history, rural & urban studies, sports, politics & society, biography, science & technology, folklore, Native Americans, literature, mythology & religion, multi-cultural studies, women's studies, legal issues, contemporary world issues & ethics.

Editor(s): Robert G Neville
Address: 35A Great Clarendon Street, Oxford OX2 6AT
Telephone: 01865 311350
Fax: 01865 311358
Email: bneville@abc-clio.lid.uk
Imprints: World Bibliographical Series, ABC-Clio Companions
Parent Company: ABC-Clio Inc, Santa Barbara, Caifornia USA
Payment Details: By negotiation
Unsolicited Manuscripts: Yes

Absolute Press

Cookery, food and wine; Outlines - series of profiles on gay and lesbian creative artists; gift books; limited travel; Streetwise maps - laminated maps of major cities in Europe and North America.

Editor(s): Jon Croft, Bronwen Douglas, Mathew Inwood
Address: Scarborough House, 29 James Street West, Bath BA1 2BT
Fax: 01225 445836
Email: sales@absolutepress.demon.co.uk
Unsolicited Manuscripts: Yes - with reply paid envelopes

Abson Books London

Language glossaries, gay issues, gardening.
Editor(s): Michael Ellison, Sharon Wright
Address: 5 Sidney Square, London E1 2EY
Telephone: 0171 790 4737
Fax: 0171 790 7346
Email: absonbooks@aol.com
Unsolicited Manuscripts: Yes

Acair Ltd

Scottish Highlands & Islands, modern & historical, Gaelic & English, children's Gaelic, educational, music, poetry & song, learners of Gaelic.

Editor(s): Norma MacLeod
Address: 7 James Street, Stornoway, Isle of Lewis HS1 2QN
Telephone: 01851 703020
Fax: 01851 703294
Email: acair@sol.co.uk
Website: www.hebrides.com/acair
Imprints: Acair
Payment Details: Payment by arrangement if published.
Unsolicited Manuscripts: Yes

Accountancy Books

Accountancy Books is the publishing arm of the Institute of Chartered Accountants in England and Wales. Providing support for the professionals in both practice and industry, we publish over 300 key titles covering the breadth of accounting, tax, auditing, company law, financial mangement and IT.

Address: 40 Bernard Street, London WC1N 1LD
Telephone: 0171 920 8991
Fax: 0171 920 8992
Email: abgbooks@icaew.co.uk
Website: www.icaew.co.uk
Imprints: Accountancy Books, Bottom Line Business Guides
Parent Company: ICAEW

Addison Wesley Longman Limited

Academic & scholarly, agricultural, archaeology, architecture & design, atlases & maps, audio books, biography & autobiography, biology & zoology, chemistry, children's books, cinema, video, tv & radio, computer science, economics, educational & textbooks, electronic, engineering, English as a foreign language, English language teaching, environment & development, gender studies, geography & geology, history & antiquarian, industry, business & management, language & linguistics, law, literature & criticism, mathematics & statistics, military & war, natural history, nautical, philosophy, photography, poetry, politics & world affairs, psychology & psychiatry, religion & theology, sociology & anthropology, veterinary science and vocational training.

Address: Edinburgh Gate, Harlow, Essex CM20 2JE
Imprints: Longman, Addison-Wesley, Scott Foresman
Parent Company: Pearson Plc
Unsolicited Manuscripts: Yes

African Books Collective Ltd

Founded in 1989, ABC is a major self-help initiative by a group of African publishers to promote their books in Europe, North America and Commonwealth countries outside Africa. It is collectively owned by its founder-member publishers. ABC is a donor organisation supported and non-profitmaking on its own behalf, and because of this, is in a position to offer its members more favourable terms than are normally available under conventional commercial distribution agreements. Titles in English and children's in Swahili are stocked. Membership has grown to 42 publishers in 12 African countries. Over 1500 titles are now stocked in ABC's UK warehouse.

Address: The Jam Factory, 27 Park End Street, Oxford OX1 1HU
Telephone: 01865 726686
Fax: 01865 793298
Email: abc@dial.pipex.com
Website: www.africanbookscollective.com
Unsolicited Manuscripts: No

Age Concern Books

Publish a range of practical handbooks aimed at the mass public, health and social care professionals, voluntary and professional organisations plus business organisations. These books are all concerned with the well-being of older people and their carers, with the exception of several titles concerned with mid-life planning. We would like to stress that the majority of our titles are specially commissioned, and that we do not publish fiction, life-stories or collections of poetry.

Editor(s): Richard Holloway
Address: Age Concern England, Astral House, 1268 London Road, London SW16 4ER
Telephone: 0181 765 7200
Fax: 0181 765 7211
Website: www.ace.org.uk
Parent Company: Age Concern England (registered charity)
Payment Details: Advances & royalties usually paid to authors
Unsolicited Manuscripts: Very rarely accepted

Air Research Publications

Publishers of specialist (non-fiction) aviation books. Especially World War 2 and military aviation history.

Editor(s): Simon Parry
Address: PO Box 223, Walton-on-Thames, Surrey KT12 3YQ
Telephone: 01932 243165
Fax: As phone
Email: air_research@morl.bogo.co.uk
Website: www.bogo.co.uk/air_research/webcat.htm
Payment Details: Royalty on sales
Unsolicited Manuscripts: Yes, and returned

Airlife Publishing Ltd

Three non-fiction imprints. Airlife: military aviation; civil aviation; military & naval history; military & naval biography; books for pilots. Waterline: practical books for cruising & racing yachtsmen; boatbuilding. Swan Hill Press: natural history; fishing; dog training; country sports; equestrian; walking & climbing; diving; art & decorative arts.

Editor(s): Peter Coles
Address: 101 Longden Road, Shrewsbury SY3 9EB
Telephone: 01743 235651
Fax: 01743 232944
Email: airlife@airlifebooks.com
Imprints: Airlife, Waterline, Swan Hill Press
Payment Details: Royalty
Unsolicited Manuscripts: Yes

Albrighton Publications

Two publications on education of minority groups in Britain: Language, Race And Education (1988); Equality And Education (1988).

Editor(s): Author for these publications: Gurbachan Singh
Address: 53 The Hollow, Littleover, Derby DE23 6GH
Telephone: 01332 764064

Ian Allen Publishing Ltd

Transport, aviation, military, sport and leisure. No fiction, poetry, children's titles, books of memories, biographies or autobiographies.

Editor(s): Peter Waller
Address: Riverdene Business Park, Molesey Road, Hersham, Surrey KT12 4RG
Telephone: 01932 266600
Fax: 01932 266601
Imprints: Ian Allan Ltd, Dial House, OPC
Parent Company: Ian Allan Group Ltd
Payment Details: Subject to contract terms agreed
Unsolicited Manuscripts: No

J A Allen & Co Ltd

Equine and equestrian publishers - non-fiction titles on any area of horse-related subjects. Prefer authoritative works by established experts in their fields. Broad academic base, also publishing some commercial titles and have a junior list which does not include fiction.

Address: Saddlewood, 51 Fourth Avenue, Frinton on Sea, Essex CO13 9DY
Telephone: 01255 679388
Fax: 01255 670848
Payment Details: Royalties paid twice-yearly
Unsolicited Manuscripts: Yes, all submissions are read with interest

Allison & Busby

Publishes biography and general non-fiction, literary fiction, crime fiction, translations and a series of writers' guides.

Editor(s): Roderick Dymott, David Shelley
Address: 114 New Cavendish Street
Telephone: 0171 636 2942
Fax: 0171 323 2023
Email: dshelley@allisonbusby.co.uk
Website: www.allisonandbusby.co.uk
Imprints: A new non-fiction imprint to be launched 1999
Parent Company: Editorial Prensa Iberica, SA, Barcelona

Alun Books/Goldleaf Publishing

Small press, limited resources, specialising in books by Welsh authors / about Welsh subjects - mostly in English.

Editor(s): S Jones
Address: 3 Crown Street, Port Talbot, West Glamorgan SA13 1BG
Telephone: 01639 886186
Imprints: Alun Books (literature: poetry & fiction), Goldleaf (local history), Barn Owl Books (children's)
Parent Company: Alun Books (founded 1977)
Payment Details: 10% royalty
Unsolicited Manuscripts: No

Amber Lane Press

Original modern play scripts - only plays that have been staged professionally will be considered; books on theatre and modern drama.

Editor(s): Judith Scott
Address: Church Street, Charlbury, Oxon OX7 3PR
Telephone: 01608 810024
Fax: As phone
Payment Details: Formal author's contract with advance and percentage royalty
Unsolicited Manuscripts: No

Amberwood Publishing Ltd

Introducing - Amberwood Publishing, founded in 1991 with the object of publishing affordable books on natural health care. All our titles are commissioned from authors who are chosen for their expertise. Each book is presented in a format suitable for the general public and students alike. All of us at Amberwood care about the information we publish. Our aim is to market factual scientifically-based literature for the benefit of the growing number of people wanting to use natural medicine.

Editor(s): Victor Perfitt
Address: Braboeuf House, 64 Portsmouth Road, Guildford, Surrey GU2 5DU
Telephone: 01483 570821
Fax: 01483 457101
Unsolicited Manuscripts: To Mrs June Crisp

AMCD (Publishers) Ltd

Key areas are China, the power sector, financial dictionaries, business books, local history (Croydon and Cheshire) and electronic books. We would like to develop our history titles: ideas for histories of the British Isles and European countries are of interest.

Editor(s): S J MacNally
Address: PO Box 182, Altrincham, Cheshire WA15 9UA
Telephone: 0161 434 5105
Fax: As phone
Email: 100625.3570@compuserve.com
Imprints: AMCD, Jensen
Parent Company: AMCD
Payment Details: Royalties twice-yearly
Unsolicited Manuscripts: One short chapter only

Amnesty International Publications

Amnesty International is a worldwide voluntary human rights movement that campaigns for the release of prisoners of conscience, fair trials for political prisoners and an end to torture, 'disappearances', political killings and the death penalty. Amnesty International works impartially to promote all human rights enshrined in the Universal Declaration of Human Rights and other international standards. The organisation publishes books relating to this work, and produces short specialist reports on human rights abuse issues, which are available on the World Wide Web.

Address: 99-119 Rosebery Avenue, London EC1R 4RE
Email: info@amnesty.org.uk
Website: www.amnesty.org.uk
Parent Company: Amnesty International UK
Unsolicited Manuscripts: To Publications Dept

Amolibros

Amolibros manages a number of imprints which are usually distributed by Gazelle Book Services. It specialises in assisting small or private publishers to produce and market their books. Popular titles managed include Outrageous Fortune by Terence Risby (author of There's A Girl In My Soup) and Thoth, published by Edru Books.

Editor(s): Jane Tatam
Address: 5 Saxon Close Watchet Somerset TA23 0BN
Telephone: 01984 633713
Fax: As phone
Email: amolibros@aol.com
Unsolicited Manuscripts: No

Anchor Books

Poetry books (themed and general); quarterly newsletter Anchors Aweigh.

Editor(s): Heather Killingray
Address: Remus House, Coltsfoot Drive, Woodston, Peterborough PE2 9JX
Parent Company: Forward Press Limited
Payment Details: On newsletter, £2.00 per letter, £10.00 per article, £5.00 per booklet review, Worm's Eye View £5.00
Unsolicited Manuscripts: Yes - for newsletter: articles, reviews, literary festival reports - call for info. For anthologies: poems up to 30 lines any subject, any form.

Andersen Press Ltd

Founded in 1976 by Klaus Flugge, Andersen Press publishes quality picture books and fiction for children. Main authors and artists on the list are David McKee, Tony Ross, Michael Foreman, Ruth & Ken Brown, Susan Varley, Colin McNaughton and Melvin Burgess. Specialises in selling foreign co-editions. Bestselling titles: Badger's Parting Gifts (Susan Varley), Elmer (David McKee), Junk (Melvin Burgess).

Editor(s): Editorial Director: Janice Thomson; Editor: Audrey Adams (Fiction)
Address: 20 Vauxhall Bridge Road, London SW1V 2SA
Telephone: 0171 840 8702 (A Adams 8700) (J Thomson 8706)
Fax: 0171 233 6263
Imprints: Tigers, Andersen Young Readers' Library, Andersen Press Paperback Picture Books
Payment Details: Royalties twice-yearly
Unsolicited Manuscripts: With SAE; 3 sample chapters and synopsis for novels

Anglia Publishing

Specialist in metal detecting and amateur archaeology. Most titles which Anglia has published relate to the identification of small metallic finds. The scope is large because metal detecting turns up a very wide variety of material: Bronze Age axes to Butlin's holiday camp enamel badges! The buyers of Anglia's titles also come from a wide spectrum, not just metal detectorists and amateur archaeologists but also museum staff, professional archaeologists and, of course, collectors. The possibilities to add to Anglia's growing lists are large indeed. New titles are eagerly sought: books and booklets, which can be as short as 10,000 words. Would someone like to write little books about pipe tampers through the ages, shotgun cartridges and bullets? Get the idea?

Editor(s): Derek Rowland
Address: The Old Mill, Lower Raydon, Ipswich IP7 5QR
Telephone: 01473 823553
Fax: As phone
Email: anglia@anglianet.co.uk
Website: www.anglia.anglianet.co.uk
Imprints: Anglia Publishing, Anglia Shoe-Box Library
Payment Details: Royalty negotiable, payable quarterly
Unsolicited Manuscripts: No - a synopsis first or a telephone call

Anglia Young Books

Cross-curricular stories for primary schools, specialising in historical fiction with support material for the literacy hour.

Editor(s): Rosemary Hayes
Address: Durhams Farmhouse, Butcher's Hill, Ickleton, Saffron Walden CB10 1SR
Telephone: 01799 531192
Fax: As phone
Email: r.hayes@btinternet.com
Imprints: Anglia Young Books
Unsolicited Manuscripts: No

Angling Publications Ltd

Books and magazines on the subject of carp fishing. Author of majority of publications is Tim Paisley.

Editor(s): Tim Paisley
Address: 272 London Road, Sheffield S2 4NA
Telephone: 0114 2580812
Fax: 0114 2582728
Website: www.completeangler.co.uk/angrb.hem

Anness Publishing

Crafts, cookery, gardening, DIY, health, hobbies, New Age, sports, stationery, children's.

Editor(s): Joanna Lorenz
Address: Hermes House, 88-89 Blackfriars Road, London SE1 8HA
Imprints: Lorenz, Hermes House, Old Forge
Unsolicited Manuscripts: No

Antique Collectors' Club

Publishers of books on art, antiques, gardening and children's classics. We also publish a magazine - ten issues a year of articles on art, antiques and collectables.

Editor(s): Brian Cotton
Address: 5 Church Street, Woodbridge, Suffolk IP12 1DS
Telephone: 01394 385501
Fax: 01394 384434
Email: accbc@aol.com
Imprints: Garden Art Press, ACC Children's Classics
Payment Details: Negotiable
Unsolicited Manuscripts: No

Anvil Press Poetry Ltd

Poetry, poetry in translation.

Editor(s): Peter Jay
Address: Neptune House, 70 Royal Hill, London SE10 8RF
Payment Details: To be negotiated if work accepted
Unsolicited Manuscripts: Yes must include SAE

Apple Press

Apple Press publish a range of non-fiction, illustrated books and children's interactive books. The principal subject areas are food and drink, art and craft, antiques and collecting and children's non-fiction. Series include the Companion series, the Apple Identifier series and the best-selling Fridge Fun(TM) range.

Address: The Fitzpatrick Building, 188-194 York Way, London N7 9QR
Telephone: 0171 700 2929
Fax: 0171 609 6695
Imprints: Apple Kids
Parent Company: Quarto Plc
Payment Details: Negotiable upon acceptance
Unsolicited Manuscripts: Yes - send to sister company Quintet Publishing at same address

Appletree Press

Appletree publishes a range of non-fiction gift books, covering subjects such as food and drink, poetry, sports histories, the history and customs of various countries. Series include the Little Cookbooks, the Little Scottish Bookshelf and the Little Irish Bookshelf.

Editor(s): Rob Blackwell, Catherine McIlvenna
Address: 19-21 Alfred Street, Belfast BT2 8DL
Telephone: 01232 243074
Fax: 01232 246756
Email: reception@appletree.ie
Website: www.appletree.ie
Unsolicited Manuscripts: Yes

Arc Publications

Arc Publications is not only committed to publishing works by new British writers, but actively seeks to promote work by internationally significant poets higherto neglected in the UK, whether in their original English or in translation. Poets submitting work should be familiar with the type of work we publish.

Editor(s): Tony Ward
Address: Nanholme Mill, Shaw Wood Road, Todmorden, Lancashire OL14 6DA
Imprints: Arc Publications
Unsolicited Manuscripts: Send representative selection, no reply without SAE

Arcadia Books Ltd

Newly-established independent publishing house whose writers include Shere Hite, John Berger, Tariq Ali, Robert Dessaix, Elisabeth Russell Taylor, Dacia Maraini, Michael De-la-Noy, Kathy Acker, Fiona Pitt-Kethley, A Sivanandan (author of the award-winning novel When Memory Dies) and Richard Zimler, author of the international bestseller The Last Kabbalist Of Lisbon. We publish in the areas of fiction (including translated fiction), biography/autobiography, travel, gay books and women's/gender studies.

Editor(s): Gary Pulsifer
Address: 15-16 Nassau Street, London W1N 7RE
Telephone: 0171 436 9898
Fax: As phone
Unsolicited Manuscripts: Only with SAE and/or return postage for ms

Archive Editions Ltd

Publishing of multi-volume, selected, facsimile documents, particularly on the 18th, 19th, 20th century history of the Middle East, but also increasingly European-oriented.

Editor(s): James Dening, Jessica Brown
Address: 7 Ashley House, The Broadway, Farnham Common, Slough SL2 3PQ
Telephone: 01753 646633
Fax: 01753 646746
Email: ArchiveEdn@aol.com

Aris & Phillips Ltd

Archaeology - Egyptology, classical (Greek & Latin) texts, Hispanic classics (Spanish and Portuguese).

Editor(s): A A Phillips, L M Phillips
Address: Teddington House, Church Street, Warminster, Wilts BA12 8PQ
Telephone: 01985 213409
Fax: 01985 212910
Email: aris.phillips@binternet.com
Website: www.arisandphillips.com
Imprints: Aris & Phillips
Unsolicited Manuscripts: Yes

Arms & Armour

Military history. General history. Air, land and sea warfare.

Editor(s): Barry Holmes
Address: Cassell Plc, Wellington House, 125 Strand, London WC2R 0BB
Imprints: Arms & Armour, Cassell
Parent Company: Cassell Plc
Payment Details: Negotiable
Unsolicited Manuscripts: No. Synopses yes

Art Sales Index Ltd

Established 1968. Results of fine art international auction sales; fine art reference books & CD-ROM. Mail order service.

Editor(s): Duncan Hislop
Address: 1 Thames Street, Weybridge, Surrey KT13 8JG
Telephone: 01932 856426
Fax: 01932 842482
Email: asi@art-sales-index.com
Website: www.art-sales-index.com
Unsolicited Manuscripts: No

Arthritis Research Campaign (ARC)

A national charity which exists to raise funds for research into arthritis and rheumatism. It produces a range of booklets and leaflets on arthritis, as well as publications for medical professionals and students.

Address: ARC Trading Ltd (Supplies), Brunel Drive, Northern Road Industrial Estate, Newark NG24 2DE
Telephone: 01246 558033
Fax: 01246 558007
Website: www.arc.org.uk
Parent Company: ARC, Copeman House, St Mary's Court, St Mary's Gate, Chesterfield S41 7TD

Articles Of Faith Ltd

Specialises in short print runs of religious books for the schools educational market.

Editor(s): C Howard
Address: Resource House, Kay Street, Bury BL9 6BU
Telephone: 0161 763 6232
Fax: 0161 763 5366
Email: edsltd@compuserve.com
Website: www.ed-dev.co.uk
Unsolicited Manuscripts: No

Aspire Publishing

Small specialist publisher of original fiction; sister company Greenzone publishes non-fiction. Both companies established 1997. Aspire aims to create opportunity for new and unknown talent, with a literary standard on a par with that of leading publishing houses; Greenzone's mission is to bring to light the truth surrounding controversial issues of national and international scale. Publications printed and produced entirely in UK as a matter of policy, and sold through diverse outlets, including service stations, grocery stores, supermarkets, as well as traditional bookstores. Trade clients include all major bookshop chains, wholesalers and library suppliers.

Editor(s): Senior Editor: Patricia Hawkes
Address: 8 Betony Rise, Exeter EX2 5RR or 9 Wimpole Street, London W1M 8LB
Telephone: 01392 252516 (Exeter); 0171 723 3773 (London)
Fax: 01392 252517
Email: aspire@centrex.force9.net
Imprints: Aspire Publishing, Greenzone Publishing
Parent Company: Xcentrex Ltd
Payment Details: Standard advance & royalties
Unsolicited Manuscripts: No - write for guidelines & include SAE

ASR Resources

Design, management, psychological and educational - with a cybernetic perspective.

Address: 465 Twickenham Road, Isleworth TW7 7DZ
Telephone: 0181 892 1933
Imprints: Resources Occasional Papers, Scohne Papers
Unsolicited Manuscripts: No

Associated University Presses/Cygnus Arts

Associated University Presses is a US based company specialising in academic and scholarly books on any subject, but mainly literary criticism and history. Will consider PhD theses if they have been converted to book-length (min 70, 000) studies. Editorial board is based in US. Cygnus Arts, an imprint established in 1996, publishes non-academic but serious studies in the humanities, particularly music, dance, cinema and cultural studies. Editorial board is based in UK.

Editor(s): Andrew Lindesay, Tamar Lindesay
Address: 16 Barter Street, London WC1A 2AH
Imprints: Cygnus Arts
Parent Company: Golden Cockerel Press
Unsolicited Manuscripts: Yes

Association For Science Education

A number of periodicals, sent free to our members, covering all phases of science education from ages 5 to 19. Priority is given to our own members' contributions but articles are accepted from anyone involved in school science education in the UK and abroad. Notes for contributors available from above address.

Editor(s): Various
Address: College Lane, Hatfield, Herts AL10 9AA
Unsolicited Manuscripts: Yes

Association For Scottish Literary Studies

The ASLS is an educational charity promoting the languages and literature of Scotland. We publish works of Scottish literature which have either been neglected or which merit a fresh presentation to a modern audience; essays, monographs and journals on the literature and languages of Scotland; and Scotnotes, a series of comprehensive study guides to major Scottish writers. We also produce New Writing Scotland, an annual anthology of contemporary poetry and prose in English, Gaelic and Scots.

Editor(s): Contact Duncan Jones
Address: c/o Department of Scottish History, 9 University Gardens, University of Glasgow, Glasgow G12 8QH
Telephone: 0141 330 5309
Fax: As phone
Email: cmc@arts.gla.ac.uk
Website: http://www.st-andrews.ac.uk/~www.se/personal/cjmm/aslhomepage.html
Imprints: ASLS
Payment Details: Approx £10 per page
Unsolicited Manuscripts: Short stories and poetry for New Writing Scotland

Association Of Teachers Of Mathematics (ATM)

ATM aims to promote ideas and encourage the sharing of teaching and learning strategies in relation to mathematics. Members receive regular jounals: Mathematics Teaching (4 issues a year, concerned with classroom approaches to mathematics teaching) and Micromath (3 issues a year, focuses on integrating ICT into mathematics classroom practice). Journals feature news, discussion and classroom ideas. ATM also publish resources for all ages. Publications include a comprehensive range of books and teaching materials. Recent publications: Questions And Prompts For Mathematics Thinking (£7.95); Teaching, Learning And Mathematics, Challenging Beliefs (£12.50); Transforming (£4.50). Free catalogue on request.

Editor(s): D Ball & B Ball (Mathematics Teaching), Sue & Peter Johston Wilder (Micromath)
Address: 7 Shaftesbury Street, Derby DE23 8YB
Telephone: 01332 346599
Fax: 01332 204357
Email: atm_maths@compuserve.com
Website: http://acorn.educ.nottingham.ac.uk//SchEd/pages/atm/

The Athlone Press

Academic publishers across the social sciences, humanities and the sciences. Anthropology, architecture, art history/theory, Asian studies, biology, business studies, chemistry, classics, climatology, cultural & media studies, education, English & world literature & literary studies, environmental sciences, film studies, history, history of science, law, museum studies, natural history, planning, performance studies, philosophy, physics, psychiatry, psychoanalysis, psychology, sociology, therapy, technology, urban studies.

Editor(s): Brian Southam, Tristan Palmer
Address: 1 Park Drive, London NW11 7SG
Telephone: 0181 458 0888
Fax: 0181 201 8115
Email: athlonepress@btinternet.com
Unsolicited Manuscripts: Yes

Aurelian Information Ltd

Internet books for beginners and office users in business and the charity sector. National charities database: the 7,500 leading national charities (and UK-based international charities) available for rental on electronic disks - floppy and CD-ROM.

Editor(s): Paul Petzold
Address: Aurelian Information Ltd Research Unit, 4a Alexandra Mansions, West End Lane, London NW6 1LU
Telephone: 0171 794 8609 (books) 0171 407 5987 (data)
Fax: As phone (books) 0171 407 6294 (data)
Website: www@dircon.co.uk/aurelian
Imprints: Internet-For-All Books (books), National Charities Database (database information)
Unsolicited Manuscripts: No - proposals only, by letter

Aureus Publishing

Primarily a leisure-driven company, Areus Publishing specialises in sports books, music (all types) and other leisure titles. Aureus is a dynamic company with an international outlook.

Editor(s): Proprietor: Meuryn Hughes
Address: 24 Mafeking Road, Cardiff CF2 5DQ
Telephone: 01222 455200
Fax: As phone
Email: meurynhughes@aureus.co.uk
Website: www.aureus.co.uk
Imprints: Aureus
Unsolicited Manuscripts: Synopis only please, typed. SAE required for reply

Aurum Press

General illustrated non-fiction: film, music, art & design, craft, sport, military history, biography.

Editor(s): Piers Burnett, Sheila Murphy, Anica Alvarez
Address: 25 Bedford Avenue, London WC1B 3AT
Telephone: 0171 637 3225
Fax: 0171 580 2469
Email: aurum@ibm.net
Unsolicited Manuscripts: Yes

Avon Books

Works on the basis of shared responsibility between author and publisher. This involves a payment or subsidy by the author as a contribution towards the cost of publishing his or her work.

Editor(s): Robin Salkia
Address: 1 Dovedale Studios, 465 Battersea Park Road, London SW11 4LR
Telephone: 0171 978 4825
Fax: 0171 924 2979
Email: enquiries@avonbooks
Website: www.avonbooks.co.uk
Payment Details: Negotiable
Unsolicited Manuscripts: Yes

AvonAngliA

Innovative publisher covering not only books, pamphlets and leaflets but postcards, posters and 'talking books' as well. Specialising in guidebooks, local history, business and transport subjects, it also owns Kingsmead Press, which concentrates on art books, Bath history and historical reprints. Small-run reprints and special productions for special opportunities include anniversaries and company histories; the full range of facilities exist including a writing service for those with a subject but no material.

Editor(s): Ian Body, Margaret Leitch
Address: 74 Ryder Street, Pontcanna, Cardiff CF1 9BU
Telephone: 01222 407336
Fax: 01222 407476
Website: www.ibody@aol.com.uk
Imprints: AvonAngliA, Kingsmead Press
Parent Company: AvonAngliA Publications & Services
Unsolicited Manuscripts: Accepted on most subjects - particularly transport, business & commerce, local history

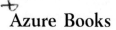

Azure Books

Publishers of books in the broad subject area of human spirituality, such as you might find in the 'mind, body, spirit' section of a bookshop. These books explore what it means to be a spiritual person in the late 20th century, taking in how we relate to ourselves, others and the world around us. Some books on the list explore the subjects of mysticism and the nature of God, and how some world religions, like Christianity, are experienced today.

Editor(s): Alison Barr
Address: 1 Marylebone Road, London NW1 4DU
Telephone: 0171 387 5282
Fax: 0171 388 2352
Email: abarr@spck.org.uk
Imprints: Azure Books
Payment Details: By negotiation
Unsolicited Manuscripts: Please send synopsis and sample chapter

M & M Baldwin

Publishers of books on local history, second world war codebreaking and inland waterway (including The Working Waterways series); also the Historical Canal Maps series.

Editor(s): Mark Baldwin
Address: 24 High Street, Cleobury Mortimer, Kidderminster DY14 8BY
Telephone: 01299 270110
Fax: As phone
Imprints: M & M Baldwin
Payment Details: Annual royalty on sales
Unsolicited Manuscripts: Yes

Ballinakella Press

Small publishing house (circa 25 books to date), we now limit our works to in-series books. Our Country House books are comprehensive architectural and historical records of the houses and families associated with them, of each Irish county. Our People And Places series of Irish family names are small but fairly comprehensive records of major Irish families or clans. We also have biographical records of characterful or historic Irish citizens or people of Irish descent. We occasionally consider books with a family history bent.

Editor(s): Hugh W L Weir, Ana Maria Hajba
Address: Whitegate, Co Clare, Ireland
Telephone: 353061 927030
Fax: As phone
Email: weir@iol.ie
Imprints: Weir's Guides
Payment Details: By arrangement
Unsolicited Manuscripts: Only for Irish topographical & historical books in series

The Banton Press

Makes reprints of esoteric and occult titles from the 4th to 20th century. Subject areas include alchemy, astrology, autobiography, biography, Celts, druids, Egypt, folklore, history, kabbala, tarot, witchcraft, religion, philosophy, symbolism and sex worship. The books are perfect bound facsimile reprints with card covers and the title page as front cover. Also some titles on the Isle of Arran with more to come this year. New titles are added on an irregular basis.

Editor(s): Mark Brown
Address: Dipping Cottage, Kildonan, Isle of Arran KA27 8SB
Telephone: 01770 820231
Fax: As phone
Email: bantonpress@compuserve.com
Website: www.gaelforce.ndirect.co.uk/bantonpress/index.htm
Imprints: Banton
Unsolicited Manuscripts: To Editor

Barefoot Books Ltd

Children's full-colour picture books: traditional myths, legends and fairytales, with a strong cross-cultural focus.

Editor(s): Publisher: Tessa Strickland
Address: PO Box 95, Kingswood, Bristol BS30 5BH
Imprints: Barefoot Beginners, Barefoot Books, Barefoot Collections, Barefoot Poetry Collections
Payment Details: Advance against royalty
Unsolicited Manuscripts: No

Barnworks Publishing

Publishers of interesting lives, local cookery books, interesting subjects and pastimes. Also vanity publishing and advice.

Editor(s): Hazel Kelly, Sue Jackson
Address: Asbury, Roydon Road, Launceston, Cornwall PL15 8DN
Telephone: 01566 777303
Fax: As phone
Imprints: Barnworks Publishing
Payment Details: Usual for payment in 3 parts, unless ms exceptional
Unsolicited Manuscripts: Yes in above subjects

Barny Books

No restrictions. We mainly work with new writers and offer both a readership & advisory service and an editing one. There is a £20 fee for the readership scheme (£10 for less than 40 pages); editing by negotiation. We are a non-profitmaking group set up to help new talent.

Editor(s): Molly Burkett
Address: Hough-On-The-Hill, Grantham NG32 2BB
Payment Details: 50/50 on profits
Unsolicited Manuscripts: Accepted for the readership & advisory service only

Basic Skills Agency

Publish teaching and learning material to help children, young people and adults improve their basic skills, which we define as 'the ability to read, write and speak in English/Welsh and use mathematics at a level necessary to function and progress at work and in society in general.' We are a not-for-profit publisher. Our publications range from readers' packs, advice and material for teachers to some multimedia products. We also work with some commercial publishers. As well as publishing teaching and learning material, we also commission and publish research into the level of need, the cause of basic skills difficulties and the effectiveness of basic skills programmes.

Address: Commonwealth House, 1-19 New Oxford Street, London WC1A 1NU
Telephone: 0171 405 4017
Fax: 0171 440 6626
Email: enquiries@basic-skills.co.uk
Website: www.basic-skills.co.uk

Batsford

Architecture, bridge, chess, crafts, design, English heritage, entertainment, fashion, film, gardening, historic Scotland, aviation, military, history, nautical.

Address: 583 Fulham Road, London SW6 5BY
Telephone: 0171 471 1100
Fax: 0171 471 1101
Email: info@batsford.com
Website: www.batsford.com
Imprints: Brassey's, Conway Maritime Press, Putnam Aeronautical, DPR Publishing
Unsolicited Manuscripts: No

Beaconsfield Publishers Ltd

Medicine, nursing, patient information; homoeopathic medicine.

Editor(s): John Churchill
Address: 20 Chiltern Hills Road, Beaconsfield, Buckinghamshire HP9 1PL
Telephone: 01494 672118
Fax: 01494 672118
Email: books@beaconsfield-publishers.co.uk
Website: www.beaconsfield-publishers.co.uk
Imprints: Beaconsfield
Payment Details: Royalty
Unsolicited Manuscripts: No

Ruth Bean Publishers

Needlecrafts: lace-making, embroidery (practical and historical). Costume and costume history and anthropology related to textiles.

Editor(s): N W & R Bean
Address: Victoria Farmhouse, Carlton, Bedford MK43 7LP
Telephone: 01234 720356
Fax: 01234 720590
Email: ruthbean@mcmail.com
Payment Details: Negotiable
Unsolicited Manuscripts: Yes

B

Belitha Press

Quality children's non-fiction for schools and library market in the UK, plus US and worldwide co-editions. Some books for pre-school children (3+) but most for ages 5-12.

Editor(s): Mary-Jane Wilkins
Address: London House, Great Eastern Wharf, Parkgate Road, London SW11 4NQ
Parent Company: C&B Publishing
Payment Details: Various
Unsolicited Manuscripts: No, but new series proposals welcome

David Bennett Books Ltd

Books for babies, toddler play books, novelty books.

Editor(s): David Bennett
Address: 15 High Street, St Albans, Herts AL3 4ED
Telephone: 01727 855878
Fax: 01727 864085
Parent Company: Collins & Brown
Payment Details: Advance plus royalty or flat fee
Unsolicited Manuscripts: No

The Berean Publishing Trust

Small Christian publishing trust promoting the truth of God's Word Rightly Divided. See Tim 2:15. The publications are the writings of our own authors.

Editor(s): Alan Schofield
Address: The Chapel of the Opened Book, 52a Wilson Street, London EC2A 2ER
Telephone: 0181 446 2762
Email: bptsales@compuserve.com
Website: http://ourworld.compuserve.com/homepages/bptsales/homepage.htm
Parent Company: The Berean Forward Movement
Unsolicited Manuscripts: No

Berghahn Books

Publishers of scholarly books in the humanities and social sciences with an emphasis on European studies and European, especially German-American, relations. Publish approximately 50 books and 10 journals a year, specifically in history, cultural studies, anthropology & sociology, politics & economics, Jewish studies, media & film studies, women's studies and military & war.

Editor(s): Marion Berghahn
Address: 3 Newtec Place, Magdalen Road, Oxford OX4 1RE
Telephone: 01865 250011
Fax: 01865 250056
Email: berghahnuk@aol.com
Website: www.berghahnbooks.com
Payment Details: Royalties paid once a year
Unsolicited Manuscripts: Yes

Berlitz Publishing Co Ltd

Publishers of self-teach language materials, pocket guides, phrase books and language travel products for children.

Address: Fourth Floor, 9-13 Grosvenor Street, London W1X 9FB
Telephone: 0171 518 8300
Fax: 0717 518 8310
Email: roger.kirkpatrick@berlitz.ie
Website: http://www.berlitz.com
Imprints: Berlitz
Parent Company: Berlitz International Inc
Unsolicited Manuscripts: No

Bible Reading Fellowship

The Bible Reading Fellowship (BRF) publishes resources for Bible reading and study, for Lent and Advent, for prayer and reflection, for individual and group use. BRF also publishes resources for children under the age of 11 (Barnabas imprint) and for 11-14-year-olds, encouraging them to a stronger commitment to build foundations to last a lifetime and beyond.

Editor(s): Sue Doggett, Naomi Starkey
Address: Peter's Way, Sandy Lane West, Oxford OX4 5HG
Telephone: 01865 748227
Fax: 01865 773150
Email: enquiries@brf.org.uk
Website: www.brf.org.uk
Imprints: Barnabas
Unsolicited Manuscripts: No

Bibliagora

Subject areas: contract bridge, philosophy and snooker. Publishers and international out-of-print book tracers.

Editor(s): David Rex-Taylor
Address: PO Box 77, Feltham, Middlesex TW14 8JF
Telephone: 0181 898 1234 / hotline: 07000 BIBLIO
Fax: 0181 844 1777
Email: biblio@bibliagora.com
Website: www.bibliagora.com
Payment Details: Negotiated
Unsolicited Manuscripts: No

BILD Publications (British Institute Of Learning Disabilities)

The British Institute of Learning Disabilities (BILD) publishes a range of materials for anyone with an interest in learning disabilites. BILD publications include: textbooks aimed at professionals and students in the field; workshop training materials and independent study materials designed and tested by leading experts and aimed at front-line staff and carers; accessible publications on a wide range of topics designed for independent use by people with learning disabilities or with support from carers or family members.

Address: Wolverhampton Road, Kidderminster DY10 3PP
Telephone: 01562 850251
Fax: 01562 851970
Email: bild@bild.demon.co.uk
Website: www.bild.org.uk
Payment Details: By negotiation
Unsolicited Manuscripts: No

Bios Scientific Publishers Ltd

Life sciences and medicine; particularly molecular biology, biochemistry, genetics, cell biology, plant biology, microscopy and anaesthesia. We publish textbooks, practical handbooks, high-level review volumes and revision guides on all the above subjects.

Editor(s): J Ray, R Offord
Address: 9 Newtec Place, Magdalen Road, Oxford OX4 1RE
Telephone: 01865 726286
Fax: 01865 200386
Email: offord@bios.co.uk
Website: www.bios.co.uk
Payment Details: Royalties and advances (discussed on a book to book basis)
Unsolicited Manuscripts: No

Birlinn Ltd

Gaelic interest, West Highland, Scottish classics, general Scottish and Scottish humour.

Address: Unit 8, Canongate Venture, 5 New Street, Edinburgh EH8 8BH
Telephone: 0131 556 6660
Fax: 0131 558 1500
Email: info@birlinn.co.uk
Website: http://www.birlinn.co.uk
Unsolicited Manuscripts: Yes

A & C Black

Children's and education books (including music) for 3-15 years, ceramics, calligraphy, drama, fishing and practical sport, theatre, travel guides, and books for writers.

Editor(s): Editorial Director: Jill Coleman
Address: 35 Bedford Row, London WC1R 4JH
Telephone: 0171 242 0946
Fax: 0171 831 8478
Email: publicity@acblack.co.uk
Imprints: Adlard Coles Nautical, Herbert Press, Christopher Helm Publishers
Parent Company: A & C Black (Publishers) Ltd
Unsolicited Manuscripts: Preliminary enquiry appreciated

Black Ace Books

We are only interested in completed full-length books. Bright ideas, proposals in synopsis form, work in progress and so on are not of interest. As far as our own list is concerned, some of the categories we definitely do not require include children's, DIY, poetry, religion, short stories. Relatively few of our books are non-fiction. Occasionally, for a really exceptional book, and provided we can devise a suitable budget, we may offer to publish work in such categories as biography, history, philosophy and psychology. Most of our output is high-quality literary fiction. Works likely to excite us would include an oustanding first novel from a new author with a fresh perspective and distinctive voice. Such works are rare. Over a recent weekend we processed approximately 140 submissions, of which only five or six had any hope of being published by any commercial publisher and only two were of potential interest to Black Ace Books.

Address: PO Box 6557, Forfar DD8 2YS
Unsolicited Manuscripts: Write for guidelines with SAE. We do not respond to cold-calls or faxes.

Black Spring Press Ltd

A small, independent publisher specialising in modern literary fiction as well as non-fiction reflecting contemporary culture. Titles include: Nick Cave's King Ink and King Ink II, And The Ass Saw The Angel; Charles Jackson's The Lost Weekend; Kyril Bonfiglioli's The Mortdecai Trilogy.

Editor(s): Directors: Simon Pettifar, Maja Prausnitz
Address: 2nd Floor, 126 Cornwall Road, London SE1 8TQ
Telephone: 0171 401 2044
Fax: 0171 401 2055
Email: bsp@blackspring.demon.co.uk
Unsolicited Manuscripts: Yes

Blackhat

Independent small-press publisher, specialising in contemporary open-field poetry. Interested in poetry and prose that test the boundaries of language and structure, while still having something actual to say. Not interested in poetry found on a newspaper reader's page. Approach at manuscript stage made by publisher to author, not other way round. Suggest writers save cost of postage, unless invited by editor. Small one-off print-runs only.

Editor(s): Lloyd Robinson
Address: 40 Ruby Street, Cardiff CF2 1LN
Imprints: Canarant (audio tapes)
Payment Details: Variable
Unsolicited Manuscripts: No. Any received not guaranteed a reply

Blackstaff Press Ltd

Leading Irish publisher with a wide range of categories - history, politics, fiction, poetry, etc - mostly of Irish interest. UK Small Publisher of the Year 1992.

Editor(s): Anne Tannahill
Address: 3 Galway Park, Dundonald, Belfast BT16 2AN
Telephone: 01232 487161
Fax: 01232 489552
Payment Details: Standard royalties
Unsolicited Manuscripts: Send synopsis and sample material with covering letter in first instance. Enclose SAE for return.

Blandford/Ward Lock

Subject areas: mind, body, spirit; UFOs, earth mysteries, unexplained phenomena; mythology; major controversial books; major illustrated books.

Editor(s): Stuart Booth
Address: Wellington House, 125 Strand, London WC2R 0BB
Telephone: 0171 420 5555
Fax: 0171 240 7261
Imprints: Blandford, Ward Lock
Parent Company: Orion Publishing Group
Payment Details: Royalty or outright fee
Unsolicited Manuscripts: Yes

Bloodaxe Books

Contemporary poetry. Note to propective authors and agents: when submitting work to Bloodaxe, please enclose SAE or International Reply Coupons. If your work is not accepted for publication, we will not be able to return it to you unless you have sent return postage. While we are pleased to consider unsolicited submissions, we cannot accept any responsibility for loss or damage to manuscripts or artwork. Please also note the following: * If you want a quick response, send a sample selection of up to a dozen poems rather than a full-length collection. If you want us to consider something other than poetry, please send a preliminary letter and synopsis rather than the book itself. * We are not publishing any more fiction. * If you do not read any contemporary poetry, we are unlikely to be interested in your work. * It is usually advisable to submit poems to magazines before thinking about putting a book together. * We regret that we aren't able to offer detailed criticism of poetry submitted for publication (we currently receive about 100 books to consider each week). There are specialist organisations offering critical services, writers' workshops and courses.

Editor(s): Neil Astley
Address: PO Box 1SN, Newcastle-upon-Tyne NE99 1SN
Unsolicited Manuscripts: Yes

Bloomsbury Publishing

Literary fiction, biography, illustrated, reference, travel in hardcover; children's, trade paperback and mass market paperback.

Editor(s): Liz Calder, David Reynolds, Rosemary Davidson, Matthew Hamilton
Address: 38 Soho Square, London W1V 5DF
Telephone: 0171 494 2111
Fax: 0171 434 1190
Website: www.bloomsbury.com

B
BMJ Books

BMJ Books has a growing list of medical titles in areas such as primary care, anaesthesia, cardiology, trauma and evidence-based medicine. We are also known for our basic guides to writing and research, such as Statistics At Square One and How To Read A Paper, and the famous ABC series for general practitioners.

Editor(s): Commissioning Editor: Mary Banks
Address: BMA House, Tavistock Square, London WC1H 9JR
Telephone: 0171 387 4499
Fax: 0171 383 6662
Email: orders@bmjbooks.com
Website: www.bmjbooks.com
Imprints: BMA Publications. Distributed titles: American Academy of Opthalmology, American College of Surgeons, Schattauer, American Academy of Pediatrics.
Parent Company: BMJ Publishing Group
Unsolicited Manuscripts: Yes - to Commissioning Editor

Bodmin Books

Founded 1972 to promote Cornish history, tradition and present attractions. Bodmin Books pioneered attention to Bodmin Moor ('72), the Bodmin Riding custom ('74); and the delights of Kynance ('76) on the Lizard in west Cornwall - and still holds the only definitive study of a nationally-known murder mystery Charlotte Dymond 1844 ('78). The occasional imprint Cotterill & Munn was launched in 1997, with the publication of the words/music pamphlet The Ballad Of '97 to commemorate the 500th anniversary of the Cornish uprising against Henry VII. This was followed by The Bodmin Community Christmas Day Party tabloid, annually since 1997; and a re-launch of the Bodmin Map, with historical notes and placename references. This imprint will continue to carry poetry, plays, etc, while Bodmin Books will continue with academic studies. Both imprints are voluntary co-operative hobbies, with authors contributing printing costs, and the company its storage space, production and promotional experience, and orders facilitation. If/when books sell, authors may be reimbursed some or all of their contribution.

Editor(s): P I Munn
Address: 4 Turf Street, Bodmin, Cornwall PL31 2DH
Imprints: Cotterill & Munn
Parent Company: Bodmin Books
Payment Details: None
Unsolicited Manuscripts: No

Bogle-L' Ouverture Press Ltd

Founded in 1969 as Bogle-L'Ouverture Publications. This company went into voluntary liquidation in 1991 and Bogle-L'Ouverture Press was founded in its place. The press provides a window to the world of black experience, mainly in the UK. We publish work across the wide spectrum of poetry, fiction, non-fiction, children's etc.

Address: PO Box 2186, London W13 9QZ
Telephone: 0181 579 4920
Fax: As phone
Unsolicited Manuscripts: Yes

The Book Castle

Publishes non-fiction of local interest (Bedfordshire, Hertfordshire, Buckinghamshire, Northamptonshire, the Chilterns), 6 titles a year. About 50 titles in print, eg Chiltern Walks series, The Hill Of The Martyr, Journeys Into Buckinghamshire.

Editor(s): Paul Bowes
Address: 12 Church Street, Dunstable, Beds LU5 4RU
Telephone: 01582 605670
Fax: 01582 662431
Payment Details: Royalty
Unsolicited Manuscripts: Yes

The Book Guild

Biography, military, health, history, literary criticism, philosophy, natural history, fiction and children's fiction.

Editor(s): John Trenhaile
Address: Temple House, 25 High Street, Lewes, East Sussex BN7 2LU
Telephone: 01273 472534
Fax: 01273 476472
Email: info@bookguild.co.uk
Website: www.bookguild.co.uk
Payment Details: Royalties paid twice-yearly
Unsolicited Manuscripts: No

B

Borthwick Institute Publications

The Institute publishes a series of studies concerned with the ecclesiastical history of the north of England and other aspects of the history or historiography of Yorkshire. Also concentrates on issuing editions and catalogues of its deposited archives and providing guides to the handwriting and contents of records.

Editor(s): Editorial board
Address: St Anthony's Hall, Peasholme Green, York YO1 7PW
Telephone: 01904 642315
Fax: 01904 633284
Website: www.york.ac.uk/inst/bihr
Imprints: Borthwick Papers, Borthwick Texts & Calendars, Borthwick Lists & Indexes, Borthwick Studies In History, Borthwick Wallets, Monastic Research Bulletin
Parent Company: University of York

Boulevard Books/The Babel Guides

Fiction in translation, the Babel Guides to fiction in translation. Innovative books in travel/world culture.

Editor(s): Ray Keenoy
Address: 8 Aldbourne Road, London W12 0LN
Website: www.raybabel.dircon.co.uk
Imprints: Boulevard, Babel
Payment Details: Bi-annual royalty payment or on commission basis
Unsolicited Manuscripts: No

Bowker-Saur

Library and information science, including series such as Guides To Information Sources, Information Services Management and British Library Research. Also business information and African studies.

Editor(s): Louise Tooms, Linda Hajdukiewicz
Address: Windsor Court, East Grinstead House, East Grinstead RH19 1XA
Telephone: 01342 326972
Fax: 01342 335612
Website: http://www.bowker-saur.com
Imprints: Headland Business Information, Bowker-Saur, Hans Zell
Parent Company: Reed Business Information
Unsolicited Manuscripts: Yes

Marion Boyars Publishers Ltd

An established literary imprint (since 1960) with specialisations in fiction, fiction in translation, cinema and avant-garde music. Famous authors include Ken Kesey, Hubert Selby Jnr, Gilbert Sorrentino, Michael Ondaatje, Yevegeny Yevtushenko, Kenzabaro Oe, Pauline Kael, Rober Creeley, Julio Cortazar, John Cage, Ingmar Bergman and Georges Bataille.

Editor(s): Ken Hollings (non-fiction); Marion Boyars (fiction)
Address: 24 Lacy Road, London SW15 1NL
Telephone: 0181 7889522
Fax: 0181 7898122
Unsolicited Manuscripts: Accepted for literary standard works (as against mass-market)

BPS Books (The British Psychological Society)

Psychology for managers, the medical professions, teachers, general public. Also psychology texts for school and undergraduate level, psychometrics, management and professional development.

Editor(s): Publisher: Joyce Collins
Editors: Susan Pacitti, Jon Reed
Address: St Andrews House, 48 Princess Road East, Leicester LE1 7DR
Telephone: 0166 254 9568
Website: http://www.bps.org.uk
Imprints: BPS Books, BPS Multimedia
Payment Details: Royalties
Unsolicited Manuscripts: No

Barry Bracewell-Milnes

Economic policy, tax policy, tax avoidance and evasion.

Editor(s): Barry Bracewell-Milnes
Address: 26 Lancaster Court, Banstead, Surrey SM7 1RR
Telephone: 01737 350736
Imprints: Panopticum
Unsolicited Manuscripts: Write first

Bradford Libraries

Publish local history items.

Address: Central Library, Prince's Way, Bradford BD1 1NN
Telephone: 01274 753600
Fax: 01274 395108
Parent Company: Bradford Council
Unsolicited Manuscripts: No

Bradt Publications

Country guides - a comprehensive selection of individual countries spanning all continents from Albania to Zanzibar. Hiking guides - to out-of-the-way places including South America and Eastern Europe. Rail and road guides - advice on travelling to and around destinations on a global scale; constantly updated. Wildlife guides - covering the natural history of areas rich in wildlife; highly illustrated.

Editor(s): Tricia Haynes
Address: 41 Nortoft Road, Chalfont St Peter, Bucks SL9 0LA
Payment Details: Royalties
Unsolicited Manuscripts: No

Brandon/Mount Eagle

Trade publisher of general & literary fiction and non-fiction. Authors include Gerry Adams and Alice Taylor. Brandon is an imprint of Mount Eagle Publications.

Address: PO Box 32, Dingle, Co Kerry, Ireland
Telephone: 353 66 9151463
Fax: 353 66 9151234
Imprints: Brandon, Mount Eagle
Parent Company: Mount Eagle Publications
Unsolicited Manuscripts: No

Nicholas Brealey Publishing

We are publishers of leading-edge books for business that inform, inspire, enable and entertain. We also focus on personal development, the international and intercultural fields and topical bestsellers that go beyond the traditional business book to look at the global picture.

Editor(s): Nicholas Brealey
Address: 36 John Street, London WC1N 2AT
Unsolicited Manuscripts: Yes

Breedon Books Publishing Co Ltd

Local history, sport, biography and autobiographies by sports personalities.

Editor(s): Anton Rippon
Address: 44 Friar Gate, Derby DE1 1DA
Telephone: 01332 384235
Fax: 01332 292755
Email: breedonbooks@netmatters.co.uk
Imprints: Breedon Sport, Breedon Heritage
Payment Details: By arrangement
Unsolicited Manuscripts: Yes if accompanied by return postage

Breese Books Ltd

Publish Sherlock Holmes pastiches. Are not presently seeking new writers or manuscripts, and do not invite telephone calls or unsolicited manuscripts.

Editor(s): Andrea de Belleroche
Address: 164 Kensington Park Road, London W11 2ER
Imprints: Breese Books
Parent Company: Martin Breese International
Payment Details: By arrangement
Unsolicited Manuscripts: No

Brewin Books

Midland regional history topics. Biographies. Transport history: railways, buses, aircraft and canals. Joint publications with trusts, local authorities etc (non-fiction topics).

Editor(s): Alan Brewin
Address: Doric House, 56 Alcester Road, Studley, Warwickshire B80 7LG
Telephone: 01527 854228
Fax: 01527 852746
Imprints: Brewin Books
Parent Company: Brewin Books Ltd
Payment Details: Usual royalties payable six-monthly
Unsolicited Manuscripts: No. But preliminary letter with synopsis acceptable

The Bridgeman Art Library

Fine art photographic library with over 100,000 art images available for publication. Representing over 750 collections from all over the world, the Bridgeman is the world's most comprehensive source of fine art images. Our picture researchers can source the images you need and send a selection of scans or transparencies to suit your brief. The library is fully digitised and a catalogue of the entire collection is available on CD-ROM. The collection covers every style, period and subject from cave painting to contemporary art.

Address: 17-19 Garway Road, London W2 4PH
Telephone: 0171 727 4065
Fax: 0171 792 8509
Email: info@bridgeman.co.uk
Website: www.bridgeman.co.uk
Parent Company: Sister office: The Bridgeman Art Library, New York, 65 East 93rd Street, New York NY10128

British Cement Association

Cement, concrete, civil and structural engineering, construction, materials science and standards.

Editor(s): Martin Clarke
Address: Century House, Telford Avenue, Crowthorne, Berks RG45 6YS
Email: cement@bca.org.uk
Website: www.bca.org.uk
Payment Details: Negotiable
Unsolicited Manuscripts: Yes

British Library Publications

The British Library has a flourishing and expanding publishing programme of approximately 40 titles per year and over 600 titles in print. The majority of the titles are bibliographies and reference works; however there is also an expanding list of general and illustrated books, based primarily on the Library's extensive historic connections.

Editor(s): David Way, Anne Young
Address: 96 Euston Road, London NW1 2DB
Telephone: 0171 412 7704
Fax: 1071 412 7768
Email: blpublications@bl.uk
Website: www.portico.bl.uk
Imprints: British Library Publications
Parent Company: The British Library

Brooklands Books Ltd

Brooklands' popular Gold Portfolio series now covers motor cycle marques, and these, together with our Road Test and new Limited Editions series provide an unparalleled source of motoring reference literature. In addition, Brooklands are the publishers of official factory manuals, parts catalogues and handbooks for Jaguar, Triumph, MG and Land Rover.

Editor(s): No editors used, books are compilations
Address: PO Box 146, Cobham, Surrey KT11 1LG
Telephone: 01932 865051
Fax: 01932 868803
Unsolicited Manuscripts: Yes

Brown, Son & Ferguson Ltd

Nautical and navigation both technical and non-technical (not biographical).

Editor(s): L Ingram-Brown
Address: 4/10 Darnley Street, Glasgow G41 2SD
Telephone: 0141 429 1234
Fax: 0141 420 1694
Email: info@skipper.co.uk
Website: www.skipper.co.uk
Payment Details: Standard royalty agreement
Unsolicited Manuscripts: Yes

Bryntirion Press

The literature arm of the Evangelical Movement of Wales, Bryntirion Press publishes books in English and Welsh for the Christian market. It publishes children's books in Welsh but not in English. Its books range from booklets to works of 300+ pages. Subjects covered include Christian doctrine, Church history, Christian living and biography.

Editor(s): Managing Editor: David Kingdon
Address: Bryntirion, Bridgend CF31 4DX
Telephone: 01656 655886
Fax: 01656 656095
Email: press@drcco.co.uk
Parent Company: Evangelical Movement of Wales
Payment Details: 5% royalty
Unsolicited Manuscripts: No - but proposals welcomed

John Burgess Publications

Writer and publisher of history books, local and regional interest.

Address: 28 Holme Fauld, Scotby, Carlisle CA4 8BC
Telephone: 019228 513173

Edmund Burke Publisher

Specialises in fine historical publications and limited editions.

Editor(s): Eamonn de Burca
Address: Cloonagashel, 27 Priory Drive, Blackrock, Co Dublin, Ireland
Telephone: 003531 2882159
Fax: 003531 2834080
Email: deburca@indigo.ie
Website: http://indigo.ie/-deburca/deburca.htm
Imprints: Edmund Burke Publisher, Caislean Burc

Burral Floraprint Ltd

Publish good-value gardening titles, from eminent horticultural authors, featuring vibrant pictures and thoroughly helpful text, at at very reasonable prices. Examples include the 128-page Shrubs For Everyone by Peter Seabrook and Making The Most Of Clematis by Raymond Evison. Most of the photographs in the books come from Floraprint International's extensive plant picture library. The same company (Burall Floraprint Ltd) is the UK's leading supplier of pictorial plant labels, as used to label plants in the majority of UK garden centres and horticultural retailers.

Address: Oldfield Lane, Wisbech PE13 2TH
Telephone: 01945 461165
Fax: 01945 474396
Email: floraprint@burall.com
Website: www.burall.com
Imprints: Floraprint
Parent Company: Burall Ltd
Unsolicited Manuscripts: No

Butterworths Ltd

Publishers of law and accountancy titles for the legal profession. The entire product range comprises books, looseleaf works, encyclopaedias, reports and periodicals, as well as our rapidly-expanding portfolio of CD-ROM and online products. Butterworths has been at the forefront of innovative publishing for nearly 180 years, demonstrating the ability to respond to the changing needs of practitioners.

Address: Halsbury House, 35 Chancery Lane, London WC2A 1EL
Telephone: 0171 400 2500
Fax: 0171 400 2842
Website: http://www.butterworths.co.uk
Imprints: Tolley, Charles Knight, Barry Rose
Parent Company: Reed Elsevier
Unsolicited Manuscripts: Yes

Cairns Publications

Books and meditation cards which seek to unfold afresh the spiritual inheritance of the Christian church and to connect that inheritance to issues of contemporary concern.

Editor(s): Jim Cotter
Address: 47 Firth Park Avenue, Sheffield S5 6HF
Telephone: 0114 243 1182
Fax: As phone
Email: cottercairns@compuserve.com
Website: http://ourworld.compuserve.com/homepages/cottercairns
Parent Company: John Hunt Publishing

Cambridge University Press

Primary and secondary school books. English language teaching. Academic publishing embraces just about every subject seriously studied in the English speaking university world.

Editor(s): Many subject specialists
Address: The Edinburgh Building, Shaftsbury Road, Cambridge CB2 2RU
Imprints: Canto. Distribute outside N America: Stanford Univ. Press, Mathematical Association of America. Distribute worldwide: CSLI, SIGS, MacKeith Press.
Parent Company: University of Cambridge
Payment Details: Varies according to the nature and level of the individual book
Unsolicited Manuscripts: Send outline proposal

C

Canongate Books Ltd

Fiction (not children's), mountaineering & travel, Scottish interest, biography, humour, art and history.

Editor(s): Eva Freischlager
Colin McLear (Payback Press)
Kevin Williamson (Rebel Inc)
Address: 14 High Street, Edinburgh EH1 1TE
Telephone: 0131 557 5111
Fax: 0131 557 5211
Email: info@canongate.co.uk
Website: www.canongate.co.uk
Imprints: Rebel Inc, Payback Press
Unsolicited Manuscripts: Yes

Capall Bann Publishing

Mind body spirit, women's studies, personal development, nautical, environmental, occult, folklore, animals, mediumship, crystals, astrology, tarot, alternative health.

Editor(s): Julia Day, Jon Day
Address: Freshfields, Chieveley, Berks RG20 8TF
Telephone: 01635 248711(editorial) / 01635 247050 (sales)
Imprints: Capall Bann
Payment Details: 10% Quarterly
Unsolicited Manuscripts: Yes

Carcanet Press Ltd

Carcanet Press publish poetry and fiction in translation from around the world. Fyfield Books is dedicated to keeping neglected English poets of the 16th-19th century in print.

Editor(s): Michael Schmidt
Address: 4th Floor, Conavon Court, 12-16 Blackfriars Street, Manchester M3 5BQ
Telephone: 0161 834 8730
Fax: 0161 832 0084
Email: pnr@carcanet.u-net.com
Website: www.carcanet.co.uk
Imprints: Fyfield Books
Unsolicited Manuscripts: No

Cardiff Academic Press

This is a small but highly efficient publishing house which welcomes manuscripts from established and new writers. No works of fiction have been published but the present list includes academic books in architecture, biography, education, history, life sciences, literature, mycology, plant biology, psychology, religious studies and theology. As a Cardiff based publisher, the Press is particularly interested in books relating to Wales: biography, culture, history, politics, religious studies and women's studies. The Press provides a European marketing and distrubution service for a number of overseas academic publishers so is well placed to arrange co-editions or distribution in overseas markets. The Press also specialises in reprints of out-of-print texts and would welcome suitable titles, with additional updated introductions.

Address: St Fagans Road, Fairwater, Cardiff CF5 3AE
Email: E-bost:drakegroup@btinternet.com
Imprints: Cardiff Academic Press, Plantin
Parent Company: Drake Group Ltd
Unsolicited Manuscripts: Yes but only biographical details and qualifications, brief synopsis, extent and target audience

C

Carlton Books

Books in all categories of popular culture, particularly sport, puzzles, quizzes & games, music, fashion, style & beauty, health & sex, television and popular science. We also publish tv tie-ins, particularly with Carlton Television.

Editor(s): Publishing Director: Piers Murray Hill
Address: 20 St Anne's Court, London W1V 3AW
Imprints: Carlton
Parent Company: Carlton Communications
Unsolicited Manuscripts: Yes, but no fiction

Jon Carpenter Publishing

Environment, sustainable economics and development, Green politics, social issues and health. Authors should send for our author information sheet before submitting any other material.

Editor(s): Jon Carpenter
Address: 2, The Spendlove Centre, Charlbury OX7 3PQ
Telephone: 01608 811969
Fax: As phone
Email: joncarpenterpublishing@compuserve.com
Payment Details: Royalties
Unsolicited Manuscripts: No

Casdec Print & Design Centre

Publishers and printers of educational non-fiction books, training materials for various bodies, and writers of open/distance learning materials. Specialise in publishing training and learning materials for universities, colleges, financial and other bodies. Publisher of the nationally-recognised Your Business Success bookkeeping and financial control system. Over 100,000 supplied to a national financial institution for use by clients.

Editor(s): T Moffat
Address: 21-22 Harraton Terrace, Birtley, Chester-le-Street, Co Durham DH3 2QG
Telephone: 0191 410 5556
Fax: 0191 410 0229

Frank Cass & Co Ltd

Publisher of academic books and journals including social science and Middle Eastern studies.

Editor(s): Andrew Humphries
Address: Newbury House, 900 Eastern Avenue, Newbury Park, Ilford IG9 7HH
Telephone: 0181 599 8866
Fax: 0181 599 0984
Email: info@frankcass.com
Website: www.frankcass.com
Imprints: Frank Cass, Woburn Press, Vallentine Mitchell

Cassell Publishers

Natural history, health, crafts, home decorating, interiors, spiritual, cookery, woodworking, gardening, personal development, science.

Editor(s): Mr Booth, Ms Washburn, Mrs Van Eesteren, Ms Churly
Address: Wellington House, 125 Strand, London WC2R 0BB
Imprints: Wardlock, Blandford
Parent Company: Orion Publishing Group
Unsolicited Manuscripts: Yes

Kyle Cathie Ltd

Cookery, wine, natural history, history, health and beauty, lifestyle, interiors and gardening. Also reference books - words, dictionaries and music.

Editor(s): Kate Oldfield, Sophie Bessemer
Address: 20 Vauxhall Bridge Road, London SW1V 2SA
Payment Details: Advance against royalty or flat fee
Unsolicited Manuscripts: No - proposals required

Catholic Institute For International Relations

Third world development, gender, peacebuilding, drugs and development, agriculture, transnational corporations, third world theology, Asia, Latin America, Europe and southern Africa.

Editor(s): Adam Bradbury
Address: Unit 3, Canonbury Yard, 190a New North Road, London N1 7BJ
Telephone: 0171 354 0883
Fax: 0171 359 0017
Email: ciir@ciir.org
Website: www.ciir.org
Unsolicited Manuscripts: No

Cavalier Paperbacks

Specialise in pony books for children but want to widen publishing programme - interested in adventure stories for boys, fictional picture books. Always interested in illustrators for covers, etc.

Editor(s): Charlotte Fyfe
Address: Burnham House, Jarvis Street, Upavon, Wilts SN9 6DU
Telephone: 01980 630379
Fax: As phone
Payment Details: 7.5% royalty
Unsolicited Manuscripts: Yes

C

CCBI Publications

Absolutely all areas that Christianity impinges upon. Eg: ecumenism, faith & order, interfaith relations, women in church and society, human sexuality, ethics, communication, racism, economics, healing, mission & evangelism and international affairs.

Editor(s): Colin Davey
Address: Inter-Church House, 35-41 Lower Marsh, London SE1 7RL
Telephone: 0171 620 4444
Fax: 0171 928 0010
Email: book_ccbi@cix.co.uk
Website: www.ccbi.org.uk
Imprints: CCBI, CEC, WCC
Parent Company: Council of Churches for Britain & Ireland
Payment Details: By negotiation
Unsolicited Manuscripts: Very rarely

CCH Editions Ltd

Part of the Wolters Kluwer group, leading international publishers of business and professional information. CCH Editions Ltd produce a wide range of tax and business law publications in a variety of formats. Loose-leaf services, books, newsletters, seminars and electronic media deliver the knowledge businesses need across a broad spectrum of subjects including personnel management, commercial and company law, taxation, European law, insolvency and auditing.

Address: Telford Road, Bicester OX6 0XD
Telephone: 01869 253300
Fax: 01869 874700
Email: marketing@cch.co.uk
Website: www.cch.co.uk
Parent Company: Wolters Kluwer
Payment Details: Negotiable
Unsolicited Manuscripts: Brief explanatory letter invited as first step

Centaur Press

Subjects in the field of humane education, animal rights and classic literature.

Editor(s): Jeannie Cohen, Elisabeth Petersdorff
Address: 51 Achilles Road, London NW6 1DZ
Telephone: 0171 431 4391
Fax: 0171 431 5088
Email: books@opengate.demon.co.uk
Website: www.opengate.demon.co.uk
Imprints: Centaur Press, Linden Press
Parent Company: Open Gate Press
Unsolicited Manuscripts: Synopses & ideas for books only

The Centre For Educational Visits & Exchanges

The Central Bureau, incorporating the UK Centre for European Education and Education Partners Overseas, forms part of the British Council. It is funded by the Education Departments of the United Kingdom and is the UK National Agency for many of the European Union Education and Training Programmes. The Bureau has over 50 years' experience publishing information guides on the theme of work, study and travel opportunities. Catalogue available.

Editor(s): Thom Sewell
Address: 10 Spring Gardens, London SW1A 2BN
Telephone: 0171 389 4004
Fax: 0171 389 4426
Email: books@centralbureau.org.uk
Website: www.britcoun.org/cbeve/
Parent Company: British Council

Centre For Economic Policy Research

A network of over 400 Research Fellows, based primarily in European universities. The Centre coordinates its Fellows' research activities and communicates their results to the public and private sectors. CEPR is an entrepreneur, developing research initiatives with the producers, consumers and sponsors of research. Established in 1983, CEPR is a European economics research organisation with uniquely wide-ranging scope and activities. CEPR is a registered educational charity, supported by various charitable trusts and banks, none of which gives prior review to the Centre's publications, nor necessarily endorses the views expressed.

Address: 90-98 Goswell Road, London EC1V 7RR
Telephone: 0171 878 2900
Fax: 0171 878 2999
Email: cepr@cepr.org
Website: www.cepr.org
Imprints: CEPR
Payment Details: Confidential
Unsolicited Manuscripts: No

Centre For Information On Language Teaching & Research (CILT)

The Centre for Information on Language Teaching & Research provides a complete range of services for language professionals in every stage and sector of education, including a list of publications designed to support teachers.

Editor(s): Head of Publications: Emma Rees
Address: 20 Bedfordbury, London WC2N 4LB
Telephone: 0171 379 5101
Fax: 0171 379 5082
Email: publications@cilt.org.uk

Chalcombe Publications

Technical publications for agriculture, specialising in animal nutrition, grass & forage crops and animal production systems.The books are for farmers, students, teachers, research workers and advisers. Complete list for 1999 available from Chalcombe Publications. 21 books in print.

Address: Painshall, Church Lane, Welton, Lincoln LN2 3LT
Telephone: 01673 863023
Fax: 01673 863108
Email: chalcombe@compuserve.com

Chambers Harrap Publishers Ltd

Dictionaries - English language and bilingual.

Address: 7 Hopetoun Crescent, Edinburgh EH7 4AY
Imprints: Chambers and Harrap
Parent Company: CEP Communications, France
Unsolicited Manuscripts: No

Chapman Publishing

Chapman New Writing series aims to present up-and-coming writers, Scottish and international (short fiction, poetry and plays). We also publish a quarterly literary magazine that includes poetry, fiction and critical work from around the world, and reviews of new publications. Previously unpublished poetry, fiction (up to 3,000 words) and critical pieces accepted.

Editor(s): Joy Hendry
Address: 4 Broughton Place, Edinburgh EH1 3RX
Telephone: 0131 557 2207
Fax: 0131 556 9565
Email: chapman-pub@ndirect.co.uk
Website: www.airstrip-one.ndirect.co.uk/chapman
Imprints: Chapman New Writers Series, Chapman Magazine
Payment Details: Copies only
Unsolicited Manuscripts: Yes if accompanied by SAE/IRC

Chartered Institute Of Bankers

Distance learning and other reference texts dealing with all aspects of the financial services industry. Mangement reports and magzines.

Editor(s): Philip Blake, Finola McLaughlin
Address: Emmanuel House, 4-9 Burgate Lane, Canterbury, Kent CT1 2XJ
Telephone: 01227 762600
Fax: 01227 497641
Email: pblake@cib.org.uk
Website: www.cib.org.uk
Imprints: CIB Publishing
Payment Details: On application
Unsolicited Manuscripts: Yes

Zelda Cheatle Press

Specialist photography publishers.

Address: 99 Mount Street, London W1Y 5HF
Telephone: 0171 408 4448
Fax: 0171 408 1444
Email: phot@zcgall.demon.co.uk
Unsolicited Manuscripts: No

Checkmark Publications

Publishes The Step By Step Guide To Planning Your Wedding by Lynda Wright (£5.95). Supplied through Gardners Books or Checkmark Publications.

Address: 2 Hazell Park, Amersham, Bucks HP7 9AB
Telephone: 01494 431289
Fax: As phone
Email: checkmark@avnet.co.uk
Unsolicited Manuscripts: No

Child's Play (International) Ltd

Independent publisher of children's educational books, games and audio-visual materials - specialising in whole-child development, learning through play, life skills and values. Founded in 1972, Child's Play is non-sectarian, non-political, non-sexist, multi-cultural and eco-friendly. We encourage children to think about the world they want to live in, and provide challenging information books alongside beautifully illustrated fiction for the 2-10 age group.

Editor(s): Sue Baker
Address: Ashworth Road, Bridgemead, Swindon SN5 7YD
Telephone: 01793 616286
Fax: 01793 512795
Email: childs-play.com
Imprints: Mission
Payment Details: Negotiable
Unsolicited Manuscripts: Yes - but no novels

The Children's Society

One of the UK's leading child care charities whose mission is to be a positive force for change in the lives of children and young people. Publishes books and reports for professionals on topics related to child welfare issues, and resources for children and young people in difficult circumstances. Does not publish general books for children.

Address: Edward Rudolf House, Margery Street, London WC1X 0JL
Telephone: 0171 841 4400
Fax: 0171 841 4500
Email: publishing@childsoc.org.uk
Website: www.the-childrens-society.org.uk
Imprints: The Children's Society
Payment Details: By negotiation
Unsolicited Manuscripts: On issues related to UK child welfare only

C

The Christadelphian Magazine & Publishing Association Ltd

Publishes magazines, pamphlets and books on Bible topics, and to promote the Christian faith.

Editor(s): M J Ashton
Address: 404 Shaftmoor Lane, Hall Green, Birmingham B28 8SZ
Telephone: 0121 777 6324
Fax: 0121 778 5024
Email: the_christadelphian@compuserve.com
Website: www.christadelphian.uk.com
Imprints: The Christadelphian, Faith Alive!

Christchurch Publishers Ltd

General book publishers. Publications include reference, fine art, architecture and fiction.

Editor(s): James Hughes, Leonard Holdsworth
Address: 10 Christchurch Terrace, London SW3 4AJ
Telephone: 0171 351 4995
Fax: As phone
Imprints: Albyn Press, Charles Skilton Ltd, Luxor Press, Tallis Press, Cavasham Communications Ltd
Parent Company: Christchurch Publications Ltd
Payment Details: By negotiation
Unsolicited Manuscripts: Letter before sending anything

Christian Focus Publications

Christian books for all ages. We are an evangelical publisher that produces board books to children's bibles for younger people and biographies to theological books for adults. For an idea of our range write for our full catalogue.

Editor(s): Malcolm Maclean (Adult), Catherine Mackenzie (Children)
Address: Geanies House, Fearn, Tain, Ross-Shire Scotland IV20 1TW
Telephone: 01862 871 005
Fax: 01862 871 699
Email: cfp@geanies.org.uk
Website: http://www.christianfocus.com
Imprints: Christian Focus, Christian Heritage, Mentor
Parent Company: Balintore Holdings
Payment Details: Negotiable royalty %, fixed fee
Unsolicited Manuscripts: Yes

Christian Music Ministries

CMM serves and resources churches, schools, bookshops and individuals through teaching, workshops, 'music in worship' seminars, musicals, training courses, day and weekend conferences and mail-order catalogue. Deals principally with the publishing, recording and marketing of music composed by Roger Jones, the Director. This includes his 16 musicals, the latest being Snakes And Ladders to be published in 1999. He has also released various collections of worship songs, Ways To Praise and Precious & Honoured being the two latest. CMM also run various Family Music Weeks during the summer which includes an annual visit to Lee Abbey in Devon.

Editor(s): Director: R W Jones
Address: 325 Bromford Road, Hodge Hill, Birmingham B36 8ET
Telephone: 0121 783 3291
Fax: 0121 785 0500
Email: roger@cmm.org.uk
Website: www.cmm.org.uk

Christian Research

Publishers of specialist reference books for leaders of churches and Christian organisations, including directories, handbooks, statistical works and an atlas. Also publish results of own research projects relating to Christian activity and behaviour. Do not consider unsolicited material. UK and worldwide.

Editor(s): Peter Brierley, Heather Wraight
Address: Vision Building, 4 Footscray Road, Eltham, London SE9 2TZ
Telephone: 0181 294 1989
Fax: 0181 294 0014
Email: 100616.1657@compuserve.com
Unsolicited Manuscripts: No

Church Pastoral Aid Society

The Church Pastoral Aid Society is a Christian charity supported by the Church of England. Dedicated to equipping church leaders, youth workers and teachers, CPAS publish approximately 20 publications a year. Housing a direct marketing operation, CPAS combines both publishing and promotion to provide moral, biblical and religious resources.

Editor(s): Rory Keegan
Address: Athena Drive, Tachbrook Park, Warwick CV34 6NG
Telephone: 01926 458 458
Fax: 01926 458459
Email: liselle@cpas.org.uk
Website: www.cpas.org.uk
Unsolicited Manuscripts: To the Editor

C

Church Society

As well as two regular quarterly publications, Churchman (a theological journal) and CrossWay (a magazine mainly for CS members), Church Society publishes pamphlets as the need arises, on vital issues facing the Church and nation, and theological works such as The Principles Of Theology by Griffith Thomas (an introduction to the 39 Articles) and An English Prayer Book (a prayer book in modern English).

Editor(s): David Phillips (CrossWay), Gerald Bray (Churchman)
Address: Dean Wace House, 16 Rosslyn Road, Watford, Hertfordshire WD1 7EY
Telephone: 01923 235111
Fax: 01923 800362
Website: http://www.churchsociety.org/

Cicerone Press

Activity guides - walking, climbing, cycling etc. We are the leading publishers in this field with 300 titles.

Editor(s): Walt Unsworth
Address: 2 Police Square, Milnthorpe, Cumbria LA7 7PY
Telephone: 015395 62060
Fax: 015395 63417
Email: info@cicerone.demon.co.uk
Website: http://www.cicerone.demon.co.uk
Payment Details: Royalties every 6 months
Unsolicited Manuscripts: No - send synopsis only

Claridge Press

Articles max 4,000 words on philosophy, history, politics from conservative viewpoint, literature, religion, art. We also publish books.

Editor(s): Roger Scruton
Address: 33 Cannonbury Park South, London N1 2JW
Imprints: Salisbury Review
Payment Details: No payment - works like an academic magazine
Unsolicited Manuscripts: Yes

T & T Clark Ltd

Theology and religion - international, non-denominational, academic and professional - books and journals. Law - Scottish, national and international, academic and professional - books and journals.

Editor(s): Geoffrey Green
Address: 59 George Street, Edinburgh EH2 2LQ

Telephone: 0131 225 4703
Fax: 0131 220 44260
Email: mailbox@tandtclark.co.uk
Website: www.tandtclark.co.uk
Imprints: T&T Clark
Payment Details: Royalties or fees
Unsolicited Manuscripts: Yes

James Clarke & Co Ltd

Religious & theological non-fiction, children's fiction & non-fiction, children's religious fiction & non-fiction, adult non-fiction and sponsored books. All the above either illustrated or non-illustrated.

Editor(s): Adrian Brink
Address: PO Box 60, Cambridge CB1 2NT
Telephone: 01223 350865
Fax: 01223 366951
Email: publishing@jamesclarke.co.uk
Website: www.jamesclarke.co.uk
Imprints: James Clarke & Co, The Lutterworth Press
Payment Details: Varies
Unsolicited Manuscripts: Yes

Class Publishing

Popular health, medicine and law.

Address: Barb House, Barb Mews, London W6 7PA
Telephone: 0171 371 2119
Fax: 00171 371 2878
Email: class.co.uk
Unsolicited Manuscripts: Almost always rejected

Clifton Press

Specialises in educational support materials for students, teachers and writers. Publish guidance notes in writing and study skills and specialise in the application of information technology for educational purposes. Also publish computer software programs in essay writing, study skills and English language.

Address: PO Box 100, Manchester M20 6GZ
Telephone: 0161 432 5811
Fax: 0161 443 2766
Email: info@mantex.co.uk
Website: www.mantex.co.uk
Payment Details: 20% royalties
Unsolicited Manuscripts: Yes

Clwyd Family History Society

Publishers of parish register transcripts and indexes, and other indexes of value to the family and local historian.

Address: Pen Y Cae, Ffordd Hendy, Gwernymynydd, Sir Y Fflint CH7 5JP
Telephone: 01352 755138
Email: dafydd@wyddgrug.freeserve.co.uk
Website: http://sentinel.ac.uk/genuki/big/wal/fln/cllwydfhs/

Co-operative Union Ltd

Co-operative philosophy; Co-operative and social history; Directory Of Co-operative Societies; statistical analysis.

Editor(s): Iain Williamson
Address: Holyoake House, Hanover Street, Manchester M60 0AS
Telephone: 0161 832 4300
Fax: 0161 831 7684
Email: info@co-opunion.org.uk
Imprints: Holyoake Books
Parent Company: Co-operative Union Ltd
Payment Details: Royalty at usual publishers' rates, generally paid as an advance
Unsolicited Manuscripts: No

Peter Collin Publishing Ltd

We publish a wide range of dictionaries for students and professionals, in English, and many other languages.

Editor(s): P H Collin and S Collin
Address: 1 Cambridge Road, Teddington, Middlesex TW11 8DT
Telephone: 0181 943 3386
Fax: 0181 943 1673
Email: general@pcp.co.uk
Website: hhtp://www.pcp.co.uk/
Payment Details: Fee for smaller glossaries, royalty for larger works
Unsolicited Manuscripts: No, but draft propasals acceptable

$\mathcal{C}$

Collins & Brown

Publishers of high-quality illustrated non-fiction for the international co-edition market - so books must have international appeal. Subject areas include crafts, gardening, practical art & photography, lifestyle & interiors, New Age, health & beauty.

Editor(s): Editorial Directors: Sarah Hoggett, Liz Dean, Kate Kirby
Address: London House, Great Eastern Wharf, Parkgate Road, London SW11 4NQ
Telephone: 0171 924 2575
Fax: 0171 924 7725
Payment Details: Negotiable
Unsolicited Manuscripts: Yes send brief synopsis first

Colourpoint Books

Educational textbooks: special emphasis on Northern Ireland curriculum. Transport: railways, buses, shipping, air transport, trams, etc. Particular interest in all Irish subjects and the Isle of Man. Will also consider English, Scottish and Welsh subjects. History: books on Irish subjects and local history photographic albums.

Editor(s): Sheila Johnston, Norman Johnston
Address: Unit D5, Ards Business Centre, Jubilee Road, Newtownards, Co Down BT23 4YH
Telephone: 01247 820505
Fax: 01247 821900
Email: info@colourpoint.co.uk
Website: http://www.colourpoint.co.uk
Payment Details: Royalties on longer works; one-off fee on shorter books depending on the length
Unsolicited Manuscripts: Yes

Colt Books Ltd

A small privately owned publishing company - a list of about 30 titles. Many of these concentrate on country and field sports matters. Also publish Bedside Book anthologies on specific subjects - fishing, shooting, bridge, racing, cricket. Rarely take anything from outside submission.

Editor(s): Linda Yeatman
Address: 9 Clarendon Road, Cambridge CB2 2BH
Telephone: 01223 357047
Fax: 01223 365866
Email: coltbooks@msn.com
Imprints: Colt Books, White Lion Books
Unsolicited Manuscripts: No

The Columba Press

Publishes a broad range of religious titles, mainly for the Roman Catholic and Anglican traditions. Specialise in pastoral resources, homiletics, counselling, liturgy, theology, scripture and spirituality, especially Celtic spirituality.

Editor(s): Sean O Boyle
Address: 55a Spruce Avenue, Stillorgan Industrial Park, Blackrock, Co Dublin, Ireland
Telephone: 353 1 2942556
Fax: 353 1 2942564
Email: sean@columba.ie
Website: www.columba.ie
Imprints: The Columba Press
Unsolicited Manuscripts: Send table of contents & sample chapter

Columbia University Press

Reference books: gay/lesbian/gender studies, social sciences/anthropology, international politics, Asian/Far Eastern studies, Middle-eastern studies, film, philosophy, psychology and natural sciences.

Address: 1 Oldlands Way, Bognor Regis, West Sussex PO22 9SA
Unsolicited Manuscripts: Yes

Community Of Poets Press

An independent press with an increasing focus on printing and publishing poetry with original artwork. Our magazine Community Of Poets is an international quarterly which seeks and publishes creative and innovative work in any genre. New voices from all communities are especially welcome and encouraged. Also publish hand-sewn collections under the Pamphlet Poets and Poems By Post imprints. Each ready-to-send poem has an original woodcut print. We hope to launch Community of Artists and Poets Press for the millennium.

Editor(s): Philip Bennetta, Susan Bennetta
Address: Hatfield Cottage, Chilham, Kent CT4 8DP
Telephone: 01227 730787
Email: cpoets@globalnet.co.uk
Imprints: Pamphlet Poets, Poems by Post
Parent Company: Community of Poets Press
Payment Details: % payment on all sales for Pamphlet Poets. Free magazine to non-subscriber contributors
Unsolicited Manuscripts: No. Prefer to see small selection of work and like to publish in magazine first

C

Compendium Publishing

Illustrated non-fiction for adults, children's books & games, hobby-based books.

Editor(s): Simon Forty
Address: 5 Gerrard Street, London W1V 7LJ
Telephone: 0171 287 4570
Fax: 0171 494 0583
Email: compendium@compuserve.com
Payment Details: By negotiation
Unsolicited Manuscripts: Yes

Computer Step

Established in 1991, the leading British publisher of computer books. All popular subject areas are covered in concise and easy-to-understand format. The main imprint is In Easy Steps and there are more of these titles in Booktrack's Top 50 best-selling list of computer books in UK than from most other publishers. Computer Step also exports, reprints and translates its work internationally. It is represented by Penguin for distribution to the book trade in UK and internationally.

Editor(s): Harshad Kotecha
Address: Southfield Road, Southam, Warwickshire CV33 0FB
Telephone: 01926 817999
Fax: 01926 817005
Email: publisher@computerstep.com
Website: http://www.computerstep.com
Imprints: In Easy Steps
Payment Details: Advance and royalties paid.
Unsolicited Manuscripts: Yes

Concept (England)

Publishers and distributors of the Allen Carmichael books. The six titles are concerned with network marketing (MLM), selling, self-development and motivation. Now some 28 editions around the world. Average sales per book have been 20,000.

Editor(s): S M Parkinson
Address: PO Box 614, Polegate, E Sussex BN26 5SS
Telephone: 01323 485434
Fax: As phone
Unsolicited Manuscripts: No

Constable & Co Ltd

History, biography, memoirs, travel, Celtic interest, guide books, mountaineering, popular science, psychology, and military history; plus crime fiction.

Editor(s): Editorial Director: Carol O'Brien
Address: 3 The Lanchesters, 162 Fulham Palace Road, London W6 9ER
Telephone: 0181 741 3663
Fax: 0181 748 7562
Website: www.constable-publishers.co.uk

Leo Cooper

Publishers of military, naval and aviation history covering most periods, especially WW1, WW2, the Falklands and Napoleonic wars.

Editor(s): Henry Wilson
Address: 47 Church Street, Barnsley, South Yorkshire S70 2AS
Telephone: 01226 734 222
Fax: 01226 734 438
Email: charles@pen-and-sword.demon.co.uk
Website: www.yorkshire-web/ps/
Imprints: Leo Cooper, Battleground Europe, Pals
Parent Company: Pen and Sword Books Ltd
Payment Details: Twice-yearly
Unsolicited Manuscripts: Yes, with synopsis

Cottage Publications

Full-colour books on Irish towns and areas, illustrated with paintings by well-known local artists and written by local historians or journalists.

Editor(s): Alison Johnston, Tim Johnston
Address: 15 Ballyhay Road, Donghadee, Co Down BT21 0NG
Telephone: 01247 888033
Fax: 01247 888063
Email: info@cottage-publications.com
Website: www.cottage-publications.com
Unsolicited Manuscripts: No

Countryside Books

Established in 1976, we publish books of local interest, almost always relating to whole English counties. Non-fiction only. Main subjects local history and outdoor activities, especially walking.

Editor(s): Nicholas Battle
Address: Highfield House, 2 Highfield Avenue, Newbury RG14 5DS
Telephone: 01635 43816
Fax: 01635 551004
Unsolicited Manuscripts: Yes, but send outline & sample chapter first

Covenant Publishing Co Ltd

Migrations of the lost 10 tribes of Israel; early Church history (British Church); history of the Royal Family.

Address: 8 Blades Court, Deodar Road, London SW15 2NU
Telephone: 0182 877 9010
Fax: 0181 861 4770
Email: admin@covpub.co.uk
Website: www.britishisrael.co.uk
Unsolicited Manuscripts: No

R & E Coward

Publish Richard Coward's mystery thrillers only.

Address: 16 Sturgess Avenue, London NW4 3TS
Telephone: 0181 202 9592
Unsolicited Manuscripts: No

Crabtree Press

The Press was incorporated in 1946 but since delimited, and now under the sole proprietorship of Ernie Trory, who uses it to publish his own extensive writings, some of which are partly autobiographical. Apart from a biography of the poet Percy Bysshe Shelley, and another of Thomas Hughes, author of Tom Brown's School Days, Crabtree Press publishes only contemporary history (1913 to date) from a Marxist viewpoint.

Address: 4 Portland Avenue, Hove, E Sussex BN3 5NP
Unsolicited Manuscripts: No

Crafthouse

Publishers of interactive CD-ROMS on diet & health, cookbooks, art & craft, travel. Under Vigara: Interactive Contact magazine (worldwide). Also Crafthouse Advertiser, an internet directory for various small companies; contains 'new writers' section where authors can display samples of their work for publishers' attention. Launch date early 1999; details on application.

Editor(s): W Nicholas
Address: 122a Cambridge Road, Southend on Sea, Essex SS1 1ER
Telephone: 01702 354621
Fax: 01702 347353
Email: crafthouse@clara.net
Website: www.crafthouse.uk.com
Imprints: Winslow, Vigara
Parent Company: Crafthouse
Unsolicited Manuscripts: Accepted with return postage

Creative Monochrome Ltd

Specialist books on the art and craft of monochrome photography.

Editor(s): Roger Maile
Address: Courtney House, 62 Jarvis Road, South Croydon, Surrey CR2 6HU
Telephone: 0181 686 3282
Fax: 0181 681 0662
Email: roger@cremono.demon.co.uk
Imprints: Creative Monochrome, Digital Photo Art, Photo Art International
Payment Details: Negotiable
Unsolicited Manuscripts: No - contact first

Crecy Publishing Ltd

Publisher of aviation and military books, with over 150 titles in the range. Majority of titles second word war biographies and autobiographies. Also distribute for a number of other publishers.

Editor(s): Nancy Rolph
Address: 1a Ringway Trading Estate, Shadowmoss Road, Manchester M22 5LH
Telephone: 0161 499 0024
Fax: 0161 499 0298
Email: books@airplan.u-net.com
Website: www.airplan.u-net.com
Imprints: Crecy, Goodall
Unsolicited Manuscripts: Yes with SAE

Crescent Moon

Crescent Moon aims to publish the best in contemporary writing in the fields of poetry, literature, painting, sculpture, media, cinema, feminism and philosophy. Also publishes a quarterly magazine, Passion, and a bi-annual anthology of new American poetry, Pagan America.

Editor(s): J Robinson
Address: PO Box 393, Maidstone, Kent ME14 5XU
Telephone: 01622 729593
Imprints: Crescent Moon, Joe's Press
Payment Details: To be negotiated
Unsolicited Manuscripts: Yes, with letter & SAE or IRCs

Cressrelles Publishing Company Ltd

Established in 1972 to publish general books, now concentrates on plays and theatre books.

Address: 10 Station Road Industrial Estate, Colwall WR13 6RN
Telephone: 01684 540154
Fax: As phone
Imprints: J Garnett Miller Ltd, Kenyon-Deane, Actinic Press
Parent Company: Cressrelles Publishing Co Ltd

Cresta Booksellers Direct

Publishers and booksellers of books and manuals concerning industrial and commercial cleaning chemicals, methods and techniques, also kitchen cleaning manuals and books on industrial housekeeping.

Editor(s): J K P Edwards, A M Edwards
Address: 14 Beechfield Road, Liverpool, L18 2EH
Telephone: 0151 722 7400
Imprints: Cresta Publishing Company

Critical Vision

Publishers of challenging, cutting-edge non-fiction. Previous books include The X Factory: Inside The American Hardcore Film Industry; Intense Device: A Journey Through Lust, Murder & The Fires Of Hell; and Slimetime: A Guide To Sleazy, Mindless Movie Entertainment. Future projects will include concise histories of horror comics and British underground comics of the sixties and seventies, as well as studies of controversial films of the last 25 years. We are always looking for thought-provoking and esoteric new work but will only consider non-fiction submissions and proposals.

Editor(s): David Kerekes
Address: Headpress, 40 Rossall Avenue, Radcliffe, Manchester M26 1JD
Fax: 0161 796 1935
Email: david.headpress@zen.co.uk
Imprints: Critical Vision
Parent Company: Headpress
Payment Details: By arrangement with author
Unsolicited Manuscripts: Yes

Crown House Publishing

Formed by The Anglo American Book Company in 1998 to publish a range of books by authors who are professionals of many years' experience, all highly respected in their own field. We specialise in the areas of psychotherapy, particularly NLP, hypnosis/hypnotherapy and personal growth, and choose our books with care for their content and character, and for the value of their contribution of both new and updated material to their particular field. The first of our books was published in 1995. From small beginnings the publishing business has grown so that up to December 1998 we have published 22 titles. All of these books fall within the category of psychology. In 1999 we plan to publish a further 15 titles.

Editor(s): David Bowman
Address: Crown Buildings, Bacyfelin, Carmarthen SA33 5ND
Telephone: 01267 211880
Fax: 01267 211882
Email: crownhouse@anglo-american.co.uk
Website: www.anglo-american.co.uk
Payment Details: 6-monthly
Unsolicited Manuscripts: Yes

G L Crowther

Author/publisher of a series of railway, tramway and waterway atlases of the UK (63 vols). They show navigable rivers; canals, locks, wharves, warehouses, towpaths; mineral tramroads; railways, locations of over 11000 railway stations including obscure and short-lived ones, tunnels, viaducts, rail-served factories, collieries and docks; horse, steam, cable and electric street tramways, termini and depots, as well as thousands of dates of use.

Address: 224 South Meadow Lane, Preston PR1 8JP
Telephone: 01772 257126

CRU Publishing Ltd

Publish directories, plant lists and databooks in the following industries: fertilizers and related chemicals - World Directory Of Fertilizer Manufacturers, World Directory Of Fertilizer Products, World Fertilizer Plant List & Atlas, Fertilizer Technology Databook, Sulphur Recovery Databook, Sulphuric Acid Databook; diamonds, jewellery and watches - World Diamond Industry Directory & Yearbook, Collecting & Classifying Coloured Diamonds, World Machinery & Technology Directory & Yearbook; metals - International Metals Databook, International Steel Databook & Atlas, Metal Monitor Annual. Also publish a number of magazines in these industries, and organise a series of conferences and seminars.

Editor(s): Adam Hives, Alex Meazzini
Address: 31 Mount Pleasant, London WC1X 0AD
Telephone: 0171 837 5600
Fax: 0171 664 4354
Email: smoore@cruint.tcom.co.uk
Website: www.cru-int.com
Parent Company: CRU International Ltd
Unsolicited Manuscripts: No

James Currey Publishers

Academic books on Africa, the Caribbean and the Third World. Approximately 30 titles published this year.

Editor(s): Douglas H Johnson, Lynn Taylor
Address: 73 Botley Road, Oxford OX2 0BS
Telephone: 01865 244111
Fax: 01465 246454
Email: jamescurrey@dial.pipex.com
Imprints: James Currey Ltd
Parent Company: James Currey Ltd
Payment Details: According to contract
Unsolicited Manuscripts: No. Write in the first instance with details of proposal

Curzon Press

Academic and university coursebooks, including reference books, mainly on Asian and Middle-eastern studies and mainly in the arts and social sciences.

Editor(s): Jonathan Price
Address: 15 The Quadrant, Richmond, Surrey TW9 1BP
Telephone: 0181 948 4660
Fax: 0181 332 6735
Email: publish@curzonpress.demon.co.uk
Imprints: Japan Library, Caucasus World
Unsolicited Manuscripts: To the Chief Editor

Dalesman Publishing Company

3 regional magazines - Dalesman, Cumbria And Lake District Magazine, Peak And Pennine. Also regional books on each of these areas about history and culture. Humour books. Walking guides for all abilities, mountain safety, potholing and mountain biking.

Editor(s): Terry Fletcher, Roly Smith
Address: Stable Courtyard, Broughton Hall, Skipton, North Yorkshire BD23 3AE
Email: editorial@dalesman.co.uk
Payment Details: Negotiable
Unsolicited Manuscripts: Yes

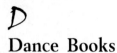

Dance Books

Dance as a theatre art.

Address: 15 Cecil Court, London WC2N 4EZ
Payment Details: By arrangement
Unsolicited Manuscripts: Yes

The C W Daniel Company

Alternative healing and the metaphysical.

Editor(s): Sebastian Hobnut
Address: 1 Church Path, Saffron Walden CB10 1JP
Telephone: 01799 526216
Fax: 01799 513462
Email: daniel_publishing@dial.pipex.com.
Website: cwdaniel.com
Imprints: Health Science Press, Neville Spearman Publishers, LN Fowler
Unsolicited Manuscripts: No

Daniels Publishing

In May 1996 Folens Publishers acquired the professional publishing lists of Daniels. The list includes PSHE, sex education, pregnancy, childcare, drugs education and self development. The packs feature photocopiable pages, selected publications contain INSET materials. The age range of the list is 5-18 and adults.

Editor(s): Colin Forbes
Address: Folens Publishers, Albert House, Apex Business Centre, Boscombe Road, Dunstable LY5 4RL
Telephone: 01582 478110
Fax: 01582 475524
Email: folens@folens.com
Website: http://www.folens.com
Parent Company: Folens Publishers
Unsolicited Manuscripts: To Colin Forbes

DARF Publishers Ltd

Facsimile reprints of travel and history of the Middle East, North Africa, and Islamic Spain; also translations of Arabic literature.

Address: 277 West End Lane, London NW6 1QS
Telephone: 0171 431 7009
Fax: 0171 431 7655
Unsolicited Manuscripts: No

D
David & Charles

Crafts, art techniques, decorative art & interiors, fine art, woodwork, photography, gardening, equestrian, country, walking, pets and natural history.

Address: Brunel House, Forde Close, Newton Abbot TQ12 4PU
Telephone: 01626 323200
Fax: 01626 323232
Imprints: Godsfield, David & Charles Children's Books, Pevensey Press
Parent Company: D&C Group Ltd
Payment Details: Royalties paid twice-yearly
Unsolicited Manuscripts: Yes, synopsis or sample chapters

Christopher Davies Publishers Ltd

Non-fiction: history, biography, natural history, and sport of Welsh interest only.

Editor(s): Christopher Davies
Address: PO Box 403, Swansea SA1 4YF
Telephone: 01792 648825
Fax: As phone
Imprints: Christopher Davies, Triskele Books
Payment Details: Royalty payments twice-yearly in April and October
Unsolicited Manuscripts: No

John Dawes Publications

Self-publisher of books about swimming pools: design, trade information etc. Catalogue available. Also consultant adviser to the Author-Publisher Network, concerned with self-publishing information and issues.

Editor(s): John Dawes, Pam Davis
Address: 12 Mercers, Hawkhurst, Kent TN18 4LH
Telephone: 01580 753346
Fax: As phone
Imprints: John Davies Publications
Payment Details: Self-payment by result
Unsolicited Manuscripts: Author-publisher primarily, but willing to discuss means of publishing mss concerned with swimming pool technology/design.

Giles de la Mare Publishers Ltd

Art & architecture, biography, history, music, general non-fiction.

Editor(s): Editor & Director: Giles de la Mare
Address: 3 Queen Square, London WC1N 3AU
Telephone: 0171 465 7607
Fax: 0171 465 7535
Email: gilesdlm@faber.co.uk
Payment Details: Royalty
Unsolicited Manuscripts: No

D

Andre Deutsch Ltd

Biography, cookery, children's, humour, history, film & tv, music, natural history, photography, sport, politics & current affairs, lifestyle, fitness.

Editor(s): Louise Dixon, Hannah Macdonald, Nicky Paris
Address: 76 Dean Street, London W1V 5HA
Fax: 0171 316 4499
Imprints: Andre Deutsch, Chameleon, Manchester United Books, Andre Deutsch Classics, Madcap
Parent Company: VCI
Unsolicited Manuscripts: No

Dickson Price Publishers Ltd

City & Guilds 224 course only.

Address: Hawthorn House, Bowdell Lane, Brookland, Romney Marsh, Kent TN29 9RW
Imprints: Dickson Price
Payment Details: By arrangement
Unsolicited Manuscripts: No

Dillons Publishing

Publish only commissioned books. Next publication The Universe And Philip Larkin by William Larkin.

Editor(s): T James
Address: 641 Castle Lane West, Bournemouth BH8 9TS
Telephone: 01202 396230
Unsolicited Manuscripts: No

Discovery Walking Guides Ltd

Walking guides/maps to popular holiday destinations. Essential to study our style, subject matter, on our website before approaching us.

Editor(s): David A Brawn, Ros Brawn
Address: 10 Tennyson Close, Northampton NN5 7HJ
Telephone: Initial contact by letter
Website: www.walking.demon.co.uk
Imprints: Warm Island Walking Guides
Payment Details: Negotiable
Unsolicited Manuscripts: No

Dolphin Book Co Ltd

Publish books of Spanish, Catalan and Latin American interest.

Address: Tredwr, Llangrannog, Llandysul SA44 6BA
Telephone: 01239 654404
Fax: 01239 654002
Unsolicited Manuscripts: No

Donhead Publishing Ltd

Donhead publishes books on building and architectural conservation, heritage and museum studies; scientific and technical books concerning the use of traditional building materials, and the conservation of those materials, looking at both the research and theory, along with the practical aspects of conservation. Would prefer it if potential authors were to contact us before sending a manuscript, either by telephone or letter to outline their ideas in order for us to assess whether it would be suitable for our list.

Editor(s): Jill Pearce
Address: Lower Coombe, Donhead St Mary, Shaftesbury SP7 9LY
Telephone: 01747 828422
Fax: 01747 828522
Email: jillpearce@donhead.u-net.com
Website: www.donhead.u-net.com
Imprints: Donhead
Unsolicited Manuscripts: Only if relevant to our list

Dorling Kindersley Ltd

Editor(s): Editorial Directors: Robin Wood (Adult); Ruth Sandys (Children's)
Address: 9 Henrietta Street, Covent Garden, London WC2E 8PS
Telephone: 0171 753 3594
Fax: 0171 753 7561
Website: www.dk.com
Parent Company: Dorling Kindersley
Unsolicited Manuscripts: No

The Dovecote Press Ltd

Non-fiction local interest, specialising in good quality well-illustrated books about individual English counties. Topography, natural history, guides, history, etc.

Address: Stanbridge, Wimborne, Dorset BH21 4JD
Telephone: 01258 840549
Fax: 01258 840958
Email: dovecote@mcmail.com
Unsolicited Manuscripts: Please enclose SAE

Downlander Publishing

Publisher of high-quality poetry only. Very few titles are accepted in any one year. Selection is rigorous. Candidates should be experienced in their craft. The house is non-profit. Currently our list is full for the next two years. A poet who is found acceptable must be prepared to contribute towards the cost of publication, simply because poetry is, while an important field in our literary heritage and development, commercially an inevitable loss-maker. Neither poet nor publisher will profit finanacially. Nevertheless, very good work should not be lost to view, or to posterity.

Editor(s): D Bourne-Jones
Address: 88 Oxendean Gardens, Lower Willingdon, Eastbourne, E Sussex BN22 0RS
Payment Details: Applicant must be prepared to meet basic production cost
Unsolicited Manuscripts: No. An initial letter with up to 5 example poems, plus SAE, please.

Downside Abbey Publications

A department of the famous Somerset Benedictine monastery Downside Abbey, it specialises in English Roman Catholic history and produces about two books a year in addition to the quarterly periodical of theology, philosophy and history The Downside Review. This latter also reviews books in its subject area.

Address: Downside Abbey, Stratton on the Fosse, Bath BA3 4RH
Telephone: 01761 235 109
Fax: 01761 235 124
Email: domcharles@downside.co.uk
Imprints: Downside Abbey
Parent Company: Downside Enterprise Ltd
Payment Details: No royalties on 1st editions
Unsolicited Manuscripts: Only after consultation

Dragon's Head Press

Independent small-press publishing project, founded in 1993 and affiliated to the Association of Little Presses. Aims to publish affordable, specialist books, booklets and periodicals devoted entirely to dragons, associated lore and related themes. Provides a forum for writers, researchers, poets and artists, as well as being an invaluable resource in its chosen literary and academic field.

Editor(s): Project Co-ordinator/Editor: Ade Dimmick
Address: PO Box 3369, London SW6 6JN
Email: dragonet@vtx.ch
Website: http://freespace.virgin.net/huw.rees/dc/
Payment Details: Negotiable
Unsolicited Manuscripts: No

Dramatic Lines

Dramatic Lines is a small independent company dedicated to the publication of dramatic material for use in schools and acting examinations. Publications include monologues, duologues, an introduction to Shakespeare through one-act plays, a resource book of drama lessons for teachers, Shakespeare rewrites, plays linked to history national curriculum and performance pieces for three and four players.

Editor(s): John Nicholas
Address: PO Box 201, Twickenham, London
Telephone: 0181 296 9502
Fax: 0181 296 9503
Imprints: Dramatic Lines
Payment Details: Negotiable
Unsolicited Manuscripts: Yes

Dublar Scripts

Publishers of pantomimes, one-act and full-length plays. Drama and comedy. Scripts aimed at the amateur theatre. Founded 1994.

Address: 204 Mercer Way, Romsey, Hants SO51 7QJ
Telephone: 01794 501277
Fax: 01794 502538
Email: dublar@hantslife.co.uk
Imprints: Sleepy Hollow Pantomimes
Unsolicited Manuscripts: All unsolicited manuscripts must be accompanied by SAE for return

Martin Dunitz Ltd

High-quality medical publishers covering areas such as dermatology, cardiology, neurology and orthopaedics. New areas include oncology, psychiatry, endocrinology and bone metabolism.

Address: The Livery House, 7-9 Pratt Street, London NW1 0AE
Telephone: 0171 482 2202
Fax: 0171 267 0159
Website: http://www.dunitz.co.uk

Eagle Publishing

Specialises in Christian books, primarily on prayer and spirituality, but also including a number of gift books incorporating classic and modern art.

Editor(s): Sue Wavre
Address: 6-7 Leapale Road, Guildford, Surrey GU1 4JX
Telephone: 01483 306309
Fax: 01483 579196
Email: eagle-indeprint@compuserve.com
Imprints: Eagle
Parent Company: Inter Publishing Services (IPS) Ltd
Payment Details: On application
Unsolicited Manuscripts: Yes

E

Earlsgate Press

Publisher of business management books.

Address: The Plantation, Rowdyke Lane, Wyberton, Boston, Lincs PE21 7AQ
Telephone: 01205 350764
Fax: 01205 359459
Email: earlsgatepress@btinternet.com
Website: www.btinternet.com/~earlsgate.press
Parent Company: Roberston Cox Ltd
Unsolicited Manuscripts: Yes but only business management

Earthscan Publications Ltd

Non-fiction publishers of books at all levels on the social, political and economic aspects of environmentally sustainable development.

Editor(s): Frances Maldermott, Ruth Coleman
Address: 120 Pentonville Road, London N1 9JN
Telephone: 0171 2780433
Fax: 0171 27811442
Email: earthinfo@earthscan.co.uk
Website: www.earthscan.co.uk
Parent Company: Kogan Page Ltd
Unsolicited Manuscripts: Yes

Ebury Press

Division of Random House UK, specialising in adult non-fiction publishing over a broad range of subjects, from cookery, gardening and lifestyle to psychology, health and personal development, and including high-quality illustrated books, film and television tie-ins, sports and popular music. Sales force of 15 reps working across the UK, supported by 25 head office sales staff, a dedicated marketing and publicity team; sales offices in the USA, Canada, Australia, New Zealand and South Africa; and a rights department selling rights in all languages throughout the world.

Editor(s): Fiona MacIntyre, Julian Shuckburgh, Denise Bates, Jake Lingwood (Ebury Press); Joanna Carreras (Vermilion); Judith Kendra (Rider Books)
Address: Random House, 20 Vauxhall Bridge Road, London SW1V 2SA
Telephone: 0171 840 8400
Fax: 0171 840 8406
Website: www.randomhouse.co.uk
Imprints: Ebury Press, Vermilion, Rider Books, Barrie & Jenkins
Parent Company: Random House UK Ltd
Unsolicited Manuscripts: Yes with return postage

Eco Logic Books

Publishers of environmental books that specialise in providing practical solutions to environmental problems.

Address: 10-12 Picton Street, Bristol BS6 5QA
Telephone: 0117 942 0165
Fax: 0117 942 0164
Unsolicited Manuscripts: No

Eddison Sadd Editions

A packaging company creating illustrated non-fiction titles as international co-editions for publisher clients. Experience in producing kits. Particularly interested in all self-help titles - New Age, health, craft, gardening, sex. Authors often need to write to fit a layout and be closely involved in design stages.

Editor(s): Ian Jackson
Address: St Chad's House, 148 Kings Cross Road, London WC1X 9DH
Payment Details: Fees when appropriate, or royalties based on net receipts
Unsolicited Manuscripts: No - synopsis first

Egmont World Ltd

Specialises in children's books for home and international markets: activity, sticker, baby, early learning, novelty, character books and annuals. Series - Mr Men; I Can Learn; Learning Rewards.

Editor(s): Nina Filipek, Stephanie Sloan
Address: Deanway Technology Centre, Wilmslow Road, Handforth, Cheshire SK9 3FB
Parent Company: Egmont Group, Denmark
Unsolicited Manuscripts: No - rarely used. No responsibility taken for the return of unsolicited submissions

E

Edward Elgar Publishing

A leading publisher in economics and related social sciences, Edward Elgar continues to commission actively, publishing 200 titles a year - monographs, reference works and advanced textbooks. In additon to economic science, we publish extensively on the politics and sociology of the national economies of Eastern Europe as well as the theory and practice of public policy.

Editor(s): Edward Elgar, Dymphna Evans
Address: Glensanda House, Montpelier Parade, Cheltenham GL50 1UA
Telephone: 01242 226934
Fax: 01242 262111
Website: http://www.e-elgar.co.uk
Imprints: EE

Elliot Right Way Books

We specialise in practical self-help instructional books covering a wide range of subjects, including: cookery, wine & beer making, weddings, speeches, letters, family finance, job search, business, health, quizzes, games & pastimes, pets, equestrian, motoring, fishing, sport and hobbies. Non-fiction only. Low prices - big sales.

Editor(s): Clive Elliot, Malcolm Elliot
Address: Kingswood Buildings, Brighton Road, Lower Kingswood, Tadworth, Surrey KT20 6TD
Imprints: Right Way, Clarion (bargain books)
Payment Details: Choice of royalty and advance or outright copyright payment
Unsolicited Manuscripts: Yes

Aidan Ellis Publishing

History, biography/autobiography, gardening, cookery, maritime; some novels.

Editor(s): Aidan Ellis, Lucinda Ellis
Address: Whinfield, Herbert Road, Salcombe, Devon TQ8 8HN
Telephone: 01548 842755
Fax: 01548 844356
Email: aidan@aepub.demon.co.uk
Website: www.demon.co.uk/aepub
Imprints: Aidan Ellis
Payment Details: Royalties
Unsolicited Manuscripts: Yes if non-fiction - synopsis and sample chapters & return postage. No fiction please.

Elmwood Press

Educational books, mainly mathematics.

Address: 80 Attimore Road, Welwyn Garden City AL8 6LP
Telephone: 01707 333232
Fax: 01707 333885
Email: elmwood@press.demon.co.uk
Unsolicited Manuscripts: Yes, for school mathematics texts

E
Emissary Publishing

Mainly humour.

Editor(s): Val Miller
Address: PO Box 33, Bicester, Oxon OX6 7PP
Imprints: Emissary
Parent Company: Manuscript Research
Payment Details: Royalties twice yearly
Unsolicited Manuscripts: No

The Eothen Press

An academic press devoted to publishing scholarly, but generally accessible, books on Turkey and Cyprus, particularly in the fields of modern history & politics, foreign policy, economics & economic history, social anthropology & sociology.

Address: 10 Manor Road, Hemingford Grey, Huntingdon PE18 9BX
Telephone: 01480 466106
Fax: As phone
Email: theeothenpress@btinternet.com
Imprints: The Eothen Press
Unsolicited Manuscripts: No

EPA Press

Publishers of guides to electrical and electronic regulations.

Address: Bulse Grange, Wendens Ambo, Saffron Walden CB11 4JT
Telephone: 01799 541207
Fax: 01799 541166

Epworth Press

Academic and theological works.

Editor(s): Gerald M Burt
Address: 20 Ivatt Way, Peterborough,Cambs PE3 7PG
Imprints: Epworth Press
Parent Company: Methodist Publishing House
Payment Details: Subject to negotiation
Unsolicited Manuscripts: Yes

The Erskine Press

Primarily Antarctic exploration. Occasional specialist interest short run books - non-fiction, biographical and autobiographical.

Editor(s): Stephen Gaston
Address: The Old Bakery, Banham, Norwich NR16 2HW
Telephone: 01953 887277
Fax: 01953 888361
Email: erskpres@aol.com
Imprints: Archival Facsimiles Ltd
Payment Details: Royalties paid every 6 months
Unsolicited Manuscripts: No

Estamp

Estamp was set up to meet the largely unfulfilled information needs of professionals and students specifically in the fields of printmaking, papermaking and book making. Our aim initally was to produce books which document what is going on in Britain today, reflecting contemporary ideas and attitudes as well as being a resource for working artists, printers and makers of all disciplines. Dedicated to expanding both the practical and aesthetic horizons, all books bearing an Estamp imprint are carefully chosen, researched and prepared. Estamp books have a unique blend of common sense and informed opinion and often represent some of our most authoritative and inspirational guidance available. We have recently begun a new series of books about particular artists and their working methods and a number of documentaries about specific practices on an international scale. Estamp continues to look for new titles.

Editor(s): Freelancers
Address: 204 St Albans Avenue, London W4 5JU
Telephone: 0181 994 2379
Fax: As phone
Email: st@estamp.demon.co.uk
Unsolicited Manuscripts: Yes

Euromoney Plc

A division of Euromoney Plc, Euromoney Books is a leading publisher of specialist financial books. Publishing over 100 titles, including textbooks, yearbooks, directories and country guides, the company provides authoritative and up-to-date information on financial products, practices and markets worldwide. Visit the website bookshop for details of new and best-selling titles, or for more information about the full range of books that Euromoney publishes contact by email.

Editor(s): Managing Editor: Christopher Garnett
Address: Nestor House, Playhouse Yard, London EC4V 5EX
Telephone: 0171 779 8860
Fax: 0171 779 8841
Email: books@euromoneyplc
Website: www.euromoneybooks.com
Imprints: Euromoney Books
Parent Company: Associated Newspapers
Unsolicited Manuscripts: To Jacqueline Grosch Lobo, Commissioning Editor

Evangelical Press

Publishers of evangelical Christian literature and Bible study material.

Address: Grange Close, Faverdale North Industrial Estate, Darlington DL3 0PH
Telephone: 01325 380232
Fax: 01325 466153
Website: www.evangelical-press.org
Payment Details: Royalty paid on publication
Unsolicited Manuscripts: Prefer outlines and contents list on first contact

E
Ex Libris Press

Illustrated paperbacks on West Country, mainly Wiltshire and Somerset; also books on various country topics and books on the Channel Islands. Also books production service.

Editor(s): Roger Jones
Address: 1 The Shambles, Bradford-on-Avon BA15 1JS
Telephone: 01225 863595
Fax: As phone
Email: roger@ex-libris.jpcinet.co.uk
Imprints: Ex Libris Press, Seaflower Books
Payment Details: 10% royalty twice-yearly
Unsolicited Manuscripts: Prefer initial letter with outline

Executive Grapevine International Ltd

A specialist information provider, we publish a series of directories on executive recruitment consultants, training and development consultants and providers of interim managers and non-executive directors. Each directory contains the leading suppliers in their respective fields and highlights the specialist areas in which they work. Comprehensive indexes assist the reader in their navigation of each directory. To complement this, we also produce a range of titles, focusing on the leading executives in the UK top companies. Organised by function, we have a dedicated edition for the following areas: chairmen chief executives and managing directors, finance executives, human resource executives, sales & marketing executives and information technology executives. All of these titles are updated on a regular basis.

Address: New Barnes Mill, Cottonmill Lane, St Albans AL1 2HA
Telephone: 01727 844335
Fax: 01727 844779
Email: executive.grapevine@dial.pipex.com
Website: www.d-net.com/executive.grapevine
Unsolicited Manuscripts: No

𝓕

Eyelevel Books

Publishers of biographical and historical titles, plus some children's material. Specialises in niche and unusual titles.

Editor(s): Jon Moore
Address: The Flat, Oldbury Grange, Lower Broadheath, Worcester WR2 6RQ
Telephone: 01905 427825
Email: books@eyelevel.enterprise-plc.com
Imprints: Eyelevel Books
Payment Details: By negotiation
Unsolicited Manuscripts: To Editor, non-returnable

Fabian Society

Britain's senior think-tank. Concerned since its foundation with evolutionary political and economic and progressive social change, the Fabian Society programme aims to explore the political ideas and reforms which will define the left of centre in the new century. We publish pamphlets and discussion papers in six programme areas: social inclusion, modernising Britain, redesigning the state, economic futures, the environmental age, and the next generation. Our quarterly magazine, Fabian Review, provides a forum for comment and analysis of the political issues behind the headlines.

Editor(s): Gavin Kelly, Rory Fisher
Address: 11 Dartmouth Street, London SW1H 9BN
Telephone: 0171 222 8877
Fax: 0171 976 7153
Email: fabian-society@geo2.poptel.org.uk
Website: www.fabian-society.org.uk
Payment Details: Negotiable
Unsolicited Manuscripts: Yes

ℱ
Famedram Publishers Ltd

Non-fiction: Scottish interest, local history, transport, arts, some cookery, football.

Address: P O Box 3, Ellon, Aberdeenshire AB41 9EA
Telephone: 01651 842429
Fax: 01651 842180
Email: famedram@artwork.co.uk
Website: www.artwork.co.uk
Imprints: Northern Books
Unsolicited Manuscripts: No

Farming Press

Countryside; farming and veterinary; tractor and transport history & technology.

Editor(s): Liz Ferretti, Hal Norman
Address: Miller Freeman UK Ltd, 2 Wharfedale Road, Ipswich IP1 4LA
Telephone: 01473 241122
Fax: 01473 242222
Email: farmingpress@dotfarming.com
Website: http://www.dotfarming.com
Parent Company: United News and Media
Unsolicited Manuscripts: No

$\mathcal{F}$

Farrand Press

A very small publisher of medicine and print history.

Editor(s): R A Farrand
Address: 50 Ferry Street, Isle of Dogs, London E14 3DT
Telephone: 0171 5157322
Fax: 0171 5373559
Email: farrandpri@aol.com
Payment Details: Royalty
Unsolicited Manuscripts: Yes

Feather Books

Publishes secular and religious books and music. Children's fiction includes the Quill Hedgehog novels. Also humorous verse and CDs/cassettes. Religious publications include Feather Books Poetry Series and works in association with Arthur James Ltd. Has a small religious drama list. Publishes a leading Anglo-American Christian poetry/prayers quarterly, The Poetry Church, 40pgs in length, £9 pa sub.

Editor(s): John Waddington-Feather, Tony Reavill, David Grundy, Paul Evans
Address: Fair View, Old Coppice, Lyth Bank, Shrewsbury SY3 0BW
Telephone: 01743 872177
Fax: As phone
Email: john@feather-books.com
Website: www.feather-books.com
Parent Company: Feather Books
Payment Details: Nil for poetry, but free copies
Unsolicited Manuscripts: With SAE, otherwise non-returnable

ℱ
Fernhurst Books

Watersports publisher specialising in 'how-to' books written by the leading expert in each field and where relevant endorsed by the authority. Books enable readers to get the very most out of their chosen sport. Covering all aspects of dinghies, catamarans, yachts and motorboats, whether racing or cruising; also seamanship, navigation, craft maintenance and equipment, plus surfing, waterskiing, sea kayaking.

Editor(s): Tim Davison
Address: Duke's Path, High Street, Arundel BN18 9AJ
Telephone: 01903 882277
Fax: 01903 882715
Email: sales@fernhurstbooks.co.uk
Website: www.fernhurstbooks.co.uk
Unsolicited Manuscripts: No, please phone and enquire

FHG Publications Ltd

Publisher of UK holiday accommodation guides, published annually. Titles include Pets Welcome, Golf Guide, Farm Holiday Guide. Paid entries accepted from owners of hotels, B&B, self-catering properties, etc.

Editor(s): Anne Cuthbertson
Address: Abbey Mill Business Centre, Seedhill, Paisley PA1 1TJ
Telephone: 0141 887 0428
Fax: 0141 889 7204
Email: 106111.3065@compuserve.com
Parent Company: IPC Magazines

Fiddle Faddle Press

Publishes the work of writing/editing/bookmaking project involving hundreds of school pupils in Hereford and Worcester. Provides a unique resource for teachers - an imaginative writing teaching package. Titles include A Donkity Crisis, Shapeshifter/ Sands, Shapeshifter/Sea (£3.99 each) and Spellbound and Spellbound 2 (£2.99 each). Librarians' comments include 'Worthy of top marks!' 'Original and pleasingly readable book.' 'Amazing and captivating storyline . . . '

Editor(s): Publisher: Ann Palmer
Address: 6 Kensington House, 53 Graham Road, Malvern WR14 2HU
Telephone: 01684 574525
Unsolicited Manuscripts: No

First & Best In Education Ltd

All primary and secondary education subjects plus school management titles.

Editor(s): Katy Charge, Julia Perkins
Address: Earlstrees Court, Earlstrees Road, Corby, Northants NN17 4HH
Telephone: 01536 399004
Fax: 01536 399012
Email: firstbest9@aol.com
Imprints: MSL
Payment Details: Royalties paid twice yearly

ℱ
First Class Books

Specialises in study guides to help people working to obtain NVQ in Care awards at level 2 and level 3.

Address: PO Box 1, Portishead, Bristol BS20 9BR
Telephone: 01823 323126
Fax: 01823 321876
Unsolicited Manuscripts: No

Fitzroy Dearborn Publishers

Reference books in the following areas: history, the arts, philosophy & religion, social sciences, science & technology, international affairs, business, banking & finance.

Editor(s): Lesley Henderson, Roda Morrison, Carol Jones, Mark Hawkins-Dady, Anne-Lucie Norton
Address: 310 Regent Street, London W1R 5AJ
Telephone: 0171 636 6627
Fax: 0171 636 6982
Email: postroom@fitzroydearborn.demon.co.uk
Website: www.fitzroydearborn.com
Unsolicited Manuscripts: Yes

Flambard Press

Flambard, founded in 1991, is particularly sympathetic to new or neglected writers and is keen to nourish developing talent. Based in the North and supported by Northern Arts, Flambard sees itself as having a role to play in the literary life of the region, but is open to all-comers and is not a regional publishing house. Flambard began as a poetry press and still concentrates on poetry, but now includes fiction in its list, both novels and collections of short stories. It is developing a crime fiction series.

Editor(s): Margaret Lewis, Peter Lewis
Address: Stable Cottage, East Fourstones, Hexham NE47 5DX
Telephone: 01434 674360
Fax: 01434 674178
Website: signatur@dircom.co.uk
Imprints: Flambard
Payment Details: Royalty for fiction. Usually fixed fee for poetry.
Unsolicited Manuscripts: We accept these, but prefer a preliminary letter. Informative letter about writer needed with manuscript.

Flicks Books

Specialist publishers of books and journals on film and cinema, and related media such as television. Our list covers fiction and non-fiction film, archival collections, histories of filmmaking in individual countries, monographs on important directors and films, reference works and directories, interviews with filmmakers, film scripts, and the reissue of out-of-print documents.

Editor(s): Matthew Stevens
Address: 29 Bradford Road, Trowbridge, Wiltshire BA14 9AN
Telephone: 01225 767728
Fax: 01225 760418
Payment Details: Royalty or fee system
Unsolicited Manuscripts: Yes

Folens Publishers

Folens is now Britain's largest publisher of teacher ideas materials and a significant publisher of curricular resources. The Dunstable site provides product creation, sales & marketing, financial and distribution services and employs over 100 staff. Growth has been rapid and sustained. We publish in excess of 1000 of our own titles and produce over 150 new titles per year for ages 4-16. Folens publish over 80 Big Books, 50 Belair books, 350 reading books, poetry, major resources for every curriculum area plus a wide range of teacher idea books.

Editor(s): Mike Gould (Secondary), Karen McCaffery (Primary)
Address: Albert House, Apex Business Centre, Boscombe Road, Dunstable, Beds LU5 4RL
Telephone: 01582 478110
Fax: 01582 475524
Email: folens@folens.com
Website: http://www.folens.com
Imprints: Framework Press, Daniels Publishing
Parent Company: Folens Publishers, Ireland
Unsolicited Manuscripts: To the appropriate editor

Folly Publications

Paperback books about castles and fortified houses up to the 17th century and parish churches up to c1800. The 32 volumes published since 1988 cover all the relevant buildings in Scotland, Wales and the Isle of Man, plus a selection of castles in Ireland. For England there are castles and churches books for Shropshire, Staffordshire, Warwickshire, Herefordshire, Worcestershire, Cumbria and Northumberland, and there are churches books only for Cheshire, Derbyshire and the Forest of Dean. Each book has an introduction and a gazetteer of up to 300 photographs by author-publisher Mike Salter plus old postcards and prints. New titles planned for 1999 are Old Parish Churches Of Cornwall and Castles Of Devon And Cornwall.

Address: Folly Cottage, 151 West Malvern Road, Malvern, Worcs WR14 4AY
Telephone: 01684 565211
Unsolicited Manuscripts: No

Food Trade Press Ltd

Books on food technology, science and processing, general food industry books, food hygiene, food engineering and historical books on food, plus directories.

Editor(s): Howard Binsted
Address: Station House, Hortons Way, Westerham, Kent TN16 1BZ
Imprints: Food Trade Press, Food Trade Review
Payment Details: 10% royalty on retail price of books
Unsolicited Manuscripts: Yes

Footprint Handbooks

Publishers of travel guides covering Latin America and the Caribbean, Africa, South Asia, Southeast Asia, Middle East and Europe. 36 guidebooks in the series and more in the pipeline.

Editor(s): Patrick Dawson
Address: 6 Riverside Court, Lower Bristol Road, Bath BA2 3DZ
Telephone: 01225 469141
Fax: 0122 469461
Email: handbooks@footprint.cix.co.uk
Website: footprint-handbooks.co.uk

Forbes Publications

Publishers of a wide range of books for teachers - at both primary and secondary level. Catalogues available on request.

Address: Abbott House, 1-2 Hanover Street, London W1R 9WB
Telephone: 0171 495 7945
Fax: 0171 495 7916
Parent Company: The Rapport Group

Forth Naturalist & Historian

The FNH Board publishes a wide variety of publications concerned with the natural and social history of central Scotland. Foremost amongst these publications is the annual journal Forth Naturalist And Historian. In addition it publishes a range of books, maps and pamphlets concerning the natural environment and the social history of the region. A recent publication is The Lure Of Loch Lomond. Its major publication was the book Central Scotland, which has also formed the basis of a CD-ROM schools resource Heart of Scotland Environment. The Board also organises an annual symposium Man And The Landscape, held each November since 1975 at the University of Stirling.

Editor(s): Editor/Sec. L Corbett
Address: University of Stirling, Stirling FK9 4LA
Telephone: 01259 215091
Fax: 01786 464994
Email: lindsay.corbett@stir.ac.uk
Website: www.stir.ac.uk/theuni/forthnat
Imprints: Agent/distributor for Clackmannanshire Field Studies Society
Payment Details: No payments have been made to contributors
Unsolicited Manuscripts: Yes

W Foulsham & Co Ltd

All non-fiction subject areas.

Editor(s): Wendy Hobson, Jane Hotson
Address: The Publishing House, Bennetts Close, Cippenham, Slough, Berkshire SL1 5AP
Imprints: Foulsham Educational, Quantum
Unsolicited Manuscripts: Yes

Four Courts Press

Founded in 1970 as a small press, and for many years published occasionally. Since 1992 the Press has been expanding steadily, with the result that it is now a significant publisher of academic books, particularly in the area of Irish studies.

Editor(s): Martin Fanning
Address: Four Courts Press, Fumbally Court, Dublin 8, Ireland
Telephone: 353 1 453 4668
Fax: 353 1 453 4672
Email: info@four-courts-press.ie
Website: www.four-courts-press.ie
Imprints: Open Air Publications
Parent Company: FCP
Unsolicited Manuscripts: Yes

ℱ
Fourth Estate Ltd

General trade publisher, independent. Publisher of the Year 1997. Literary fiction. Commercial fiction. General non-fiction: biography, autobiography, history, travel, popular science, popular culture. Humour. Illustrated non-fiction: cookery.

Editor(s): Virginia Bonham Carter, Louise Haines, Andy Miller, Katie Owen, Nicholas Pearson, Christopher Potter, Clive Priddle, Caroline Upcher
Address: 6 Salem Road, London W2 4BU
Telephone: 0171 627 8993
Fax: 0171 792 3176
Email: general@4thestate.co.uk
Imprints: 4th Estate Paperbacks, Guardian Books
Unsolicited Manuscripts: No

Framework Press

In June 1996 Folens Publishers acquired the Framework Press list. Folens Framework INSET materials, handbooks and packs are aimed at secondary teachers and managers. Framework resources address key issues in teaching, management and other related issues; they are excellent value for money in comparison to the cost of using outside trainers. The packs and INSET materials are photocopiable.

Editor(s): Colin Forbes
Address: Folens Publishers, Albert House, Apex Business Centre, Boscombe Road, Dunstable, Beds LU5 4RL
Telephone: 01582 478110
Fax: 01582 475524
Email: folens@folens.com
Website: www.folens.com
Parent Company: Folens Publishers
Unsolicited Manuscripts: To the Editor

F

Free Association Books

Psychotherapy, psychiatry, psychoanalysis, counselling, social welfare, addiction studies, organisational studies, child and adolescent studies, women's studies, cultural and social studies, philosophy, health and complementary medicine.

Editor(s): Publisher: Trevor Brown; Editors: Donald Most, David Stonestreet
Address: 57 Warren Street, London W1P 5PA
Telephone: 0171 388 3182
Fax: 0171 388 3187
Email: fab@fitzrovia.demon.co.uk
Website: Yes
Imprints: Fab, Free Association Books, Fitzrovia
Payment Details: Standard academic terms
Unsolicited Manuscripts: Yes

Samuel French Ltd

Scripts of stage plays only, intended for performance by amateur and professional theatre companies and therefore accompanied by stage directions, lighting, sound effects, plots etc. Seldom text books and no screenplays or scripts for other media.

Address: 52 Fitzroy Street, Fitzrovia, London W1P 6JR
Telephone: 0171 387 9373
Fax: 0171 387 2161
Email: theatre@samuelfrench-london.co.uk
Website: www.samuelfrench-london.co.uk
Imprints: French's Acting Editions
Parent Company: Samuel French Inc, New York
Unsolicited Manuscripts: Yes

The Frogmore Press

Publishes the bi-annual literary magazine The Frogmore Papers (founded 1983) as well as occasional anthologies and collections by individual poets, most recently Other Lilies by Marita Over. The Frogmore Poetry Prize will be awarded for the thirteenth consecutive year in 1999. Previous winners include Tobias Hill, John Latham, Caroline Price and Mario Petrucci.

Editor(s): Jeremy Page
Address: 42 Morehall Avenue, Folkstone, Kent CT19 4EF
Imprints: Crabflower Pamphlets (1989-1997)
Unsolicited Manuscripts: No

David Fulton Publishers Ltd

David Fulton Publishers, established in 1987, has over 350 titles in print, covering the full range of education and teaching from 3 to 19 years. The Fulton list has a distinctive focus on textbooks for student teachers and practical, professional books for teachers, coordinators and managers in mainstream and special schools. We are always interested in ideas for new books. Prospective authors should contact John Owens at our London address.

Editor(s): John Owens, Alison Foyle (Special Education)
Address: 26-27 Boswell Street, London WC1N 3JD
Telephone: 0171 405 5606
Fax: 0171 831 4840
Email: mail@fultonbooks.co.uk
Website: www.fultonbooks.co.uk
Payment Details: Royalty (no advances) paid twice a year
Unsolicited Manuscripts: No

FunFax Ltd

Children's books - from pre-school to early teens, non fiction activity and novelty.

Editor(s): Lisa Telford
Address: Tide Mill Way, Woodbridge, Suffolk IP12 1AN
Imprints: FunFax, MicroFax, Quiz Quest, The Lettermen, Mad Jack, Funpax, DK Stickers.
Parent Company: Dorling Kindersley Ltd
Payment Details: Flat fee no royalties
Unsolicited Manuscripts: No

Gallery Of Photography

Editor(s): Tanya King
Address: Meeting House Square, Temple Bar, Dublin 2, Ireland
Telephone: 353 1 6714654
Fax: 353 1 6709293
Email: gallery@irish-photography.com
Website: www.irish-photography.com
Payment Details: Negotiable
Unsolicited Manuscripts: No

G
Garnet Publishing Ltd

Subject areas art, architecture, photography, travel guides, cookery, fiction: all based on regions and different countries, especially the Middle East. 160 titles in all.

Editor(s): Emma Hawker
Address: 8 Southern Court, South Street, Reading, Berkshire RG1 4QS
Telephone: 0118 959 7847
Fax: 0118 959 7356
Email: enquiries@garnet-ithaca.demon.co.uk
Imprints: Ithaca Press
Unsolicited Manuscripts: Please send synopsis and CV to Editorial Dept

Gateway Books

Alternative health, alternative science, cosmic questions, healing, self-help and psychology. Gateway publishes books which try to represent different ways of understanding the unfolding new spiritual and social changes of the coming millennium.

Editor(s): Submissions Editor: Mari Bartholomew
Address: The Hollies, Wellow, Bath BA2 8QJ
Unsolicited Manuscripts: No - synopsis only

Geddes & Grosset Ltd

Publishers of popular reference & children's books. Packagers of children's and general books. Publishers of books used as incentives.

Editor(s): Mike Miller
Address: David Dale House, New Lanark, Scotland ML11 9DJ
Telephone: 01555 665000
Fax: 01555 665694
Imprints: Geddes & Grosset, Tarantula Books
Parent Company: DC Thomson & Co Ltd, Dundee
Payment Details: Royalty or fee
Unsolicited Manuscripts: Yes

Robert Gibson & Sons Ltd

Educational publishers of primary and secondary school books.

Address: 17 Fitzroy Place, Glasgow G3 7SF
Telephone: 0141 248 5674
Fax: 0141 221 8219
Email: robert.gibsonsons@btinternet

𝒢 Ginn & Co

Publishes materials for the teaching of a variety of subjects in primary schools. Provides a comprehensive range of resources offering solutions for teachers and schools throughout the UK and beyond. Aims to provide high quality materials and sevice to primary schools through a wide variety of resources to meet teachers' changing needs.

Editor(s): Publishers: Catherine Baker (literacy), Ruth Burdett (mathematics & foundation)
Address: Linacre House, Jordan Hill, Oxford OX2 8DP
Telephone: 01865 888000
Fax: 01865 314222
Email: services@ginn.co.uk
Website: www.ginn.co.uk
Parent Company: Reed Elsevier

Glas Publishers UK

Has been publishing the work of mainly present-day Russian writers in English translation since 1992. Authors range from Aleshkovsky to Zinik by way of Makanin and Pelevin. 'The texts and voices out of Russia come through with formidable insistence.' George Steiner.

Editor(s): Natasha Perova, Arch Tait
Address: Dept of Russian, University of Birmingham, Birmingham B15 2TT
Telephone: 0121 414 6047
Fax: As phone
Email: a.l.tait@bham.ac.uk
Website: www.bham.ac.uk/russian/glascover.html
Imprints: Glas New Russian Writing
Parent Company: Glas Publishers, Moscow
Payment Details: By agreement
Unsolicited Manuscripts: By contemporary Russian prose writers, in Russian or translation

Global Books Ltd

Publishers of Simple Guides, increasingly popular 'briefing' books currently including series on language, religions and customs & etiquette of countries worldwide. Imprints also include Global Oriental, with titles relating principally to Japan in the subject areas of memoirs & biographies, history, popular literature & poetry, travel, and Renaissance Books which features titles on contemporary social issues.

Editor(s): Paul Norbury
Address: PO Box 219, Folkestone, Kent CT20 3LZ
Telephone: 01303 226799
Fax: 01303 243087
Email: globook@aol.com
Imprints: Global Oriental, Renaissance Books
Unsolicited Manuscripts: No, introductory letter first please

Gomer Press

Founded in 1992, Gomer Press publishes a wide range of literature and non-fiction - all with a Welsh background or relevance - biography, history, aspects of Welsh culture. Books in English for children are published under the Pont imprint - all with a Welsh background or relevance. Also Welsh language literature, non-fiction and children's books.

Editor(s): Mairwen Prys Jones, Gordon Jones, Bethan Matthews
Address: New Road, Llandysul, Ceredigion SA44 4BQ
Telephone: 01559 36234
Fax: 01559 363758
Email: gwasg@gomer.co.uk
Website: www.gomer.co.uk
Imprints: Pont
Unsolicited Manuscripts: No, preliminary letter required

The complete guide to book publishers in the UK & Ireland   137

G Adam Gordon

Small publishing firm specialising in transport titles, especially relating to tramways.

Editor(s): Adam Gordon
Address: Priory Cottage, Chetwode, Nr Buckingham MK18 4LB
Telephone: 01280 848650
Unsolicited Manuscripts: Yes

Gospel Standard Trust Publications

The Trust publishes books that commend the free and sovereign grace of God. Writers are usually invited to write on given subjects. Titles cover the interest of the very young child and the serious theologian.

Editor(s): B A Ramsbottom
Address: 12b Roundwood Lane, Harpenden, Herts AL5 3EW
Telephone: 01582 765448
Fax: 01582 469148
Email: gospelstandardpublications@btinternet.co
Imprints: Gospel Standard Trust Publications
Payment Details: By agreement
Unsolicited Manuscripts: No

Gower Publishing Co Ltd

Gower is widely recognised as one of the world's leading publishers on management and business practice. Its programmes range from 1000-page handbooks through practical manuals to popular paperbacks. These cover all the main functions of management: human resource development, sales and marketing, project management, finance, etc. Gower also produces training videos and activities manuals on a wide range of management skills, and publishes a well-regarded list of titles on library and information management.

Editor(s): Julia Scott, Josephine Goodenham, Jonathan Norman
Address: Gower House, Croft Road, Aldershot, Hants GU11 3HR
Telephone: 01252 331551
Fax: 01252 344405
Email: proposals@gowerpub.com
Website: www.gowerpub.com

Graham & Whiteside Ltd

Publishes high-quality printed and electronic data on major companies throughout the world.The Major Companies Series Of Directories are long established, the oldest having been published annually for the past 22 years. Our databases of 80,000 companies are updated rigorously by teams of editors and researchers, who contact every company directly to obtain information.This accurate and comprehensive series has become established as an essential business reference tool for many of the leading national and international coroporations and institutional and business libraries.

Editor(s): Refer to individual titles
Address: Tuition House, 5-6 Francis Grove, London SW19 4DT
Telephone: 0181 947 1011
Fax: 0181 947 1163
Email: sales@major-co-data.com
Website: www.major-co-data.com
Parent Company: The Thomson Corporation
Unsolicited Manuscripts: No

G
W F Graham (Northampton) Ltd

Extensive range of excellent value, low-priced mass market children's activity books, and importers of fibre-tip pens. WF Graham is experienced in organising the design and print of customer-specific special interest and branded books and activity book packs. Has an established reputation as suppliers to large publishing houses, international airlines and high volume mass market outlets. Lines are continually reviewed and added to, with high gloss finish a regular feature. We export worldwide and can arrange foreign language overlays as required.

Address: 2 Pondwood Close, Moulton Park, Northampton NN3 6RT
Telephone: 01604 645537
Fax: 01604 648414

Graham-Cameron Publishing

We act as packagers for other publishers usually acting on their initiatives. For this reason, please don't send us mss or proposals. We are also agents for over 40 illustrators of children's and educational books.

Editor(s): Helen Graham-Cameron, Mike Graham-Cameron
Address: The Studio, 23 Holt Road, Sheringham, Norfolk NR26 8NB
Imprints: Graham-Cameron Illustration
Unsolicited Manuscripts: No

g

Grandreams Ltd

Children's book publishers. Novelty books, story books, pop-ups, annuals, colouring & activity. Minimum order £500 net in UK.

Address: 435-437 Edgware Road, London W2 1TH
Telephone: 0171 724 5333
Fax: 0171 724 5777
Imprints: Goodnight Sleeptight
Unsolicited Manuscripts: No

Grant Books

Specialists in golf books; publishers of limited edition golf books and golf club histories.

Address: The Coach House, New Road, Cutnall Green, Droitwich WR5 0PQ
Telephone: 01299 851 588
Fax: 01299 851 446
Email: grantbooks@globalnet.co.uk
Website: www.grantbooks.co.uk
Unsolicited Manuscripts: On golf subjects but not fiction or instructional

Granta Books

Small independent publisher of fiction and non-fiction, including biography, travel writing and current affairs.

Editor(s): Frances Coady, Neil Belton
Address: 2/3 Hanover Yard, Noel Road, London N1 8BE
Telephone: 0171 704 9776
Fax: 0171 354 3469
Email: info@granta.com
Website: www.granta.com
Unsolicited Manuscripts: Yes - looked at

Green Books

Environment, eco-spirituality, politics and cultural issues. No fiction or children's books. Publish around eight new books per year.

Editor(s): John Elford
Address: Foxhole, Dartington, Totnes, Devon TQ9 6EB
Email: greenboooks@gn.apc.org
Website: www.greenbooks.co.uk
Imprints: Green Books, Resurgence Books, Green Earth Books
Payment Details: Twice-yearly royalties
Unsolicited Manuscripts: No, brief synopsis intitially please

W Green - The Scottish Law Publisher

W Green, the Scottish law publishing company of Sweet, Maxwell, publishes an unrivalled collection of books, periodicals and encyclopaedias on Scots law, as well as digital products.

Address: 21 Alva Street, Edinburgh EH2 4PS
Telephone: 0131 225 4879
Fax: 0131 225 2104
Website: www.wgreen.co.uk
Parent Company: Thomson Corporation

Greenhill Books

Military History.

Editor(s): Lionel Leventhal, Kate Ryle, Jonathan North
Address: Park House, 1 Russell Gardens, London NW11 9NN
Imprints: Greenhill Books
Parent Company: Lionel Leventhal Ltd
Payment Details: Royalties
Unsolicited Manuscripts: Preliminary letter with information about project in advance of submission

Gresham Books Ltd

Specialised publisher offering hymn books, prayer books and service books in limited editions for schools and churches; schools histories have recently been added to the range of publications. Gresham Books continue to offer a reprint service and books on or about wood engraving; music books continue in their list.

Editor(s): Mary Green
Address: The Gresham Press, PO Box 61, Henley On Thames, Oxon RG9 3LQ
Telephone: 0118 940 3789
Fax: As phone
Email: greshambks@aol.com
Website: www.gresham-books.co.uk
Imprints: Gresham Books
Payment Details: Negotiable
Unsolicited Manuscripts: No

Grevatt & Grevatt

Small print runs in the following areas: descriptive linguistics; poetry; religious studies, especially Hinduism. Privately funded, so generally no royalties unless more than 500 copies are sold. Authors receive 2-10 complimentary copies.

Editor(s): S Y Killingley
Address: 9 Rectory Drive, Newcastle Upon Tyne NE3 1XT
Imprints: Grevatt & Grevatt, S Y Killingley
Unsolicited Manuscripts: No. All enquiries must include SAE

Grub Street

Cookery, health, aviation, military history.

Editor(s): John Davies, Anne Dolamore
Address: The Basement, 10 Chivalry Road, London SW11 1HT
Telephone: 0171 924 3966
Fax: 0171 738 1009
Unsolicited Manuscripts: Yes, but must include return postage

Guild Of Pastoral Psychology

We publish some lectures to do with Depth Psychology of C G Jung and spirituality. These are in booklet form - £2 - £3 plus postage. Only lectures given to the Guild are considered.

Editor(s): Guild Committee
Address: 164 Ilbert Street, London W10 4DQ
Telephone: 0181 964 1559
Fax: As phone

g Gwasg Gwenffrwd

Academic; reference; bibliograpies; Africa; Latin America; Pacific Islands; Czechoslovakia; poetry; labour history; Wales and Welsh; linguistics; anthropology; history and mission history.

Editor(s): H G A Hughes
Address: Fron Gelyn, Llandyrnog, Denbigh LL16 4LY
Imprints: Astic, Bronant, Translations Wales, Hanes Gweithwyr Cymru, Hyddgen, South Seas Studies
Payment Details: By agreement
Unsolicited Manuscripts: No all work commissioned

Gwasg Y Dref Wen

Welsh language, children's books and books for adult Welsh learners.

Address: 28 Church Road, Whitchurch, Cardiff CF4 2EA
Telephone: 01222 617860
Fax: 01222 610507
Imprints: Dref Wen
Unsolicited Manuscripts: Yes

Peter Halban Publishers

Publishers of general non-fiction, including biography, politics, history, with concentration on Jewish subjects and Middle East. While fiction is considered, very few titles are published annually. NB all trade orders to Littlehampton Book Services, Centre Warehouse, Columbia Building, Faraday Close, Durrington, Worthing BN13 3HD.

Editor(s): Martine Halban, Peter Halban
Address: 42 South Molton Street, London W1Y 1HB
Telephone: 0171 491 1582
Fax: 0171 629 5381
Email: peterhalbanpublishers@compuserve.com
Unsolicited Manuscripts: Synopsis and letter essential

Robert Hale Ltd

General adult fiction (not sf, romances, category crime or horror). General adult non-fiction, crafts, mind body and spirit, practical reference, gemmology, bridge, sport, military, music, angling and photography.

Address: Clerkenwell House, 45/47 Clerkenwell Green, London EC1R 0HT
Telephone: 0171 251 2661
Fax: 0171 490 4958
Imprints: Nag Press
Payment Details: Royalties paid half-yearly
Unsolicited Manuscripts: Yes, synopsis and specimen copies first

Halsgrove Publishing

Non-fiction publishers & distributors, specialising in southern England, local studies, art, national history.

Editor(s): Steven Pugsley, Simon Butler
Address: Halsgrove House, Lower Moor Way, Tiverton, Devon EX16 6SS
Telephone: 01884 243242
Fax: 01884 243325
Email: steven@halsgrove.com
Imprints: Devon Books, Dorset Books, Somerset Books, Exmoor Books, Country Magazines, Redcliffe, Halsgrove
Parent Company: DA Atkin (Exmoor) Ltd

Hamlyn Octopus

Music, film, style, fashion, cookery, art and craft, interiors, gardening, beauty, sex, health, New Age, sport, pet care, natural history, history, reference and graphic novels.

Address: Michelin House, 81 Fulham Road, London SW3 6RB
Imprints: Hamlyn Octopus
Parent Company: Octopus Publishing Group

Hanbury Plays

Publishers of plays, sketches, monologues and plays for all-women casts.

Editor(s): Brian J Burton
Address: Keeper's Lodge, Broughton Green, Droitwich WR9 7EE
Telephone: 01905 23132
Fax: As phone
Imprints: Hanbury Plays
Payment Details: Negotiable, but no charge to authors for publications accepted
Unsolicited Manuscripts: No - synopsis first

Hansib Publications Ltd

Publishers of books that are of interest to African, Asian and Caribbean people. History, politics, culture,sports, tourism & investments, biographical.

Editor(s): Arif Ali
Address: Tower House, 141-149 Fonthill Road, London N4 3HF
Telephone: 0171 281 1191
Fax: 0171 263 9656
Email: hansib@resolutions.netkonect.co.uk
Payment Details: For discussion
Unsolicited Manuscripts: Yes

ℋ

Happy Cat Books

Children's books for under 5's: board books, sticker books, picture books with simple texts.

Editor(s): Martin C West
Address: Fieldfares, Mill Lane, Bradfield, Essex CO11 2UT
Telephone: 01255 870902
Fax: As phone
Email: mcwest@happycat.co.uk
Payment Details: Fee basis
Unsolicited Manuscripts: No

Happy Walking International Ltd

Short Circular Walks; Long Circular Walks; Challenge Walks; Coast Walks. Derbyshire Heritage series; Nottinghamshire Heritage series; Ghosts & Legends series; Cycling Around series; Marathon Walk series. John Merrill Walk Guides.

Address: Unit 1, Molyneux Business Park, Whitworth Road, Darley Dale, Matlock, Derbyshire DE4 2HJ
Telephone: 01629 735911
Fax: As phone
Email: john.merrill@virgin.net
Website: www.happywalkinginternational.co.uk
Parent Company: Happy Walking Ltd
Payment Details: Agreement is 10% royalty
Unsolicited Manuscripts: Yes

Harden's Guides

Producers of quality consumer guides to London and the UK, with a particular emphasis on restaurant guides. Leading publishers of quality corporate gifts.

Editor(s): Richard Harden, Peter Harden
Address: 14 Buckingham Street, London WC2N 6DF
Telephone: 0171 839 4763
Fax: 0171 839 7561
Email: mail@hardens.com

Harlequin Mills & Boon Ltd

Romance novels in varying lengths. Tipsheets available with SAE, or on website.

Editor(s): Editorial Director: K Stoeker
Address: Eton House, 18-24 Paradise Road, Richmond, Surrey TW9 1SR
Telephone: 0131 288 2800
Website: www.romance.com
Imprints: Mills & Boon, Silhouette, Mira
Parent Company: Harlequin Enterprises Ltd
Payment Details: Advance against royalties
Unsolicited Manuscripts: Prefer query first

ℋ
Adam Hart (Publishers) Ltd

Independent publishing company founded in 1992 to publish books on Elizabethan and Renaissance history, especially the historical research of the historian A D Wraight. To date four substantial historic works have been published, and two more are due for publication in 1999.

Editor(s): A D Walker-Wraight, Y M Hart
Address: The Rose, 10 Idmiston Road, London SE27 9HG
Telephone: 0181 670 5182
Fax: As phone
Website: www. author.co.uk/marlowe.htm

The Harvill Press

Independent publisher, chiefly of literature in translation. Also publishes illustrated monographs in the fields of ethnography, ethnology, natural history, gardening and sailing.

Editor(s): Guido Waldman, Ian Pindar, Sophie Henby-Price, Victoria Mather
Address: 2 Aztec Row, Berners Road, London N1 0PW
Telephone: 0171 704 8766
Fax: 0171 704 8805
Website: www.harvill-press.com
Imprints: Panther
Unsolicited Manuscripts: Yes, but outline and specimen chapter first

Hawthorns Publications Ltd

Children's illustrated story books; children's fiction and non-fiction; school aid books; biography; history.

Address: Pond View House, 6A High Street, Otford, Sevenoaks, Kent TN14 5PQ
Telephone: 01959 522325
Fax: 01959 522368
Imprints: Pond View Books
Payment Details: Royalties paid twice-yearly
Unsolicited Manuscripts: Yes must be supplied with SAE

Hayes Press

Christian publisher of hymn books, doctrinal, gospel and calendars.

Address: Essex Road, Leicester LE4 9EE
Telephone: 01162 461682
Fax: 01162 740200
Email: hayespress@aol.com

ℋ
Haynes Publishing

Authoritative books on cars, motorcycles, motorsport and other wheels-related subjects, including biographies, together with an extensive range of car and motorcycle service and repair manuals. Also a limited number of maritime titles.

Editor(s): Editorial Director: Darryl Beach; Eds: Flora Myer, Alison Roelich
Address: Sparkford, Nr Yeovil, Somerset BA22 7JJ
Telephone: 01963 440635
Fax: 01963 440023
Email: sales@haynes-manuals.co.uk
Website: www.haynes.com
Imprints: Haynes, Patrick Stephens Ltd, G T Foulis & Co, Oxford Illustrated Press
Payment Details: Normal royalty terms
Unsolicited Manuscripts: Yes, but prefer synopsis only first

Hazleton Publishing

Widely recognised as the world's leading motorsport publisher. Our range of motorsport annuals dates back to 1951 with the birth of Autocourse, now in its 48th year of publication, dedicated to reviewing the Formula 1 season. Motocourse, 27th year, reviews the two-wheeled world championships, with Rallycourse, now in its 17th year, covering the World Rally Championships. Our range also includes a technical series and a history series, both on motorsports.

Editor(s): Peter Lovering
Address: 3 Richmond Hill, Richmond, Surrey TW10 6RE
Telephone: 0181 948 5151
Fax: 0181 948 4111
Email: hazleton@hazleton.uk.com
Imprints: Autocourse, Motocourse, Rallycourse
Unsolicited Manuscripts: No

Headline Book Publishing Ltd

Fiction: saga, historical, romance, literary, thriller, crime, horror. Non-fiction: sport, humour, cookery, reference, biography, travel & guides, autobiography, popular culture, crafts & hobbies, gardening, health & beauty.

Editor(s): Publishing Directors: Jane Morpett (Fiction); Heather Holden-Brown (Non-fiction)
Address: 338 Euston Road, London NW1 3BH
Imprints: Headline, Headline Delta, Feature, Headline Liaison, Review.
Parent Company: Hodder Headline Plc
Payment Details: Negotiable
Unsolicited Manuscripts: Synopsis & 5 chapters only; return postage

Health Education Authority

The Health Education Authority is England's leading provider of health promotion. It is the national centre of excellence for health education research and expertise and, through its campaigns, publications and work with health professionals, encourages the public to adopt a healthier lifestyle. Resources are produced in the following health categories: alcohol; cancer; coronary heart disease; drugs; folic acid; food & nutrition; HIV, AIDS & sexual health; immunisation; oral health; popular health books; physical activity and smoking. Resources produced for specific groups: minority ethnic groups, older people, pregnancy, parenting & child health and women's health.

Editor(s): Chris Owen, Delphine Verroest, Liz Niman, Flair Milne, Michele Appleton, Susannah Blake, Andrea Horth (New media).
Address: Trevelyan House, 30 Great Peter Street, London, SW1P 2HW
Imprints: HEA
Unsolicited Manuscripts: No

ℋ
Heart Of Albion Press

Books, booklets and computer-readable publications on local history (especially Leicestershire), folklore, mythology and archaeology.

Editor(s): R N Trubshaw
Address: 2 Cross Hill Close, Wymeswold, Loughborough LE12 6UJ
Telephone: 01509 880725
Email: albion@gmtnet.co.uk
Website: www.gmtnet.co.uk/albion/
Imprints: Heart of Albion Press
Payment Details: Contact Editor
Unsolicited Manuscripts: Future publications will be CD-ROM only so conventional mss not of interest

Heinemann Educational

Educational textbooks, and other publications for the primary, secondary and further education sectors. Very closely targeted to the needs of the curriculum. Most authors are teachers, examiners, advisers or other educational professionals.

Address: Halley Court, Jordan Hill, Oxford OX2 8EJ
Imprints: Heinemann, New Windmills
Parent Company: Reed Educational and Professional Publishing Ltd
Unsolicited Manuscripts: Yes if appropriate to the market

William Heinemann

Fiction and general non-fiction.

Editor(s): Lynne Drew, Victoria Hipps, Maria Rejt, Ravi Mirchandani
Address: 20 Vauxhall Bridge Road, London SW1V 2SA.
Parent Company: Random House
Unsolicited Manuscripts: No

Helm Information

Ornithology and natural history.

Editor(s): Nigel Redman
Address: The Banks, Mountfield, Nr Robertsbridge TN32 5JY
Telephone: 01580 880561
Fax: 01580 880541
Imprints: Pica Press
Unsolicited Manuscripts: No

Christopher Helm (Publishers) Ltd

Ornithology.

Editor(s): Robert Kirk
Address: 35 Bedford Row, London WC1R 4JH
Telephone: 0171 404 5630
Fax: 0171 404 7706
Email: ornithology@acblack.co.uk
Parent Company: A & C Black
Payment Details: Advances against royalties and flat fees
Unsolicited Manuscripts: Yes

Ħ
Hendon Publishing Co

44-page books - landscape, mainly photographs - with small amount of text.
As It Was series: old photos of towns as they used to be late 1800's-1940/50's.

Editor(s): Dorothy Nelson
Address: Hendon Mill, Nelson, Lancashire BB9 8AD
Parent Company: Hendon Trading Co Ltd
Payment Details: Royalties agreed individually
Unsolicited Manuscripts: No

Ian Henry Publications Ltd

Local history of Essex, Suffolk, Norfolk, Cambridge and London - every aspect, but
not autobiographies of childhood memories. Sherlock Holmes pastiche novels (in
the literary style of Conan Doyle) and material on SH and ACD. Transport history -
rail, road, sea and air. Cooking for allergies.

Editor(s): Ian Wilkes
Address: 20 Park Drive, Romford, Essex RM1 4LH
Telephone: 01708 749119
Fax: As phone
Imprints: Ian Henry
Payment Details: P/A agreement
Unsolicited Manuscripts: No

The Herb Society

Exists for amateurs and professionals alike with a keen interest in any aspect of herbs. We produce a quarterly magazine Herbs, which covers topics such as culinary, medicinal, aromatic, history, future and cultivation of herbs.

Editor(s): Barbara Segall
Address: Deddington Hill Farm, Warmington, Banbury OX17 1XB
Telephone: 01295 692000
Fax: 01295 692004
Email: herbsociety.co.uk
Website: www.herbsociety.co.uk
Parent Company: The Herb Society
Unsolicited Manuscripts: Yes

Highfield Publications

Publishers of food hygiene training aids to all sections of the food industry throughout the world. Publications, training videos and educational material.

Address: Vue Pointe, Spinney Hill, Sprotbrough, Doncaster DN5 7LY
Telephone: 01302 850007
Fax: 01302 311112
Email: jayne@highfieldpublications.com
Website: www.highfieldpub.u-net.com

ℋ
Highgate Publications (Beverley) Ltd

A company established in 1985 which has issued over 100 publications, the majority relating to East Yorkshire, some to Yorkshire as a whole, and a small number of wider than local interest. Highgate is interested in publishing good quality, readable books.

Editor(s): John Markham
Address: 4 Newbegin, Beverley, E Yorks HU17 8EG
Telephone: 01482 886017
Fax: As phone
Imprints: Highgate Publications
Payment Details: Quarterly 10% of net price
Unsolicited Manuscripts: Preliminary letter required. Not interested in autobiograpies except in rare circumstances

Hilmarton Manor Press

Publishers, distributors and mail order booksellers of art and antique reference books.

Editor(s): Charles Baile De Laperierre
Address: Calne, Wiltshire, SN11 8SB
Telephone: 01249 760208
Fax: 01249 760379
Email: hilmartonpress@lineone.net
Imprints: Hilmarton Manor Press
Unsolicited Manuscripts: No

Hippopotamus Press

Founded in 1974 and specialises in first collections of new verse by those that have had the usual magazine appearances and are ready for book publication. We also publish occasional larger books of selected poems by those that we feel are unfairly neglected. Recently we have added a few titles of criticism and literary essays. Our current list consists of 70% first collections, 15% of second and third books from these authors, 10% selected poems, the remaining 5% is prose. We only publish a narrow range of contemporary verse, so it is important to read some of our authors before submitting a collection.

Editor(s): Roland John, Anna Martin
Address: 22 Whitewell Road, Frome, Somerset BA11 4EL
Fax: 01373 466653
Imprints: Outposts Poetry Quarterly Magazine
Parent Company: Hippopotamus Press
Payment Details: 7½% Royalty
Unsolicited Manuscripts: Yes

Historical Publications Ltd

We specialise in topographical and transport books, hardback only.

Editor(s): John Richardson
Address: 32 Ellington Street, London N7 8PL
Telephone: 0171 607 1628
Fax: 0171 609 6451
Payment Details: By negotiation
Unsolicited Manuscripts: Syopsis only

Hodder & Stoughton Educational

We publish books for schools, colleges of further education, universities and general interest. Subject areas include: science, mathematics, information technology, tests and assessment, psychology, business studies, child care, teacher education, geography, beauty therapy, history, religious education, PSE and English.

Editor(s): Various
Address: 338 Euston Road, London NW1 3BH
Telephone: 0171 873 6000
Fax: 0171 873 6299
Website: www.educational.hodder.co.uk
Imprints: Teach Yourself
Parent Company: Hodder Headline PLC
Unsolicited Manuscripts: No

Hodder Children's Books

All Hodder's books are designed to hook children into the reading habit and hold them there. Several formats: Picture Books - Picture story books illustrated in full colour, approx 1,000 words, aimed at 2-5 year olds. My First Read Alone - 48-64 pages,1,000-1,500 words, for very young, early readers: ilustrated, simple and fun stories. Read Alone - B format (197 x 130mm approx.) 64 pages, 2-4,000 words; for children who are beginning to read on their own. Story Books - B format, 96-128 pages, 8-12,000 words; for young, confident readers aged 7-9, who want a satisfying read. Novels - 20-50,000 words, for children of 8 and upwards, on any theme; a strong original story and good characters, as well as particular relevance to children, are most important. Information Books - For ages 6-8, 7-11, teen - must work in standard paperback format, 64, 96 or 128 pages, with black and white line artwork; looking for original, accessible, child-centred approaches. We also offer an extensive list of classics by authors like Enid Blyton, Joan Aiken, Helen Cresswell.

Editor(s): Editorial Director: Margaret Conroy
Address: 338 Euston Road, London NW1 3BH
Telephone: 0171 873 6000
Fax: 0171 873 6024
Imprints: My First Read Alone, Read Alone, Story Book, Signature, Hodder Home Learning
Parent Company: Hodder Headline Plc
Payment Details: Subject to contract
Unsolicited Manuscripts: Yes, please include SAE for ms return. Absolutely no poetry or rhyming texts.

H
Hollis Directories Ltd

Offer a range of publications providing information for marketing communications specialists. Publishers of Willings Press Guide (previous year's edition available at half-price), Hollis UK Press & Public Relations Annual, Hollis Europe, Marketing Handbook and other similar titles. Catalogue available.

Editor(s): Publishing Director: Rosemary Sarginson
Address: Harlequin House, Teddington, Middx TW11 8EL
Telephone: 0181 977 7711
Fax: 0181 977 1133
Email: gary@hollis-pr.co.uk
Website: www.hollis-pr.uc.uk

Honeyglen Publishing Ltd

Small publisher specialising in history, biographies, belles-lettres and selected fiction.

Editor(s): Nadia Poderegin, Jelena Poderegin-Harley
Address: 56 Durrels House, Warwick Gardens, London W14 8QB
Telephone: 0171 602 2876
Fax: As phone
Unsolicited Manuscripts: Please send synopsis and sample chapter first. Must fit within our subject range.

Honno

Small publishing press dedicated to giving women from Wales the opportunity to see their work in print. Although we do publish longer pieces of fiction and children's books, our emphasis is on anthologies and collections by various writers. The press is registered as a community co-operative, and any profit goes towards the cost of future publications.

Address: Honno Editorial Office, The Theological College, King Street, Aberystywyth SY23 2LT
Telephone: 01970 623 150
Fax: As phone
Email: gol.honno@virgin.net
Imprints: Honno Modern Fiction, Honno Children's Books, Honno Autobiography, Honno Classics
Unsolicited Manuscripts: Yes, with a Welsh connection

Hope UK

Drug education leaflets, booklets and prevention manuals published. For children and young people and those working/caring for them. Hope UK is a drug education charity which concentrates on prevention issues and includes alcohol and tobacco in its brief.

Editor(s): Martin Perry, George Brinton
Address: 25F Copperfield Street, London SE1 0EN
Telephone: 0171 928 0848
Fax: 0171 401 3477
Email: enquries@hopeuk.org

ℋ
Horizon Scientific Press

Publisher of a wide range of books and journals for the scientific community, mainly in the subjects molecular biology and microbiology. Publisher of The Journal Of Molecular Microbiology And Biotechnology.

Address: PO Box 1, Wymondham, Norfolk NR18 0EH
Telephone: 01953 601106
Fax: 01953 603068
Email: mail@horizonpress.com
Website: www.horizonpress.com
Imprints: Horizon Scientific Press

How To Books Ltd

Practical reference books in the following subject areas: student handbooks, jobs & careers, living & working abroad, business basics, successful writing, mind, body, spirit, and family reference.

Editor(s): Giles Lewis
Address: 3 Newtec Place, Magdalen Road, Oxford OX4 1RE
Telephone: 01865 793 806
Fax: 01865 248 780
Email: info@howtobooks.co.uk
Website: www.howtobooks.co.uk
Imprints: Pathways
Parent Company: Oxford Publishing Ventures
Payment Details: Royalties by negotiation
Unsolicited Manuscripts: Yes

John Hunt Publishing

Books across the spectrum of Christian publishing, with an extensive children's illustrated list. Publishes 50 new titles a year.

Editor(s): J Hunt
Address: 46a West Street, New Alresford, Hants SO24 9AU
Telephone: 01962 736880
Fax: 01962 736881
Email: johnhunt@compuserve.com
Imprints: Arthur James Ltd, Hunt & Thorpe
Payment Details: Various
Unsolicited Manuscripts: Yes

Hutton Press Ltd

Yorkshire local interest and maritime interest.
Editor(s): Charles F Brook

Address: 130 Canada Drive, Cherry Burton, Beverley HU17 7SB
Telephone: 01964 550573
Fax: As phone
Unsolicited Manuscripts: Yes

H

Hydatum

Design & publishing.

Editor(s): Farel Bradbury
Address: 70 Silverdale Road, Royal Tunbridge Wells TN4 9HZ
Telephone: 01892 540 178
Fax: As phone
Imprints: Hydatum, Golf Metropolitan
Unsolicited Manuscripts: No

Hymns Ancient And Modern Ltd

Publishes hymn books for churches, schools and other institutions. All types of religious books, both general and educational. Imprints: The Canterbury Press Norwich - General religious books, liturgical, prayer and guides. Religious And Moral Education Press (RMEP) - Religious, personal and social education books for primary, middle and secondary schools (including assembly material) and teachers'/administrative books. G J Palmer & Sons Ltd - publisher of Church Times weekly newspaper (ideas welcome, no mss). The Sign; Home Words - monthly nationwide parish magazine inserts. Also, Hart Advertising - advertising agency offering specialist service to religious and charitable organisations.

Editor(s): John Bowden, Christine Smith, Mary Mears
Address: St Mary's Works, St Mary's Plain, Norwich, Norfolk NR3 3BH
Telephone: 01603 612914
Fax: 01603 624483
Website: (Church Times) www.churchtimes.co.uk
Imprints: The Canterbury Press Norwich, RMEP, G J Palmer & Sons Ltd
Payment Details: Standard advances and royalties paid annually
Unsolicited Manuscripts: Yes (Canterbury, SCM & RMEP)

IC Publications Ltd

A major publishing force in the Middle East and in Africa. From its offices in London and Paris, IC publishes three magazines and a yearbook in English and thirteen newsletters in French.

Editor(s): Alan Rake
Address: 7 Coldbath Square, London EC1R 4LQ
Telephone: 0171 713 7711
Fax: 0171 713 7970
Email: icpubs@dial.pipex.com
Website: www.africasia.com/icpubs
Imprints: IC Publications Ltd
Payment Details: By negotiation
Unsolicited Manuscripts: By negotiation

ICSA Publishing Ltd

The official publishing company of the Institute of Chartered Secretaries and Administrators (ICSA). Publishes a range of looseleaf and book products for managers in the private, public and voluntary sectors, including Company Secretarial Practice, The Charities Manual and the One Stop series.

Editor(s): Clare Grist Taylor
Address: 16 Park Crescent, London W1N 4AH
Telephone: 0171 612 7020
Fax: 0171 323 1132
Email: icsapub@icsa.co.uk
Payment Details: On application
Unsolicited Manuscripts: No

I
IFLA Offices For UAP & International Lending

Universal availability of publications. International lending. Document delivery and conference proceedings.

Editor(s): Various
Address: c/o The British Library, Boston Spa, Wetherby, West Yorkshire LS23 7BQ
Unsolicited Manuscripts: No

Impart Books

Impart Books operate in the fields of education, accounting and Christian publishing. They mostly publish books which are written or produced in-house; exceptionally, they do publish books by authors outside the organisation. They specialise in producing educational books in co-operation with publishers outside the United Kingdom for printing and publication in those countries. Most of such books are produced to assist the countries concerned rather than to obtain a profit.

Address: Gwelfryn, Llanidloes Road, Newtown, Powys SY16 4HX
Telephone: 01686 623484
Fax: 01686 623784
Unsolicited Manuscripts: No - only after permission

Imperial College Press

Established to produce high-level books and journals in both printed and electronic formats. ICP is a joint publishing venture between Imperial College and World Scientific Publishing, bringing together into one company the experience of an internationally-recognised institution of higher education in engineering, science and medicine, and that of an established medical publisher. The Press gives special emphasis to research areas and educational subjects in which the College has particular strengths. Authors are sought from the College and elsewhere.

Editor(s): John Navas, Aileen Parlane
Address: Room 203, Electrical Engineering Building, Imperial College, London SW7 2BT
Telephone: 0171 594 9568
Fax: 0171 589 2790
Email: edit@icpress.demon.co.uk
Website: www.icpress.demon.co.uk
Parent Company: World Scientific Publishing Co (PTE) Ltd, Singapore

Incorporated Council Of Law Reporting For England & Wales

Not-for-profit publishers of The Law Reports, which are always cited in precedence. Also publishers of The Weekly Law Reports, The Industrial Cases Reports, The Consolidated Index Of Law Reports and The Statues And Public General Acts. All law reports are written by barristers who attend the cases reported, and the texts of judgements are judicially reviewed prior to publication. Circulation is worldwide. A registered charity established in 1865.

Editor(s): Robert Williams
Address: 3 Stone Buildings, Lincoln's Inn, London WC2A 3XN
Telephone: 0171 242 6471
Fax: 0171 831 5247
Email: postmaster@iclr.co.uk
Website: www.lawreports.co.uk
Imprints: The Law Reports, The Weekly Law Reports, The Industrial Cases Reports
Unsolicited Manuscripts: N/A

Independent Writers Publications Ltd

Book publishing - fiction, historical novels.

Editor(s): Alfred Shmueli
Address: 97 Geary Road, Dollis Hill, London NW10 1HS
Fax: 0181 452 0721
Unsolicited Manuscripts: No

The Industrial Society

Leading independent training organisation, and publisher of business books and reports. More than 100 titles, from practical pocket guides to in-depth research reports, the publications cover topics from self development and careers to people management and employment law. Regular subscription reports focus on best practice in UK organisations as a benchmark for users. New titles for 1999 include two new series: The Business Skills Healthcheck Series and The Insider Career Guides. Individual titles include High Flying and Flying Start, essential guides for those new to work and to management; Office Politics and The Tall Poppy, practical guides to personal and professional fulfilment. For a full book catalolgue call our National Sales Unit on 0121 410 3040.

Editor(s): Susannah Lear
Address: Robert Hyde House, 48 Bryanston Square, London W1H 7LN
Telephone: 0171 479 2000
Fax: 0171 723 7375
Email: infoserv@indusoc.demon.co.uk
Website: www.indsoc.co.uk
Imprints: IS Publishing
Unsolicited Manuscripts: Synopsis first please

Insights

Insights is published by the English Tourist Board. It is a bi-monthly subscription service providing the latest information on the tourism market, in an easy-to-use format. It combines the analysis and interpretation of trends and opportunities in the tourism industry with the experience of tourism experts who comment on market developments and give practical advice on marketing and management.

Editor(s): Anna Ryland
Address: Thames Tower, Blacks Road, London W6 9EL
Telephone: 0181 563 3362
Fax: 0181 563 5058
Email: aryland@bta.org.uk
Website: www.visitbritain.com
Parent Company: ETB/BTA
Payment Details: Depends on type of report: £350-600, in-depth market profiles, max £1,000
Unsolicited Manuscripts: Yes

Institute Of Food Science & Technology

The UK independent professional qualifying body for food science and technology, and a registered educational charity. IFST publishes two journals, the International Journal Of Food Science & Technology (bi-monthly) and Food Science & Technology Today (quarterly). Also publishes books and pamphlets: Addition Of Micronutrients To Food ('97); Guide To Food Biotechnology ('96) Listing of Codes Of Practice Applicable To Foods ('93); Shelf Life Of Foods ('93); Guidelines To Good Catering Practice ('92); Food Hygiene Training ('92); Food & Drink - Good Manufacturing Practice ('98); Guidelines For The Handling Of Chilled Foods ('90).

Editor(s): P Goodenough (IJFST); H Y Paine (FSTT)
Address: 5 Cambridge Court, 210 Shepherds Bush Road, London W6 7NJ
Telephone: 0171 603 6316
Fax: 0171 602 9936
Email: ifst@easynet.co.uk
Website: www.easynet.co.uk/ifst/
Payment Details: N/A
Unsolicited Manuscripts: Yes

I

The Institute Of Irish Studies, The Queen's University Of Belfast

The aim of the Institute is to encourage interest and to promote and co-ordinate research in those fields of study which have a particular Irish interest, and it is an important multidisciplinary centre. The publications department reflects the growth and diversity of Irish studies today. The list includes a range of academic or semi-academic books, focused on aspects of Irish studies including archaeology, anthropology, biography, botany, cultural studies, history, history of science, local studies, politics, language, literature, proverbs, religion, transport, women's studies. There are two major series, The Ordnance Survey Memoirs Of Ireland (40 vols) and Northern Ireland Place-names (7vols).

Editor(s): Margaret McNulty
Address: Queen's University Belfast, 8 Fitzwilliam Street, Belfast BT9 6AW
Telephone: 01232 273235
Fax: 01232 439238
Email: lispubs@clio.arts.pub.ac.uk
Website: www.qub.ac.uk/listnd/lls.html
Parent Company: The Queen's University of Belfast
Unsolicited Manuscripts: Yes - academic work only. Please write in the first instance.

Institute Of Management

Publisher of books, checklists, CD-ROMs, on over 200 management-related topics. I M publishes independently and in association with Hodder & Stoughton and Butterworth Heinemann.

Editor(s): D Darke
Address: Management House, Cottingham Road, Corby NN17 1TT
Telephone: 01536 204222
Fax: 01536 201651
Email: deni.darke@imgt.org.uk
Website: www.inst-mgt.org.uk

The Institute Of Personnel And Development

Business and management texts for students and practitioners of training, development and personnel, and line managers.

Editor(s): Commissioning Editors: Richard Goff, Anne Cordwent
Address: IPD House, Camp Road, London SW19 4UX
Email: publishing@ipd.co.uk
Website: www.ipd.co.uk
Imprints: IPD
Payment Details: Royalty agreement by negotiation
Unsolicited Manuscripts: Outline with SAE please for initial consideration

Institute Of Physics Publishing

One of the world's leading science publishers. The company publishes books, journals and magazines in physics and related subject areas. Within the books programme, produces reference works for industry and academia, research monographs, graduate textbooks, high level undergraduate textbooks, and popular science books. The author base is international. Subjects: astronomy & astrophysics; condensed matter physics; high energy physics; history of physics; materials science; mathematical physics; measurement & instrumentation; medical physics; nuclear physics; optics; plasma physics; sensors and smart materials.

Editor(s): Penelope Barber, Kathryn Cantley, Gillian Lindsey, Robin Rees, Jim Revill, Michael Taylor
Address: Dirac House, Temple Back, Bristol BS1 6BE
Telephone: 0117 930 1147
Fax: 0117 930 1186
Email: margaret.ogorman@iopublishing.co.uk
Website: www.bookmark.iop.org
Parent Company: Institute of Physics
Payment Details: Royalty as agreed
Unsolicited Manuscripts: Yes: to Margaret O'Gorman (Publisher)

I
The Institution of Chemical Engineers

The IChemE sets out to publish books and journals which allow engineers and scientists to improve their professional skills and performance. Subjects: environment; safety and loss prevention; contract and project management; process design and operation; dust handling; process control; biotechnology; oil, gas and energy.

Editor(s): Various
Address: 165-189 Railway Terrace, Rugby CV21 3HQ
Telephone: 01788 578214
Fax: 01788 560833
Email: iandrews@icheme.org.uk
Website: www.icheme.org
Imprints: IChemE
Payment Details: Royalties on discussion
Unsolicited Manuscripts: No

The Institution of Electrical Engineers

The Institution of Electrical Engineers (IEE) is the professional association representing 135,000 electrical, electronics, communications and information engineers worldwide. Its activities include organising conferences, maintaining standards (such as the IEE wiring regulations), regulating professional engineers and providing technical and information services. As such it is a large technical publisher, producing books, magazines and journals - as well as electronic publications - for a global, professional and postgraduate audience.

Editor(s): Dir of Publishing: R Mellors-Bourne
Address: Publishing Dept, Michael Faraday House, Six Hills Way, Stevenage SG1 2AY
Telephone: 01438 313311
Fax: 01438 313465
Email: books@iee.org.uk
Website: www.iee.org.uk
Imprints: Peter Peregrinus Ltd
Unsolicited Manuscripts: Yes but only in restricted subject area

Intellect Books

Digital creativity, writing & language, computers & humanity and learning & education - all edited by Masoud Yazdani. Arts & media (inc film & television), culture & heritage - all edited by Robin Beecroft. Our European Studies series crosses all our subject areas and is edited by Keith Cameron.

Editor(s): Masoud Yazdani, Robin Beecroft, Keith Cameron
Address: EFAE, Earl Richards Road North, Exeter EX2 6AS
Telephone: 01392 475110
Fax: As phone
Email: books@intellect-net.com
Website: www.intellect-net.com
Payment Details: Standard contract
Unsolicited Manuscripts: Yes

Intermediate Technology Publications Ltd

Publishes and distributes books and periodicals at practical and policy levels on appropriate technology, Third World development, water & sanitation, agriculture, enterprise development, small-scale construction & manufacture, energy and workshop equipment. Contact us for a free catalogue.

Address: 102-105 Southampton Row, London WC1B 4HH
Telephone: 0171 436 9761
Fax: 0171 436 2013
Email: orders@itpubs.org.uk
Website: www.oneworld.org/itdg/publications.html
Parent Company: Intermediate Technology Development Group

I

International Maritime Organisation (IMO)

IMO is a specialised agency of the United Nations dealing with maritime safety and the prevention and control of marine pollution. IMO's publishing activities include the production and sales of numerous texts (conventions, codes, regulations, recommendations,etc) both in print and in electronic form. IMO has some 250 titles in English; they are translated into French and Spanish, and an increasing number also into Arabic, Chinese and Russian.

Address: 4 Albert Embankment, London SE1 7SR
Telephone: 0171 735 7611
Fax: 0171 587 3241
Email: publications.sales@imo.org
Website: www.imo.org

International Masters Publishers

An international direct marketing company specialising in high-quality continuity series. Our family information and education department embraces a range of publications designed to broaden knowledge in an entertaining and accessible way. Our cookery publications cater for every kind of cook, from the busy mother to the gourmet. Home and hobby publications are designed to help people make the most of their increasing leisure time. Our health products promote a healthy lifestyle as well as addressing more indepth medical issues. All of our fact files and books combine clear step-by-step photography and concise factual text with expert hints and tips. We are constantly updating our products and developing new ones.

Editor(s): Kay Turner, Kim Cooper, Cornelia Philipp, Mark Cockerton, Leslie Robb, Debbie Myatt
Address: Winchester House, 259-269 Old Marylebone Road, London NW1 5RW
Tel: 0171 753 9200
Fax: 0171 723 9191
Unsolicited Manuscripts: No

INTES International (UK) Ltd

English language editions of one of the most popular adventure/humour comic books in the world: The Greatest Adventures Of Spike And Suzy is suitable for children aged 7-12 years.
Editor(s): Ellie Shepherd
Address: 384 Lanark Road, Edinburgh EH13 0LX
Telephone: 0131 477 2223
Fax: 0131 441 4680
Email: eshep31245@aol.com
Website: www.cs.vuin/~hartskam/swenghome.html
Imprints: INTES International

Irish Academic Press

Book publisher interested in following subject areas: Irish history, military history, Irish culture and heritage, arts and literature. Two new series: New Directions In Irish History and Women In Irish History. New manuscript and reprint ideas in the Press' subject areas welcomed.

Editor(s): Linda Longmore
Address: Northumberland House, 44 Northumberland Road, Ballsbridge, Dublin 4, Ireland
Telephone: 353 1 6688244
Fax: 353 1 6601610
Email: info@iap.ie
Website: www.iap.ie
Imprints: Irish Acadmic Press, Irish University Press
Unsolicited Manuscripts: Yes - send to Editor

I

Iron Press

Iron Press enters its 26th year with as strong a committment as ever to the principles of small press publishing. Still unimpressed with literary competitions, marketing junkets or overhyped nonentities, Iron continues its policy of discovering the best new talent in the North East region, the rest of the country and sometimes the world. We bring out three or four new titles a year - single collections of poetry and fiction, international anthologies and contemporary plays.

Editor(s): Peter Mortimer
Address: 5 Marden Terrace, Cullercoats, North Shields, Tyne & Wear NE30 4PD
Telephone: 0191 2531901
Fax: As phone
Imprints: Iron Press
Payment Details: By agreement
Unsolicited Manuscripts: Contact Editor first

Isis Publishing Ltd

Publishers of large-print and audio books.

Editor(s): Veronica Babington Smith
Address: 7 Centremead, Osney Mead, Oxford OX2 0ES
Telephone: 01865 250333
Fax: 01865 790358
Email: audiobooks@isis-publishing.co.uk
Imprints: Isis Large Print, Isis Audio Books

Islamic Texts Society

The Islamic Texts Society publishes books from the Islamic heritage mostly in the form of translations of original Arabic texts. Subjects covered: Qur'an, Hadith, philosophy, science etc. Quinta Essentia is an imprint in which we publish books that discuss Islam, but where it is not the dominant theme. Subjects: comparative religion.

Editor(s): Fatima Azzam
Address: 22a Brooklands Avenue, Cambridge CB2 2DQ
Telephone: 01223 314387
Fax: 01223 324342
Email: mail@its.org.uk
Website: www.its.org.uk
Imprints: Islamic Texts Society, Quinta Essentia
Payment Details: Royalties 7.5% of net receipts
Unsolicited Manuscripts: Yes

Ithaca Press

Established 1973, publishes academic books, mainly on the Middle East, in the fields of history, politics & international relations, economics, social anthropology, religion and literature. Extensive backlist. Has expanded in recent years to include subjects of more general interest such as women's studies, legal studies and biography. Ithaca Press Paperbacks was launched in 1996 to reach a wider audience, including in particular students of social sciences. Important Ithaca Press series are Middle East Monographs, co-published with St Anthony's College, Oxford; the Oriental Institute Monographs, co-published with the Oriental Institute; and the Durham Middle East Monographs, co-published with the Centre for Islamic and Middle Eastern Studies, University of Durham. Strong links are also maintained with the School of Oriental and African Studies, University of London.

Editor(s): Emma Hawker
Address: 8 Southern Court, South Street, Reading RG1 4QS
Telephone: 0118 959 7847
Fax: 0118 959 7356
Email: enquiries@garnet-ithaca.demon.co.uk
Parent Company: Garnet Publishing Ltd

J
Jane's Information Group

The world's leading provider of defence, geopolitical, transport and law enforcement information to governments, militaries, businesses and universities worldwide. Jane's publishes over 200 titles annually in all formats both electonic and in hard copy.

Editor(s): Too many to list
Address: Sentinel House, 163 Brighton Road, Coulsdon, Surrey CR5 2NH
Telephone: 0181 700 3700
Fax: 0181 763 1005
Email: info@janes.co.uk
Website: www.janes.com
Parent Company: The Thomson Corporation
Unsolicited Manuscripts: Synopsis first; write initially to Claire Brunavs for appropriate editor

Janus Publishing Company

Art, biography & autobiography, crime, economics, fiction, history, humour, music, medical, military & war, nautical, the occult, philosophy, poetry, politics & world affairs, science, science fiction, self-help, religion & theology, travel.

Editor(s): Sandy Leung
Address: Edinburgh House, 19 Nassau Street, London W1N 7RE
Telephone: 0171 580 7664
Fax: 0171 636 5756
Email: publisher@januspublishing.co.uk
Website: www.januspublishing.co.uk
Imprints: Janus, Empiricus
Parent Company: Janus Publishing Company
Payment Details: Janus - mostly subsidised; Empiricus - no subsidies
Unsolicited Manuscripts: Yes

Jarrold Publishing

Travel guides mostly UK; leisure: gardening and cookery; gift books, mainly heritage titles. All books have a high photographic content and some artwork.

Editor(s): Donald Greig
Address: Whitefriars, Norwich, Norfolk NR3 1TR
Parent Company: Jarrold and Sons Ltd
Payment Details: Fees and royalties
Unsolicited Manuscripts: Approach in writing first

J H Jolly (Editorial) Ltd

Both a book publisher and a book packager - putting titles together for other publishers. Encompassing in-house editing, design, photography and pre-press. Non-fiction, illustrated, arts-related.

Address: Yelvertoft Manor, Yelvertoft, Northamptonshire NN6 6LF
Telephone: 01788 823868
Fax: 01788 823915
Payment Details: By individual arrangement

John Jones Publishing Ltd

Publishes paperback books for the tourist market in Wales and on the Celtic and Tudor periods. Publishes about 5 books a year. Most on the list are re-publications.

Editor(s): J Jones
Address: Unit 12 Clwydfru Business Centre, Ruthin, N Wales LL15 1NJ
Telephone: 01824 705272
Fax: As phone
Email: johnjonespublishing.cld@virgin.net
Website: www.johnjonespublishing.cld.uk
Imprints: John Jones Publishing
Payment Details: Royalties
Unsolicited Manuscripts: Enquiring letter first with SAE

Jordan Publishing Ltd

Jordan Publishing have now been producing practical legal books for over 100 years. During that time our Jordans imprint has established a respected reputation for a whole range of company law, commercial law, property, agricultural law, charities, private client work, education, crime and specialist insolvency titles. Under our Family Law imprint there are an extensive range of journals, law reports and reference works. A prime source of legal update and information for family lawyers.

Address: 21 St Thomas Street, Bristol BS1 6JS
Telephone: 0117 9230600
Fax: 0117 9250486
Email: ryoung@jordanpublishing.co.uk
Website: www.jordanpublishing.co.uk
Imprints: Jordans, Family Law
Unsolicited Manuscripts: Yes

Richard Joseph Publishers Ltd

Specialist publishers of reference books for the antiquarian and secondhand book trade. Interested in new titles on related subjects.

Editor(s): Alison Howard
Address: Unit 2, Monks Walk, Farnham, Surrey GU9 8HT
Telephone: 01252 734347
Fax: 01252 734307
Email: rjoe01@aol.com
Website: www.members.aol.com/rjoe01/sheppards
Imprints: Sheppard
Unsolicited Manuscripts: No, always write first

S Karger AG

Founded in 1890, Karger is an independent medical publisher based in Basel, Switzerland. We publish 80 journals and about 60 new books a year, primarily in highly specialised medical research.

Editor(s): Peter Lawson
Address: 58 Grove Hill Road, Tunbridge Wells TN1 1SP
Telephone: 01892 533534
Fax: 01892 533735
Email: lawson_karger@compuserve.com
Website: www.karger.com
Imprints: Karger
Parent Company: S Karger AG, Basel
Unsolicited Manuscripts: No

K
Karnak House

Specialists in African and Caribbean studies only. Subjects published are history, education, linguistics, languages, egyptology, prehistory, anthropology, sociology and politics. Fiction only - no memoirs, biographies or autobiographies.

Editor(s): A S Saakana
Address: 300 Westbourne Park Road, London W11 1EH
Telephone: 0171 243 3620
Fax: As phone
Imprints: Karnak House
Unsolicited Manuscripts: Yes but synopsis & sample chapter only, plus SAE

Richard Kay (Publications)

Publishes books the majority of which have a Lincolnshire association; also a few with a more general historical interest, and a few titles of medico-political and economico-political concern. Books in and about Lincolnshire dialect including a 10,000-word dictionary. Life in Lincolnshire and Vernacular History series. Local history - academic and nostalgic.

Editor(s): Richard Allday
Address: 80 Sleaford Road, Boston, Lincolnshire PE21 8EU
Telephone: 01205 353231
Imprints: Richard Kay, History Of Boston Project
Payment Details: Royalties where apppropriate paid annually
Unsolicited Manuscripts: Initial letter preferred

K

Keepdate Publishing

Traditional and new media publishers.
Editor(s): Managing Editor: J Hinves
Address: 21 Portland Terrace, Newcastle Upon Tyne NE2 1QQ
Telephone: 0191 2819444
Fax: 0191 2813105
Website: www.newsworth.com

Kegan Paul International Ltd

We are probably the leading publishers of books on all aspects of the Middle East, Asia, Africa, Japan, the Pacific and South America, from the most general to the most specialist.

Editor(s): Editorial Director: Kaori O'Connor
Address: PO Box 256, 121 Bedford Court Mansions, Bedford Ave, London WC1B 3SW
Telephone: 0171 580 5511
Fax: 0171 436 0899
Email: books@keganpau.demon.co.uk
Website: www.demon.co.uk/keganpaul/
Unsolicited Manuscripts: Yes

Kenilworth Press Ltd

Leading publisher of instructional equestrian books, including the official book of the British Horse Society, and the famous Threshold Picture Guides.

Editor(s): Lesley Gowers
Address: Addington, Buckingham, MK18 2JR
Telephone: 01296 715101
Fax: 01296 715148
Email: mail@kenilworthpress.co.uk
Imprints: Kenilworth, Threshold
Payment Details: Royalties
Unsolicited Manuscripts: Yes

Kensington West Productions

Publishes sports, leisure, photography, business and children's titles. Children's imprint 3 R's Books specialises in titles that are both fun and educational.

Editor(s): Julian West
Address: 5 Cattle Market, Hexham, Northumberland NE46 1NJ
Telephone: 01434 609933
Fax: 01434 600066
Email: kwp@kensingtonwest.demon.co.uk
Website: www.@kensingtonwest.demon.co.uk
Imprints: Kensington West Productions, 3 R's Books
Unsolicited Manuscripts: No, please send outline of proposal by post

The King's England Press

Formed in 1989 to reprint Arther Mee's King's England series of 1930s guidebooks to the English counties. Due this year are Surrey and Cambridgeshire. Also available - Notts, Derbys, Durham, Essex, Herts, Lincs, Warwicks, Staffs, Leics & Rutland, West Yorks. Press also publishes children's poetry by Gez Walsh (The Spot On My Bum) and Andrew Collett (Always Eat Your Bogies), plus other books on local history & folklore. See website or send for free catalogue.

Editor(s): Steve Rudd
Address: 21 Commercial Road, Goldthorpe Industrial Estate, Goldthorpe, Rotherham S63 9BL
Telephone: 01226 270258
Fax: 01709 897787
Email: sales@kingsengland.demon.co.uk
Website: www.kingsengland.demon.co.uk

Laurence King Publishing

Publisher of fine illustrated books on graphic design, architecture, interior design, decorative arts and textiles.

Editor(s): Philip Cooper, Jo Lightfoot, Jane Tobin, Laura Church
Address: 71 Great Russell Street, London WC1B 3BN
Telephone: 0171 831 6351
Fax: 0171 831 8356
Email: enquiries@calmann-king.co.uk
Website: www.laurence-king.com
Parent Company: Calmann & King Ltd
Payment Details: Royalties paid twice-yearly
Unsolicited Manuscripts: Yes

Kingfisher Publications

Non-fiction: children 0-16 years. Exciting, visual books, coupled with solid information that should be provided in a stimulating way to satisfy young enquiring minds. Fiction: children 0-16 years. Rich variety of titles with opportunities to share the joy of reading with every child.

Editor(s): Gill Denton (non-fiction), Ann-Janine Murtagh (fiction)
Address: New Penderel House, 283-288 High Holborn, London WC1V 7HZ
Imprints: Kingfisher Non-Fiction, Kingfisher Fiction
Parent Company: Vivendi
Unsolicited Manuscripts: No

Jessica Kingsley Publishers

Professional and academic level books on special needs, arts therapies, social work, psychiatry, psychology. Books for professionals and parents on autism, Asperger's syndrome and related conditions. An independent company founded in 1997.

Editor(s): Jessica Kingsley, Helen Parry
Address: 116 Pentonville Road, London N1 9JB
Telephone: 0171 833 2307
Fax: 0171 837 2917
Email: post@jkp.com
Website: www.jkp.com
Payment Details: Royalties
Unsolicited Manuscripts: No, but proposals for books in our subject areas welcome - send outline, contents & author CV

Kingsway Publications

Bibles, religious books.

Editor(s): Richard Herkes
Address: Lottbridge Drove, Eastbourne, East Sussex BN23 6NT
Parent Company: Kingsway Communications
Unsolicited Manuscripts: No

Kluwer Academic-Plenum Publishers

Plenum Publishing is now part of Kluwer Academic Publishers. The UK company, based in London, provides an editorial base for new journals and books at postgraduate, research and professional levels in life sciences, physical sciences and social sciences.

Editor(s): Ken Derham, Joanna Lawrence
Address: New Loom House, 101 Back Church Lane, London E1 lLU
Telephone: 0171 264 1910
Fax: 0171 264 1919
Email: mail@plenum.co.uk
Website: www.plenum.co.uk
Imprints: Plenum Press, Kluwer Academic-Plenum Publishers
Parent Company: Kluwer Academic-Plenum Publishers, New York
Payment Details: Royalty on sales negotiable according to type of book
Unsolicited Manuscripts: Yes

K

Knockabout Comics

Humorous adult comic strip collections; graphic novels; political and humorous; drug information, use and abuse, sociology.

Editor(s): George Rayburn, Tony Bennett
Address: Unit 24, 10 Acklam Road, London W10 5QZ
Telephone: 0181 969 8645
Fax: 0181 968 7614
Email: knockcomic@aol.com
Imprints: Knockabout, Crack Editions, Fanny
Parent Company: Toskanex Ltd
Unsolicited Manuscripts: No. Outlines accepted

Kogan Page Ltd

Business & management, marketing, HRM, training & development, careers, study skills, personal development, personal finance, education for schools and HE, health care management, transport & logistics.

Editor(s): Philip Mudd, Pauline Goodwin
Address: 120 Pentonville Road, London N1 9JN
Telephone: 0171 278 0433
Fax: 0171 837 6348
Email: kpinfo@kogan-page.co.uk
Website: www.kogan-page.co.uk
Payment Details: Royalties or flat fee
Unsolicited Manuscripts: No - proposal required

The Latchmere Press

Provide practical case studies on how to stimulate and maintain success in purposeful teaching and learning. Our Quality In Education series of books feature articles written by seasoned professionals who have succeeded at the chalkface - and whose successes have been reecognised nationally. Titles: Striving For Quality In Schools (£9.95); Maintaining Excellence In Schools (£10.95); The Disabled Child, The Family & The Professional (£11.95); Literacy And Numeracy: Crusade For Standards (£10.95); Partnerships For School Effectiveness (£13.95).

Editor(s): Tony Evans, Carol Kay, Angela Cornforth
Address: 6 Dundalk Road, London SE4 2JL
Telephone: 0171 639 7282
Fax: 0181 853 0724

Law Pack Publishing Ltd

Self-help law and the Internet.

Editor(s): Jamie Ross
Address: 10-16 Cole Street, London SE1 4YH
Telephone: 0171 357 0367
Fax: 0171 357 0347
Email: mailbox@lawpack.co.uk
Website: www.lawpack.co.uk
Imprints: Take Note
Payment Details: Royalty basis
Unsolicited Manuscripts: Yes

$\mathcal{L}$
Law Society Publishiing

A commercial publishing business existing within The Law Society of England and Wales. Publish practical handbooks, guides and legal reference material designed to enable solicitors and other law practitioners to carry out their work more effectively. Main publishing areas: litigation (including ADR/PI), commerce, employment law, human rights, practice management, IT, professional conduct, property & conveyancing, crime, environmental law, family & social welfare, partnerships, wills & probate and legal reference.

Editor(s): Steven Reed, Angela Atcheson, Dominic Shryane
Address: 113 Chancery Lane, London WC1A 1PL
Telephone: 0171 320 5876
Fax: 0171 404 1124
Email: steven.reed@lawsociety.org.uk
Website: www.lawsociety.org.uk
Imprints: Law Society Publishing
Parent Company: The Law Society of England and Wales
Payment Details: Royalties (negotiable)
Unsolicited Manuscripts: Yes

Lawrence & Wishart

Politics, cultural studies, history, media, education, classic political theory and earth science.

Editor(s): Sally Davison
Address: 99A Wallis Road, London, E9 5LN
Unsolicited Manuscripts: Yes

LDA

Truly effective materials for primary and special educational needs, including everything you need to implement literacy and numeracy hours. Subjects include: language, listening, handwriting, spelling, reading (assessment, dyslexia, phonolgical awareness), behaviour & self-esteem, motivation, maths, numeracy and science.

Address: Abbeygate House, East Road, Cambridge CB1 1DB
Telephone: 01223 357744
Fax: 01223 460557
Email: ldamarket@aol.com
Parent Company: Living and Learning (Cambridge) Ltd
Payment Details: Authors usually paid a royalty

Learning Materials Ltd

A popular company with teachers, devoted to publishing materials for children with special educational needs, giving excellent support in literacy and numeracy. The majority of books are photocopiable and provide much-needed differentiation within the classroom. In addition to English and mathematics, subjects covered include history, science, thinking skills and life skills. Several taped series are available to help in the development of listening skills. New publications include: More Reading For Meaning; Support For Basic Spelling; Looking And Thinking Big Books.

Editor(s): Barbara Mitchelhill
Address: Dixon Street, Wolverhampton WV2 2BX
Telephone: 01902 454026
Fax: 01902 457596
Email: LearningMaterials@btinternet.com
Website: www.btinternet.com/~learningmaterials
Payment Details: By negotiation
Unsolicited Manuscripts: Enquire first

Learning Together

Practice tests for 9-12 year olds in reasoning (verbal and non-verbal), English, maths and science. Target group is end of Key Stage 2.

Editor(s): Stephen McConkey, Tom Maltman
Address: 18 Shandon Park, Belfast BT5 6NW
Telephone: 01232 402086
Fax: 01232 425852

Legal Action Group

An independent self-financing education trust founded in 1972. Its purpose is to promote equal access to justice. It publishes a monthly journal Legal Action, the quarterly Community Care Law Reports and a range of law and practice books for legal practitioners and advisers.

Address: 242 Pentonville Road, London N1 9UN
Telephone: 0171 833 2931
Fax: 0171 837 6094
Email: lag@lag.org.uk
Website: www.lag.org.uk
Payment Details: Royalties twice-yearly
Unsolicited Manuscripts: Considered, but prefer synopsis & draft chapter

Leirmheas

Current affairs, history politics, law, Ireland, literary criticism, economics, science.

Editor(s): Daltun O Ceallaigh
Address: PO Box 3278, Dublin 6, Ireland
Telephone: 4976944
Imprints: Leirmheas

Lennard Publishing

General non-fiction but only where projects are underwritten by sponsorship or a guaranteed order for a large proportion of the print run.

Editor(s): Adrian Stephenson
Address: Windmill Cottage, Mackerye End, Harpenden, Herts AL5 5DR
Email: orders@lenqap.demon.co.uk
Parent Company: Lennard Associates Ltd
Payment Details: By negotiation
Unsolicited Manuscripts: No

ℒ
Letts Educational

Educational books for use at home and in school for 3-18 year olds. We also publish undergraduate textbooks in business and computing, and books to help trainee teachers meet requirements of the new ITTNC.

Address: Aldine House, Aldine Place, London W12 8AW
Telephone: 0181 740 2266
Fax: 0181 743 8451
Email: mail@lettsed.co.uk
Parent Company: BPP Holdings Plc
Payment Details: Royalties
Unsolicited Manuscripts: No

John Libbey & Co Ltd

John Libbey has been publishing medical books and journals for the past eighteen years. The company has achieved a reputation for well produced, timely publications - made available at realistic prices. Many titles are published with leading researchers, professional institutions and pharmaceutical companies, and based on proceeding conferences. Our specialised subjects are; epilepsy, obesity, nutrition, neurology and nuclear medicine.

Address: 13 Smiths Yard, Summerley Street, London SW18 4HR
Telephone: 0181 9472777
Fax: 0181 9472664
Email: libbey@earlsfield.win-uk.net
Imprints: John Libbey, Eurotext

L

Libertarian Alliance

The Libertarian Alliance is a radical pro-free market and civil libertarian group. It campaigns for social and economic freedom by means of regular conferences and seminars, speeches to university, political, civic, business and trade union groups, and frequent appearances on television and radio. It also gives evidence and presentations to government and parliamentary inquiries. Publishes a quarterly magazine Free Life, and a wide range of serial publications - leaflets, pamphlets and monographs - on all aspects of economic, political, social, moral and sexual freedom from classical liberal, libertarian, free market and anarcho-capitalist persepectives. There are currently over 400 items in print.

Address: 25 Chapter Chambers, Esterbrooke Street, London SW1P 4NN
Telephone: 0171 821 5502
Fax: 0171 834 2031
Email: la@capital.demon.co.uk
Website: www.freespace.virgin.net/old.whig/fl.htm
Unsolicited Manuscripts: Yes

Library Association Publishing

Reference, bibliography, information studies, information technology, librarianship, library management and training. Formats include book, CD-ROM, training packages.

Address: 7 Ridgmount Street, London WC1E 7AE
Telephone: 0171 636 7543
Fax: 0171 636 3627
Email: lapublishing@la-hq.og.uk
Website: www.la-hq.org.uk
Parent Company: Library Association
Unsolicited Manuscripts: No

L

Libris

Literary publisher specialising in German-language literature in English translation, and in studies of German literature and its authors.

Editor(s): Nicholas M Jacobs
Address: 10 Burghley Road, London NW5 1UE
Telephone: 0171 482 2340
Fax: 0171 485 4220
Imprints: Libris
Payment Details: By negotiation
Unsolicited Manuscripts: No

Lion Publishing

Publishes Christian books for general readers, both children and adults.

Editor(s): Rebecca Winter, Philip Law, Maurice Lyon, Sarah Medira, Su Box, Lois Rock
Address: Peter's Way, Sandy Lane West, Oxford OX4 5HG
Telephone: 01865 747550
Fax: 01865 747568
Email: custserv@lion-publishing.co.uk
Website: www.lion-publishing
Payment Details: Royalties paid twice a year
Unsolicited Manuscripts: To Charlotte Stewart

Little, Brown & Company (UK)

General fiction and non-fiction hardback and paperback. Non-fiction includes - biographies & autobiographies, politics, current affairs, popular science and history. Fiction includes - thrillers, crime, SF & fantasy, women's fiction and literary fiction.

Editor(s): Alan Samson, Barbara Boote, Hilary Hale, Richard Beswick, Lennie Goodings, Julia Charles, Tim Holman
Address: Brettenham House, Lancaster Place, London WC2E 7EN
Telephone: 0171 911 8000
Fax: 0171 911 8100
Email: Email:.uk@littlebrown.com
Imprints: Little Brown, Warner, Abacus, Virago, Orbit
Parent Company: Time Entertainment Inc
Unsolicited Manuscripts: No

The Littman Library Of Jewish Civilization

Established 1965, the Library publishes scholarly works that explain and perpetuate the Jewish heritage. Following the guidelines laid down by its founder, it publishes works of scholarship that reflect objectivity, fresh research, and new insight, and that are as far as possible definitive in their field. The Library also publishes translations of Hebrew and Aramaic classics so as to make the Jewish religious and literary heritage more accessible to English-speaking readers.

Editor(s): Connie Webber
Address: PO Box 645, Oxford OX2 6AS
Telephone: 01235 868104
Fax: 01235 868104
Email: connie01@globalnet.co.uk
Unsolicited Manuscripts: Yes

$\mathcal{L}$
Liverpool University Press

Academic and scholarly books in the fields of archaeology, architecture, art & art history, contemporary culture & society, history (all periods and areas of the world), literary criticism (English, American, French, Iberian, Latin American), environmental studies, science fiction criticism, poetry studies, sociology, veterinary science.

Editor(s): Robin Bloxsidge
Address: 4 Cambridge Street, Liverpool L69 3BX
Telephone: 0151 794 2231
Fax: 0151 794 2235
Email: robblo@liv.ac.uk
Website: www.liverpool-unipress.co.uk
Imprints: Liverpool University Press
Parent Company: The University of Liverpool
Payment Details: Royalties paid annually; advances negotiable
Unsolicited Manuscripts: Yes

LLP Limited

Publishers & information providers to the international shipping, transportation, legal, insurance, energy and financial markets. Publish reference and professional books and directories for these markets. 200 backlist titles and up to 50 new titles each year.

Address: 69-77 Paul Street, London EC2A 4LQ
Telephone: 0171 553 1000
Fax: 0171 553 1107
Website: www.llplimited.com
Parent Company: Informa Group Plc
Unsolicited Manuscripts: To Reference Publishing Division

Logaston Press

Concentrates on publishing books on history, social history and archaeology concerning central or South Wales, Welsh Borders, and/or West Midlands. Looking, especially, for authors to help develop series on history of pubs, and Monuments In Landscape series. Discuss ideas/synopsis first before considering chapters/manuscript.

Editor(s): Andy Johnson, Ron Shoesmith
Address: Logaston, Woonton, Almeley, Herefordshire HR3 6QH
Telephone: 01544 327344
Imprints: Logaston Press
Payment Details: By mutual agreement, normally on publication
Unsolicited Manuscripts: Send outline idea first, manuscript by request only

Loizou Publications

History: Greece, Cyprus, Balkans. Literature: Greek and English. Info communication technology.

Editor(s): L Loizou
Address: 29 Doveridge Gardens, London N13 5BJ
Telephone: 0171 240 1968
Fax: 0171 836 2522
Email: L4books@aol.com
Parent Company: Zeno Publishers

L
Lonely Planet Publications

Independent travel guidebook publisher. Over 400 books including regional, country & city guides, pictorial books, atlases, phrasebooks, walking & diving guides.

Editor(s): Katharine Leck
Address: 10a Spring Place, London NW5 3BH
Telephone: 0171 428 4800
Fax: 0171 428 4828
Email: go@lonelyplanet.co.uk
Parent Company: Lonely Planet Publications Australia
Payment Details: Dependent on contract
Unsolicited Manuscripts: No

Richard R Long

Publication of short runs of national curriculum science guides and safety signs. Offers service to education to publish similar books.

Editor(s): Richard R Long, Jo Long
Address: Lindum Lodge, 37 Nettleham Road, Lincoln LN2 1RW
Telephone: 01522 522836
Imprints: Richard R Long

LTP (Language Teaching Publications)

LTP is an independent publisher specialising in innovative materials for the ELT market. LTP has an exceptional business English and teacher training list which continues to grow alongside general English products. Established titles include The Lexical Approach; Implementing The Lexical Approach; Dictionary Of Selected Collocations; Business Matters and The Working Week. New titles in 1999 include Idioms Organiser; Teaching Collocation; Grammar With Laughter.

Editor(s): M Lewis, J Hill
Address: 114a Church Road, Hove, E Sussex BN3 2EB
Telephone: 01273 736344
Fax: 01273 775361
Email: lanteapub@aol.com
Unsolicited Manuscripts: Accepted with contents page, rationale, 3 sample units/chapters

Lucis Press Ltd

Lucis Press publishes books of esoteric philosophy, a continuation of the Ageless Wisdom presented as a guide to the merging of spiritual values and goals with the challenges of modern living. The teaching of the Tibetan Master, Djwhal Khul, written by Alice Bailey, encompasses a wide range of subjects including the new psychology of the soul, education, discipleship, astrology, healing, intuition, karma and telepathy. Other author's titles include the Agni Yoga series.

Editor(s): Sarah McKechnie
Address: 3 Whitehall Court, Suite 54, London SW1A 2EF
Telephone: 0171 839 4512
Fax: 0171 839 5575
Email: london@lucistrust.org
Website: www.lucistrust.org/
Parent Company: Lucis Publishing, New York

$\mathcal{L}$
Lucky Duck Publishing

Specialise in books for teachers and parents which present a positive approach to behaviour management. Our catalogue includes books, videos and teaching materials about self-esteem, bullying, circle time, circle of friends, emotional curriculum, parenting skills and equal opportunities. We have published a number of first-time authors, and provide a supportive editorial service to assist in the production of user-friendly materials. Visit the website for more information.

Editor(s): George Robinson, Barbara Maines
Address: 34 Wellington Park, Clifton, Bristol BS8 2UN
Telephone: 0117 9732881
Fax: As phone
Email: publishing@luckyduck.co.uk
Website: www.luckyduck.co.uk
Payment Details: 10% of net sales
Unsolicited Manuscripts: No

M

Macmillan Publishers Ltd

Macmillan Publishers, founded in 1843, publish approximately 1400 titles a year. Unsolicited proposals and synopses are welcome in all divisions of the company, which are:

Macmillan Press Ltd, publishing textbooks and monographs; Macmillan Education, publishing international education titles; Macmillan Heineman ELT, publishing ELT titles; Macmillan, publishing biographies, autobiographies, crafts, hobbies, economics, gift books, health & beauty, history, humour, natural history, travel, philosphy, politics & world affairs, psychology, theatre & drama, gardening, cookery, encyclopedias; Pan, publishing fiction and non-fiction paperbacks; Papermac, publishing serious non-fiction; Picador, publishing literary and general fiction and non-fiction; Sidgwick & Jackson, publishing military & war and music; Macmillan Children's Books and Campbell Books, publishing novels, board books, picture books; Macmillan Reference Ltd, publishing works of reference in academic, professional and vocational subjects; Boxtree, publishing books linked to, and about, television, film, popular culture, humour and sport.

Address: 25 Eccleston Place, London SW1W 9NF
Telephone: 0171 881 8000
Fax: 0171 881 8001
Imprints: Macmillan, Pan, Papermac, Sidgwick & Jackson
Parent Company: Holtzbrinck
Payment Details: Royalties are paid annually or twice-yearly depending on contract
Unsolicited Manuscripts: Yes

M
Macmillan Reference Ltd

Art, music, politics, current affairs, economics, finance, science

Editor(s): Gina Fullerlove, Margot Levy, Sara Lloyd
Address: 25 Eccleston Place, London SW1W 9NF
Telephone: 0171 881 8000
Fax: 0171 881 8001
Website: www.macmillan-reference.co.uk
Imprints: Grove's Dictionaries
Parent Company: Macmillan Ltd
Payment Details: Vary
Unsolicited Manuscripts: Yes

Magi Publications

Children's picture books, 4-7 years, pre-school and novelty books 0-4 years.

Editor(s): Linda Jennings
Address: 22 Manchester Street, London W1M 5PG
Telephone: 0171 486 0925
Fax: 0171 486 0926
Email: info@magi.publication.demon.co.uk.
Website: www.littletiger.okukbooks.com
Imprints: Little Tiger Press
Payment Details: To be agreed with author
Unsolicited Manuscripts: Yes, welcomed, but please phone first

Magna Large Print Books

Family saga, doctor/nurse, mystery, suspense/adventure, romance, romantic/suspense, westerns, thrillers, general fiction, historical romance and a small amount of non-fiction. Please note: we only publish large-print books which have already been published in ordinary print.

Editor(s): Diane Allen
Address: Magna House, Long Preston, Nr Skipton, North Yorkshire BD23 4ND
Telephone: 01729 840225
Fax: 01729 840683
Imprints: Magna, Dales and Story Sound
Parent Company: The Ulverscroft Group
Unsolicited Manuscripts: No

Mainstream Publishing Co Ltd

Mainstream publishes a wide variety of non-fiction books covering sport, health, biography, autobiography, current affairs, art, photography and illustrated books. The company was founded by its current directors in 1978 and now publishes 80-90 titles per year. Manuscripts should not be submitted in the first instance - a covering letter and detailed synopsis will do.

Editor(s): Bill Campbell
Address: 7 Albany Street, Edinburgh EH1 3UG
Telephone: 0131 557 2959
Fax: 0131 556 8720
Email: mainstream.pub@btinternet.com
Imprints: Mainstream
Unsolicited Manuscripts: No

$\mathcal{M}$
Management Books 2000 Ltd

Management guides, handbooks and directories, covering all types of business book from career development to technical reference. Also interested in general non-fiction titles of particular topical relevance.

Editor(s): N Dale-Harris
Address: Cowcombe House, Cowcombe Hill, Chalford, Gloucester GL6 8HP.
Telephone: 01285 760722
Fax: 01285 760708
Email: m.b.200@virgin.net
Website: www.mb2000.com
Imprints: Management Books 2000, Mercury Business Books
Payment Details: Advance/Royalties
Unsolicited Manuscripts: Yes

Management Pocketbooks Ltd

Pocket-size (A6 landscape), succinct, factual text, and high visual content distinguish Management Pocketbooks. More than 40 titles in the series, which broadly fall into the following categories: training, personal deveopment, management, sales & marketing, and finance. Flagship The Trainer's Pocketbook has sold over 40,000 copies. The pages of a Pocketbook resemble an overhead transparency: a heading denotes the subject of the page; the text is often presented as bullet-points; acronyms, mnemonics and other memory trigger devices are used; and illustrations are included wherever possible. Thumb logos enable reader to identify the chapter they are reading. Many of the Pocketbook authors are trainers and present their own training materials in a similar way. The books are £6.99 and when discounted (for multiple copies) they can be used as inexpensive course material, either before, during or after the training event. ISBN series prefix 1 870471.

Editor(s): Ros Baynes, Sue Kerr, Adrian Hunt
Address: 14 East Street, Alresford, Hants SO24 9EE
Telephone: 01962 735573
Fax: 01962 733637
Email: pocketbks@aol.com
Website: http://members.aol.com/pocketbks
Payment Details: 10% of net receipts
Unsolicited Manuscripts: To Ros Baynes

Manchester University Press

Art history, history, theology & religion (ed Graham). Economics & business studies, international law, politics (ed Viinikka). Architecture, design, film & media, foreign language texts, literary studies, music, philosophy & theory, photography (ed Frost). We also publish a number of journals.

Editor(s): Vanessa Graham (history), Nicola Viinikka (economics), Matthew Frost (humanities)
Address: Oxford Road, Manchester M13 9NR
Telephone: 0161 273 5539
Fax: 0161 274 3346
Email: mup@man.ac.uk
Website: www.man.ac.uk/mup
Imprints: Mandolin
Payment Details: Royalties
Unsolicited Manuscripts: Yes

Maney Publishing

Maney is one of the few remaining independent publishers of quality in an era of declining production standards and the increasing concentration of publishing in the hands of international conglomerates. Since 1945 Maney has offered academic societies, their editors and authors outstanding service in the publication of their books and journals: that process continues with the development of our journal publishing imprint Maney Publishing and our new monograph imprint Northern Universities Press. We publish in the areas of archaeology, architecture, history, decorative arts, literature & language and more recently the biomedical sciences.

Editor(s): Michael Gallico
Address: Hudson Road, Leeds LS9 7DL
Telephone: 0113 249 7481
Fax: 0133 248 6983
Email: maney@maney.co.uk
Website: www.charlesworth.com/maney/new/
Imprints: Northern Universities Press, Maney Publishing
Parent Company: W S Maney & Son Ltd
Unsolicited Manuscripts: Yes

M
Mango Publishing

Works by Caribbean-heritage writers with a focus on literature and poetry.

Editor(s): Joan Anim-Addo
Address: 64 Broxholm Road, West Norwood, London SE27 0BT
Telephone: 0181 480 7771
Fax: As phone
Imprints: Mango Publishing
Payment Details: By arrangement
Unsolicited Manuscripts: Yes

Manson Publishing Ltd

Medicine, veterinary medicine, biological & agricultural sciences and earth sciences. All our books are distributed through Oxford University Press.

Address: 73 Corringham Road, London NW11 7DL
Telephone: 0181 905 5150
Fax: 0181 201 9233
Email: manson@man-pub.demon.co.uk
Imprints: Manson Publishing Ltd, The Veterinary Press
Unsolicited Manuscripts: No

Map Collector Publications Ltd

Specialist publishers of books about early maps and their history.

Editor(s): Valerie G Scott
Address: 48 High Street, Tring, Herts HP23 5BH
Telephone: 01442 824977
Fax: 01442 827712
Email: gp86@dial.pipex.com
Website: www.mapcollector.com
Unsolicited Manuscripts: No

Peter Marcan Publications

Small publisher of information directories: Outlets For Specialist New Books In The UK; The Marcan Handbook Of Arts Organisations; Greater London History And Heritage Handbook; Art Historians And Specialists In The UK. Also pictorial albums and prints on London history and topography.

Address: PO Box 3158, London SE1 4RA
Telephone: 0171 357 0368

M

Marcham Manor Press

Specialist publisher interested in PhD level academic publications in the field of history and church history c1520-1690 and c1750-1850.

Editor(s): Gervase Duffield
Address: Appleford, Abington, Oxon OX14 4PB
Telephone: 01235 848319
Imprints: Marcham Books, Sutton Courtenay Press
Parent Company: Appleford Publishing Group
Unsolicited Manuscripts: Only in our field

Market House Books Ltd

Compilers and packagers of reference books, including the Collins English Dictionary, the Macmillan Encyclopedia, the Larousse 6-volume Thematic Encyclopedia, the Oxford Paperback Encyclopedia and over 150 other reference books. Established 1970.

Editor(s): Alan Isaacs, John Daintieth, Elizabeth Martin
Address: Market House, Market Square, Aylesbury, Bucks HP20 1TN.
Telephone: 01296 484911
Fax: 01296 437073
Email: mhb-aylesbury@compuserve.com
Unsolicited Manuscripts: For reference books only

Marshall Cavendish Books

International packagers of popular illustrated books. Subject areas include crafts, gardening, cookery, home improvement, sex, health, children's/family reference and the arts. Established international publisher of high quality reference series Cultures Of The World, Festivals Of The World, Culture Shock! Also publishes a general trade list: natural history, cofee-table albums, cookery, professional business and biographies of Asian leaders.

Editor(s): Publishing Mgr: Shova Loh
Address: 119 Wardour Street, London W1V 3TD
Telephone: 0171 565 6047
Fax: 0171 734 1936
Email: te@corp.tpl.com.sg
Website: www.timesone,com.sg/te
Imprints: Marshall Cavendish Books, Marshall Cavendish Continuity Sets, Times Editions, Times Books International, Les Editions Du Pacifique
Parent Company: Times Publishing Group

Marshalle Publications

Alternative or complementary medicine, biblical diseases and medicines, homeopathy, murder and poisoning by arsenic, history of the Hebrews from 12C BC. History, short stories, Westcountry stories including Tamerton Treacle Mines. Amusing incidents.

Editor(s): Mervyn Madge
Address: Chelfham House, Saltburn Road, Plymouth PL5 1PB
Telephone: 01752 361832

M
Martin Books

Food, cookery and health.

Editor(s): Susanna Clarke, Anna Hitchin
Address: Grafton House, 64 Maids Causeway, Cambridge CB5 8DD
Telephone: 01223 366733
Fax: 01223 461428
Parent Company: Simon & Schuster UK Ltd
Unsolicited Manuscripts: No

Kevin Mayhew Publishers

Adult books: liturgy and worship resources, prayer and spirituality, parish outreach/ pastoral care, inspirational books, sacramental, humour, instant art, hymn books and worship song books. Children's and young people's books: worship resources, books of prayers, gift books, Palm Tree Bible Stories, Palm Tree Bible Puzzle Books, Palm Tree Bible Colouring Books, story books, instant art, drama resources, youthwork resources.

Editor(s): Helen Elliot, Jonathan Bugden
Address: Buxhall, Stowmarket, Suffolk IP14 3DJ
Telephone: 01449 737978
Fax: 01449 737834
Email: kevinmayhewltd@msn.com
Imprints: Palm Tree Press
Payment Details: Royalties paid
Unsolicited Manuscripts: Yes

B McCall Barbour

Publishers of Christian books, greeting cards, calendars and gift items etc. Also wholesale distributors for Bibles, books etc, from various other publishers. British agents for Zondervan Publishers, Living Stories Inc, AGM Publishers, Riverside/World Bibles, Dake's Bibles, Kirkbride Bibles, Sword of the Lord Publishers and Schoettle Publishers as well as Thomas Nelson Bibles and Books. Singspiration Music and Peterson Music also sole distributors. This firm is a family business established in 1900 and is strictly evangelical.

Editor(s): T C Danson-Smith
Address: 28 George IV Bridge, Edinburgh EH1 1ES
Telephone: 0131 225 4816
Fax: As phone
Payment Details: By arrangement
Unsolicited Manuscripts: No

McCrimmon Publishing Co Ltd

Religious education and music for schools and parishes. Religious clipart on CD ROM. Religious posters and cards.

Editor(s): Eileen Burzynska
Address: 10-12 High Street, Great Wakering, Southend-on-Sea, Essex SS3 0EQ
Telephone: 01702 218956
Fax: 01702 216082
Email: mcrimmons@dial.pipex.com
Payment Details: Royalty only
Unsolicited Manuscripts: No

M
Medici

Publishes illustrated children's picture books drawing on the themes of art, nature and biblical stories.

Address: Grafton House, Hyde Estate Road, London NW9 6JZ
Telephone: 0181 205 2550
Fax: 0181 205 2552
Unsolicited Manuscripts: No - send synopses with specimen illustrations only

Melrose Press Ltd

The International Biographical Centre of Cambridge has been producing a full range of biographical directories for more than thirty years. These directories cover vast interest and geographical areas and are specially designed to provide easy access to detailed biographical information from many varied, prominent individuals. All IBC titles are compiled without political, racial or religious bias and are of genuine international interest.

Editor(s): Jon Gifford
Address: 3 Regal Lane, Soham, Ely, Cambs CB7 5BA
Imprints: International Biographical Centre (IBC)
Unsolicited Manuscripts: Yes biographical data only

The Menard Press

The Menard Press will celebrate its thirtieth birthday in 1999 with a group of new books, including new translations of Rilke and Nerval, and Itinerary, the intellectual autobiography of the Mexican poet Octavio Paz, its third book by a Nobel Prize winner. The Menard Press, which specialises in literary translation (mainly of poetry), is a smaller version of presses such as Carcanet and Bloodaxe but it rarely publishes texts submitted in the usual way, rather it seeks out work of the kind its faithful readers have come to expect over many years of sporadically intensive activity. Around half of the 150 published books are still in print. In addition to translated poetry and other literary texts it has published major essays on the nuclear issue, and a number of testimonies by survivors of Nazism. Its worldwide trade distributors are Central Books, apart from North America, where Small Press Distribution is used.

Editor(s): Anthony Rudolf
Address: The Menard Press (Anthony Rudolf), 8 The Oaks, Woodside Avenue, London N12 8AR
Telephone: 0181 446 5571
Fax: As phone
Imprints: The Menard Press
Unsolicited Manuscripts: No

Mercat Press

Non-fiction Scottish interest titles, no novels or poetry.

Editor(s): Tom Johnstone, Sean Costello
Address: 53 South Bridge, Edinburgh EH1 1YS
Fax: 0131 557 8149
Email: sean.costello@jthin.co.uk (or) tom.johnstone@jthin.co.uk
Website: www.jthin.co.uk/merchome.htm
Imprints: Mercat Press
Parent Company: James Thin Ltd
Payment Details: Annual royalty on copies sold
Unsolicited Manuscripts: Yes - preferably sample chapters and synopsis

ℳ
Mercier Press/Marino Books

One Cork-based imprint (Mercier) and one Dublin-based imprint (Marino). Mercier specialises in history, folklore, heritage & Irish studies, politics. Marino in fiction, popular, business, biography.

Editor(s): Mary Feeman (Mercier), Jo O'Donoghue (Marino)
Address: 5 French Church Street, Cork, Ireland
Telephone: (01)6615299 / (021)275040
Fax: (01)6618583 / (021)274969
Email: books@mercier.ie
Website: www.indigo.ie/usrs/mercier/
Imprints: Mercier, Marino
Parent Company: Mercier Press
Unsolicited Manuscripts: Send complete ms & return postage (not UK postage)

Merlin Press Ltd

Radical history and social studies. Letters and synopses only please.

Editor(s): P Eve
Address: 2 Rendlesham Mews, Rendlesham, Woodbridge, Suffolk IP12 2SZ
Telephone: 01394 461313
Fax: 01394 461314
Email: merlinpres@aol.com
Imprints: Seafarer Books, Greenprint
Payment Details: Royalties on copies sold
Unsolicited Manuscripts: No

Merrell Holberton Publishers Ltd

High quality illustrated books on art, design, textiles, architecture, crafts and exhibitions.

Address: 42 Southwark Street, London SE1 1UN
Telephone: 0171 403 2047
Fax: 0171 407 1333
Imprints: Merrell Holberton
Unsolicited Manuscripts: All correspondence to Hugh Merrell, Publisher

Merrick & Day

Publishers of specialised books on curtain design and interior make-up techniques for designers and curtain makers.

Address: Southfield, Redbourne, Gainsborough, Lincs DN21 4QR
Telephone: 01652 648814
Fax: 01652 648104
Email: merrick.day@drapes.u-net.com
Website: www.drapes.u-net.com

Merrow Publishing Co Ltd

Publishers of textile books. Titles include Handbook Of Textile Fibres Vol 1&2 and Weaving: Conversion Of Yarn To Fabric.

Editor(s): J G Cook
Address: 22 Abbey Road, Darlington DL3 8LR
Telephone: 01325 351661
Fax: As phone
Unsolicited Manuscripts: No

M
Merton Priory Press Ltd

Independent publisher of academic and mid-market history, especially local history and industrial & transport history. Unsolicited manuscripts welcome, especially from young academic historians seeking publication of a first book based on a PhD thesis. Representation available throughout England and Wales.

Editor(s): Philip Riden
Address: 67 Merthyr Road, Whitchurch, Cardiff CF4 1DD
Telephone: 01222 521956
Fax: 01222 623599
Imprints: Merton Priory Press
Payment Details: Royalties half-yearly, normally 10% retail
Unsolicited Manuscripts: Yes, as above

Methodist Publishing House

Popular religious hymn books, serious theology, religious music and drama, Bible study material and the DISCIPLE Bible study course.

Editor(s): Brian Thornton, Susan Hibbins
Address: 20 Ivatt Way, Peterborough PE3 7PG
Imprints: Foundery Press
Parent Company: The Methodist Church
Payment Details: Subject to negotiation
Unsolicited Manuscripts: Yes

Metra Martech

Metra Martech specialises in economic, technical and management reports. Typically these sell in low quantities (100s) and with a high price. People who buy and read the reports are senior managers, planners, technical directors and special interest libraries all over the world. Title examples: Business Opportunities In China; Use Of Countertrade; European Centres Of Expertise In Advanced Materials; Sensors Technology Research; The German Building Market. Authors should either be experts in their own right, or able and willing to grasp the subject and create a report out of our background research. We publish about 3 titles a year. The main business of the company is management consultancy and specialist market research. We have a multilingual team.

Editor(s): Peter Gorle
Address: Glenthorne House, Hammersmith Grove, London W6 0LG
Telephone: 0181 563 0666
Fax: 0181 563 0040
Email: research@metra-martech.com
Website: www.metra-martech.com
Imprints: Metra, Metra Martech, Martech Publications
Parent Company: Relion Plc
Payment Details: Negotiable

M
Metro Publishing Ltd

Two imprints: Metro Books - non-fiction: lifestyle, health, self-help, popular psychology, childcare, travel, popular science, humour, cookery, gardening, biography. Richard Cohen Books - literary non-fiction: biography, autobiography, popular science. Was 1998 Small Publisher of the Year.

Editor(s): Freelance
Address: 19 Gerrard Street, London W1V 7LA
Telephone: 0171 734 1411 (Metro); 0171 439 1948 (RCB)
Fax: 0171 734 1811
Email: metro@metro-books.demon.co.uk
Imprints: Metro Books, Richard Cohen Books
Unsolicited Manuscripts: No

Micelle Press

Technical books and monographs on the science of cosmetics, toiletries, fragrances, detergents and emulsions, and the ingredients and techniques used in the preparation of these products. Natural materials - their sources and applications.

Editor(s): Janet Barber
Address: 10-12 Ullswater Crescent, Weymouth, Dorset DT3 5HE
Telephone: 01305 781574
Fax: As phone
Email: tony@wdi.co.uk
Website: www.wdi.co.uk/micelle
Imprints: Micelle Press
Payment Details: By negotiation
Unsolicited Manuscripts: Send synopsis or sample chapter first

Middleton Press

Specialists in railway, tramway and trolleybus photographic albums for England. Also military subjects in southeast England.

Editor(s): J C V Mitchell
Address: Easebourne Lane, Midhurst, West Sussex GU29 9AZ
Telephone: 01730 813169
Fax: 01730 812601
Imprints: MP
Payment Details: Negotiated
Unsolicited Manuscripts: No

Midland Publishing Ltd

Aviation and railways.

Address: 24 The Hollow, Earl Shilton, Leicester LE9 7NA
Telephone: 01455 847256
Fax: 01455 841805
Email: midlandbooks@compuserve.com
Unsolicited Manuscripts: No

M

MidNag (Mid Northumberland Arts Group)

Publishing programme centres on literature and visual arts.

Editor(s): Managing Editor: G S Payne
Address: Wansbeck Square, Ashington, Northumberland NE63 9XL
Telephone: 01607 814444 x262
Fax: 01670 857743
Imprints: MidNag
Parent Company: Mid Northumberland Arts Group
Payment Details: On application
Unsolicited Manuscripts: No

Milestone Publications

Milestone Publications is the publishing and bookselling division of Goss & Crested China Ltd. We only publish books on Goss & Crested china and English heraldic porcelain.

Editor(s): Nicholas Pine
Address: 62 Murray Road, Horndean, Waterlooville, Hants PO8 9JL
Telephone: 01705 597440
Fax: 01705 591975
Email: info@gosschinaclub.demon.co.uk
Website: www.gosschinaclub.demon.co.uk
Imprints: Milestone, Milestone Publications
Parent Company: Goss & Crested China Ltd
Unsolicited Manuscripts: Should never be sent

M

Harvey Miller Publishers

History of art, reference works; particularly medieval art & history, and 17th century studies.

Editor(s): Elly Miller, Jean-Claude Peissel, Sarah Kane
Address: K101 Tower Bridge Business Complex, 100 Clements Road, London SE16 4DG
Telephone: 0171 252 1531
Fax: 0171 252 3510
Email: sarah.kane@gbhap.com
Website: www.gbhap.com
Parent Company: G+B Arts International
Unsolicited Manuscripts: No

J Garnet Miller Ltd

Plays and theatre books.

Address: 10 Station Road, Industrial Estate, Colwall WR13 6RN
Telephone: 01684 540154
Fax: As phone
Parent Company: Cressrelles Publishing Co
Unsolicited Manuscripts: Yes

M

Mind Publications

Mental health, self-help, psychiatric drug information, complementary therapies, advocacy and mental health legislation.

Editor(s): Anny Brackx
Address: Granta House, 15-19 Broadway, Stratford, London E15 4BQ
Parent Company: Mind
Unsolicited Manuscripts: No

Minerva Press Ltd

Founded in 1997, the Minerva imprint dates back to 1792. Publishes fiction and non-fiction; biography, poetry, children's and religious books. Specialises in new authors; publishes around 250 titles a year. No 'adult' or sexually explicit material. Unsolicited manuscripts, synopses and ideas for books welcome.

Address: 6th Floor, Canberra House, 315-317 Regent Street, London W1R 7YB
Telephone: 0171 580 4114
Fax: 0171 580 9256
Email: mail@minerva-press.co.uk
Website: www.minerva-press.co.uk
Parent Company: Hybeck Holdings Ltd
Payment Details: Royalties twice-yearly
Unsolicited Manuscripts: Yes

Mitchell Beazley

Antiques, the arts, crafts, interior design, architecture, gardening, sex & health, wine, cookery and reference books.

Address: 2-4 Heron Quays, London E14 4JP
Telephone: 0171 531 8400
Fax: 0171 531 8650
Website: www.mitchell-beazley.co.uk
Parent Company: Octopus Publishing Group Ltd

Monarch Publications

All Christian literature excluding children's material, fiction and poetry.

Editor(s): Tony Collins
Address: Broadway House, The Broadway, Crowborough, East Sussex TN6 1HQ
Telephone: 01892 652364
Fax: 01892 663329
Email: monarch@dial.pipex.com
Imprints: Monarch Marc
Unsolicited Manuscripts: Yes

M

Moorleys Print & Publishing Ltd

All following of the Christian faith only: drama scripts; school assemblies; adult verse; children's recitations; prayers and meditations; humorous monologues; Bible study notes for small groups.

Editor(s): S Moorley
Address: 23 Park Road, Ilkeston, Derbyshire DE7 5DA
Email: 106545.413@compuserve.com
Payment Details: Royalties
Unsolicited Manuscripts: No

Morrigan Books

Established 1978, specialises in Ireland interest non-fiction titles, particularly history, folklore, mythology, autobiography, New Age and occult interest. Titles with a Celtic theme are also relevant.

Editor(s): Gerry Kennedy
Address: Gore Street, Killala, Co Mayo, Ireland
Telephone: 096 32555
Fax: As phone
Email: admin@atlanticisland.ie
Website: www.atlanticisland.ie
Imprints: Morrigan, Atlantic Island, Heritage Guides
Parent Company: Morigna Mediaco Teo
Payment Details: On contract
Unsolicited Manuscripts: Preliminary letter & IRC first

Multi-Sensory Learning

Special needs titles including a fully structured, integrated and cumulative literacy skills programme.

Editor(s): Philippa Attwood
Address: Earlstrees Court, Earlstrees Road, Corby, Northants NN17 4HH
Telephone: 01536 399003
Fax: 01536 399012
Email: firstbest9@aol.com
Parent Company: First & Best In Education
Payment Details: Royalties
Unsolicited Manuscripts: No

Multilingual Matters Ltd

Academic publishers in the fields of applied linguistics, translation studies and tourism. Also parents and teachers' guides and general information on bilingualism.

Address: Frankfurt Lodge, Clevedon Hall, Victoria Road, Clevedon BS21 7HH
Telephone: 01275 876519
Fax: 01275 343096
Email: multi@multilingual-matters.com
Website: www.multilingual-matters.com
Imprints: Channel View Books

M
John Murray (Publishers) Ltd

School books, success study books, history, biography, travel, art & architecture, politics, current affairs, war & military.

Editor(s): Grant McIntyre, Caroline Knox, Gail Pirkis
Address: 50 Albemarle Street, London W1X 4BD
Telephone: 0171 493 4361
Fax: 0171 499 1792
Payment Details: Royalties paid twice-yearly
Unsolicited Manuscripts: No

Peter Nahum At The Leicester Galleries Ltd

Illustrated art books and pamphlets. Eg of titles: Burne-Jones, The Pre-Raphaelites And Their Century; Michael Rothenstein's Boxes; Henri Gaudier-Brzeska - A Sculptor's Drawings; Fairy Folk In Fairy Land (William Allingham's fairy poem illustrated by Peter Nahum).

Editor(s): Peter Nahum
Address: 5 Ryder Street, London SW1Y 6PY
Telephone: 0171 930 6059
Fax: 0171 930 4678
Email: peternahum@netserve.net
Parent Company: The Leicester Galleries

National Academy Press

Publishes the reports issued by the National Academy of Science, the National Academy of Engineering, the Institute of Medicine and the National Research Council, all operating under a charter granted by the Congress of the United States of America. Subjects: science, technology, engineering, medicine and health.

Address: 12 Hid's Copse Road, Cumnor Hill, Oxford OX2 9JJ
Telephone: 01865 865466
Fax: 01865 862763
Email: nap@opp.i-way.co.uk
Website: www.nas.edu
Imprints: Joseph Henry Press
Parent Company: National Academy Press
Unsolicited Manuscripts: No

National Association For The Teaching Of English (NATE)

Academic research focused on the teaching of English 5-18+. Case studies of classroom practice. Materials to support the teaching of English. Classroom resources.

Editor(s): Ann Shreeve
Address: NATE, 50 Broadfield Road, Sheffield S8 0XJ
Telephone: 0114 225 5419
Fax: 0114 225 5296
Email: nate.hq@campus.bt.com
Website: www.nate.org.uk
Imprints: NATE, NATE/YPS(Shared Reading at KS 2, Classic Reading 11-16, post-16)
Payment Details: No advance, royalties on sales by agreement
Unsolicited Manuscripts: No

National Children's Bureau

The National Children's Bureau works to identify and promote the well-being and interests of all children and young people across every aspect of their lives. It collects and disseminates information about children and promotes good practice in children's services through research, policy and practice development, membership, publications, conferences, training and an extensive library and information service.

Address: 8 Wakley Street, London EC1V 7QE
Telephone: 0171 843 6028/6029
Fax: 0171 278 9512
Email: booksales@ncb.org.uk
Website: www.ncb.org.uk
Imprints: National Children's Bureau
Unsolicited Manuscripts: Publication proposal form also needs to be completed

National Christian Education Council

Bible reading notes, group bible study notes, worship anthologies, prayer anthologies, Teddy Horsley series for young children, Holiday Club material, all-age worship and learning material and a Christian education journal. Books on different aspects of family life.

Editor(s): Elizabeth Bruce
Address: 1020 Bristol Road, Selly Oak, Birmingham B29 6LB
Telephone: 0121 472 4242
Fax: 0121 472 7575
Email: ncec@ncec.org.uk
Website: www.ncec.org.uk
Imprints: NCEC, IBRA (International Bible Reading Association)
Unsolicited Manuscripts: Yes

National Coaching Foundation (NCF)

The NCF publishes material in various formats for the education and information of sports coaches. Primary medium is books and periodicals, but beginning to deliver electronically. Most material produced is distributed by Coachwise, the trading arm of the NCF, but also by governing bodies of sport. The NCF welcomes authors writing on sports science or coaching issues in generic or sports-specific contexts. The NCF also commissions authors with special interest in these areas for in-house projects.

Editor(s): Bill Galvin, Anne Simpkin
Address: 114 Cardigan Road, Headingley, Leeds LS6 3BJ
Telephone: 0113 2744802
Fax: 0113 2755019
Email: bgalvin@ucf.org.uk
Website: www.ncf.org.uk
Parent Company: National Coaching Foundation
Payment Details: Negotiable
Unsolicited Manuscripts: To Bill Galvin, Head of Publications

National Extension College

Distance learning courses, NVQ training materials, open learning packs, training resources, consultancy & staff development packs. NEC is a self-financing educational trust and is one of the UK's most successful open learning providers.

Address: 18 Brooklands Avenue, Cambridge CB2 2HN
Telephone: 01223 450200
Fax: 01223 313586
Email: info@nec.ac.uk
Website: www.nec.ac.uk
Imprints: NEC
Unsolicited Manuscripts: No

National Library Of Scotland

Publishes bibliographies, facsimiles, catalogues, literary and historical books mainly of Scottish interest. Tends to publish in partnership with commercial publishing houses.

Editor(s): Head of Public Programmes: Kenneth Gibson
Address: George 1V Bridge, Edinburgh EH1 1EQW
Telephone: 0131 226 4531
Fax: 0131 622 4803
Email: enquiries@nls.uk
Website: www.nls.uk
Unsolicited Manuscripts: Send outline & covering letter in first instance

National Portrait Gallery

Publishers of books on art, biography and cultural history; exhibition catalogues and educational material; as well as posters, postcards and unusual gifts and stationery.

Editor(s): Publishing Manager: Jacky Colliss Harvey; Senior Editor: Lucy Clark; Sales & Marketing: Pallavi Vadhia
Address: Publications Department, 2 St Martin's Place, London WC2H 0HE
Telephone: 0171 306 0055 ext266
Fax: 0171 306 0092
Email: pvadhia@npg.org.uk
Website: www.npg.org.uk

The Natural History Museum - Publishing Division

Academic & scholarly; biology & zoology; fine art & art history; geography & geology; natural history; scientific & technical.

Editor(s): Head of Publishing: June Hogg; Editorial Manager: Trudy Brannan; Production Manager: Lynn Millhouse; Assistant Editor: Catharine Baden-Daintree
Address: Cromwell Road, London SW6 5BD
Telephone: 0171 938 9048
Fax: 0171 938 8709
Email: publishing @nhm.ac.uk
Website: www.nhm.ac.uk
Imprints: The Natural History Museum - Publishing Division
Unsolicited Manuscripts: No

Need2Know

Need2Know publishes a distinctive series of self-help non-fiction for the general reader. Subjects fall within the consumer/health/personal relationship areas. Current titles include A Parent's Guide To Dyslexia, Make The Most Of Your Retirement, The Facts About The Menopause, Make The Most Of Being A Carer, It's Up To You - Your Blueprint For A Better Life. We are open to ideas and proposals for new titles, especially from experts/practitioners in their subject. Will read and comment on manuscript submissions.

Editor(s): Anne Sandys
Address: Remus House, Coltsfoot Drive, Woodston, Peterborough PE2 9JX
Telephone: 01733 898103
Fax: 01733 313524
Parent Company: Forward Press Ltd
Payment Details: Advance, 15% royalties
Unsolicited Manuscripts: Yes

Network Educational Press Ltd

The company focuses its activity on the quality of teaching and learning in mainstream education, working with teachers and their managers in three ways: publishing high-quality, accessible and practical books; producing quality educational conferences; providing in-service training for teachers. All these activities draw upon current practical research, particularly that on how the brain functions, and then present the outcomes in ways that can be applied directly to the classroom. Examples of titles: Accelerated Learning In Practice (Smith); Accelerated Learning In The Classroom (Smith); Effective Learning Activities (Dickenson); Raising Boys' Achievement (Pickering); Effective Provision For Able And Talented Children (Teare).

Editor(s): Gina Whisker, Carol Thompson, Chris Griffin
Address: Box 635, Stafford ST16 1BF
Telephone: 01785 225515
Fax: 01785 228566
Email: enquiries@networkpress.co.uk
Website: www.networkpress.co.uk
Unsolicited Manuscripts: Yes, considered

New Beacon Books

Small specialist publisher. Areas of interest: Caribbean, Africa, Black Britain, Black Europe.

Editor(s): John La Rose
Address: 76 Stroud Green Road, London N4 3EN
Telephone: 0171 272 4889
Fax: 0171 281 4662
Unsolicited Manuscripts: No

New City

Publishers of religious books.

Editor(s): Callan Slipper
Address: 57 Twyford Avenue, London W3 9PZ
Telephone: 0181 993 6944
Fax: As phone
Email: newcity@mcmail.com
Unsolicited Manuscripts: To Editor

New Clarion Press

Workers' co-operative publishing non-fiction books on current affairs and social policy for the intelligent general reader and college market. Our publications are written from a reformist perspective. We do not yet publish fiction, but are open to persuasion.

Editor(s): Chris Bessant
Address: 5 Church Row, Gretton, Cheltenham GL54 5HG
Telephone: 01242 620623
Fax: As phone
Email: chrisbessant@clarion.prestel.co.uk
Payment Details: Royalty
Unsolicited Manuscripts: Synopsis in first instance

New Era Publications UK Ltd

New Era publish the works of L Ron Hubbard only. However, the L Ron Hubbard Writers Of The Future Contest is a quarterly contest for new sf/fantasy writers. Full details available on request.

Address: Saint Hill Manor, East Grinstead RH19 4JY
Telephone: 01342 314846
Fax: 01342 314857
Parent Company: New Era Publications International
Unsolicited Manuscripts: No

New European Publication Ltd

Publish books on a wide range of European affairs as well as other matters. Publish and edit World Review and New European. Also work with Adamantine Press and I B Tauris, although those are not New European imprints. All books distributed through Central Book.

Editor(s): Richard Body, John Coleman
Address: 14-16 Carroun Road, London SW8 1JT
Imprints: NEP

New Holland (Publishers) Ltd

International co-edition publishers of illustrated reference books for the international market. Subjects published: interiors; DIY and home decoration; soft furnishings; outdoor DIY and gardening; needlecrafts; crafts (including mosaics, stained glass, ceramics, etc); food and drink; cake decorating; art and design; gift books. Our international travel and wildlife programme covers numerous destinations and includes: travel guides, maps and atlases; large-format illustrated travel titles; walking guides; diving, climbing and golf guides; large-format underwater and sports titles; natural history field and pocket guides; large-format wildlife and 'wildplaces' titles.

Editor(s): Yvonne McFarlane, Charlotte Parry-Crooke
Address: 24 Nutford Place, London W1H 6DQ
Telephone: 0171 724 7773
Fax: 0171 724 6184
Email: postmaster@nhpub.co.uk
Imprints: New Holland,Struik, Southern, Zebra
Parent Company: Struik Publishers
Payment Details: By negotiation
Unsolicited Manuscripts: Yes

New Island Books

Founded in 1992, New Island Books has continued the innovative and often polemical publishing tradition of its predecessor Raven Arts Press. Recent successes include Are You Somebody by Nuala O'Faolain; The Secret World Of The Irish Male by Joe O'Connor; Our Father: A Tribute To Dermot Morgan by Don, Bobby & Ben Morgan; Lie Of The Land by Fintan O'Toole.

Editor(s): Executive Editor: Dermot Bolger; Managing Editor: Ciara Considine
Address: 2 Brookside, Dundrum Road, Dublin 14, Ireland
Telephone: 3531 2989937
Fax: 3531 2982783
Imprints: New Island Books, Brookside
Payment Details: Twice a year
Unsolicited Manuscripts: With SAE. Fiction & non-fiction; no original poetry or short stories

New Living Publishers

Pentecostal/evangelical publisher. Only publish own material.

Address: 164 Radcliffe New Road, Whitefield, Manchester M45 7TU
Telephone: 0161 7661166
Fax: As phone
Email: theway@ministrybl.freeserve.co.uk
Unsolicited Manuscripts: No

New Playwrights' Network

Publishes plays for amateur performance.

Editor(s): L G Smith
Address: 10 Station Road, Colwall, Worcs WR13 6RN

New World Press

High-quality general non-fiction and educational books, covering literature, science, culture, philosophy, spirituality. Write to Sales Department for current lists. Bimonthly journal New World covering similar subjects and short stories.

Editor(s): Matt Fopson
Address: 24 Grange Court, Grange Road, Sutton, Surrey SM2 6RR
Telephone: 0181 643 3967
Fax: 0181 287 2350
Imprints: New World, Knightscross
Unsolicited Manuscripts: No unsolicited mss. Typewritten synopses considered; please allow 6-8 weeks for a response.

Nexus Special Interests

Hobby and leisure in the core subject areas of modelling, model engineering, radio control modelling, workshop practice, home brewing, and military modelling.

Address: Nexus House, Azalea Drive, Swanley, Kent BR8 8HU
Telephone: 01322 660070
Fax: 01322 616309
Parent Company: Nexus Media
Payment Details: Standard authors' contract advance & royalties
Unsolicited Manuscripts: Yes

NIACE

The National Organisation for Adult Learning publishes books and journals on policy and practice in adult education. Our aim is to promote adult learning for all people, regardless of age, race, gender, disability, social or economic background. We do this by organising conferences, through publishing, research and development work. We seek to influence government, business, trade unions, adult education providers.

Editor(s): Senior Publications Officer: Virman Man
Address: 21 De Monfort Street, Leicester LE1 7GE
Telephone: 0116 204 4200
Fax: 0116 285 4514
Imprints: NIACE
Parent Company: NIACE
Payment Details: By negotiation

NMS Publishing Ltd

Scottish history and culture, Scottish literary anthologies, art, archaeology, geology, museum studies science and technology.

Editor(s): Helen Kemp
Address: Royal Museum, Chambers Street, Edinburgh EH1 1JF
Telephone: 0131 247 4026
Fax: 0131 247 4012
Email: cmw@nms.ac.uk
Payment Details: Royalties
Unsolicited Manuscripts: Synopsis and sample chapter only

No Exit Press

Leading independent publisher of crime and noir fiction.

Address: 18 Coleswood Road, Harpenden, Herts AL5 1EP
Telephone: 01582 761264
Fax: 01582 712244
Email: info@noexit.co.uk
Website: www.noexit.co.uk
Unsolicited Manuscripts: No

North York Moors National Park

Publish booklets on walking in the North York Moors as well as booklets on local history and natural history of interest to visitors to the area. Also publish planning documents and strategies relevant to the area work and research papers relating to archaeology, the environment, etc.

Editor(s): Jill Renney
Address: The Old Vicarage, Bondgate, Helmsley, York YO62 5BP
Telephone: 01439 770657
Fax: 01439 770691
Email: info@northyorkmoors-npa.gov.uk
Website: www.northyorkmoors-npa.gov.uk

Northcote House Publishers Ltd

Established in 1985, publishes up to 30 titles each year in the fields of: literary criticism (Writers & Work series); education and education management (Resources In Education); careers and self-development (Starting Out . . .); and a small number of education dance and drama titles. In addition to the above, a series of studies of specific works of literature is in preparation, aimed at A level and higher education students in both English and Modern Languages.

Editor(s): Brian Hulme
Address: Plymbridge House, Estover Road, Plymouth, Devon PL6 7PY
Telephone: 01752 202368
Fax: 01752 202330
Imprints: Northcote House
Parent Company: Northcote House Publishers Ltd
Payment Details: Annual royalty by contract
Unsolicited Manuscripts: Well argued proposals in the above subjects with good marketing credentials welcome

W W Norton & Co

Independent publisher of quality trade and academic books. Subject areas include biology; business books; history; music; nautical; biography; poetry; politics & current affairs; sport; photography; and art & architecture. Norton's college list includes textbooks in literature & criticism; classical studies; music; history; economics; psychology & science.

Editor(s): All editorial work undertaken in the US
Address: 10 Coptic Street, London WC1A 1PU
Telephone: 0171 323 1579
Fax: 0171 436 4553
Email: office@wwnorton.co.uk
Website: www.wwnorton.com
Imprints: Liveright Publishing Corporation, The Countryman Press
Parent Company: W W Norton & Co Inc, 500 Fifth Avenue, New York NY10110

Nottingham University Press

Agriculture, medicine, geography, food science, law, sports and engineering. Other subject areas also considered.

Editor(s): D J A Cole
Address: Manor Farm, Main Street, Thrumpton, Nottingham NG11 0AX
Telephone: 0115 9831011
Fax: 0115 9831003
Imprints: Castle Publications
Unsolicited Manuscripts: Yes

Oakwood Press & Oakwood Video Library

Established 1931. Family-owned company specialising in transport topics - buses, trams, canals, and especially railways. Producing books of interest to railway historians and enthusiasts alike. Catalogue available.

Editor(s): Various
Address: PO Box 13, Usk NP5 1YS
Telephone: 01291 690505
Fax: 01291 690606
Unsolicited Manuscripts: Yes

O

Oasis Books

Publishers of short fiction and poetry - no novels. Look for work that takes linguistic and imaginative risks and which would not normally find a home with mainstream publishers. Our programme for 1999 is full. Also publish Oasis Magazine - 6 issues a year - looks for a wide range of excellent writing that concentrates on originality of thought, expression and imagination.

Editor(s): Ian Robinson
Address: 12 Stevenage Road, London SW6 6ES
Telephone: 0171 736 5059
Imprints: Oasis Books
Payment Details: Copies only
Unsolicited Manuscripts: Yes but not for 1999

Oberon Books

Theatre books, play texts and translation of plays.

Editor(s): James Hogan, Cathy Herbert, Humphrey Gudgeon
Address: 521 Caledonian Road, London N7 9RH
Telephone: 0171 6073637
Fax: 0171 6073629
Email: oberon.books@btinternet.com
Imprints: Oberon Modern Playwrights, Absolute Classics
Unsolicited Manuscripts: Yes

OCLC Forest Press

A division of OCLC Online Computer Library Centre. Publishes the DDC (Dewey Decimal Classification) in 4 volumes. (£220 + p&p).

Editor(s): Joan S Mitchell
Address: OCLC Europe, 7th Floor, Tricorn House, 51-53 Hagley Road, Edgbaston, Birmingham B16 8TP
Telephone: 0121 456 4656
Fax: 0121 456 4680
Email: europe@oclc.org
Website: www.oclc.org/europe

The Octagon Press

Philosophy, psychology, Sufism, eastern classics and travel. We do not accept any manuscripts which we have not ourselves commissioned under any circumstances.

Editor(s): G R Schrager
Address: PO Box 227, London N6 4EW
Telephone: 0181 348 9392
Fax: 0181 341 5971
Email: octagon@octagonpress.com
Website: www.octagonpress.com
Unsolicited Manuscripts: No

O
Octopus Publishing Group

The group comprises the following, with specialist areas as noted: Hamlyn Octopus (cookery, gardening, craft, sport, film tie-ins, rock 'n' roll); Mitchell Beazley (antiques, gardening, craft & interiors, wine); Millers (antiques & collectibles); Conran Octopus (lifestyle, cookery, gardening); Philips (atlases, maps, encyclopaedias); Bounty (promotional publishing); Brimax. All are adult illustrated reference publishers, with the exception of Brimax, a publisher of illustrated children's books.

Editor(s): Publishers: Laura Bamford (Hamlyn); Jane Aspden (Mitchell Beazley/ Millers); Carolyn Proud (Conran Octopus); John Gaisford (Philips); Mark Newman (Bounty/Brimax)
Address: 1-4 Heron Quays, London E14 9
Telephone: 0171 531 8400
Fax: 0171 531 8650
Website: www.octopus-publishing.co.uk
Parent Company: Octopus Publishing Group
Unsolicited Manuscripts: Yes

Old Bailey Press

Publisher of the largest integrated student law library of textbooks, casebooks, statutes and revision workbooks, providing busy students with a complete package of study materials in a wide range of subjects. Currently undergoing a period of growth and development, Old Bailey Press has recently launched three new series - 150 Leading Cases, 101 Questions And Answers and Law In Practice. The launch of the Law In Practice series marks a significant expansion into the field of practitioner texts. These concise guides, in keeping with our ethos, are competitively priced and cover recent developments in key areas of mainstream practice. A primary aim of the texts is to enable busy practitioners and students on professional law courses to keep readily abreast of current developments in law and practice. The series also includes a number of specialist texts on some of the fast-emerging areas of contemporary legal practice.

Editor(s): Editorial Director: Cedric Bell; Legal Editor: Helen O'Shea
Address: 200 Greyhound Road, London W14 9RY
Telephone: 0171 385 3377
Fax: 0171 381 3377
Email: hlt@holborncollege.ac.uk
Website: www.holborncollege.ac.uk
Parent Company: The HLT Group Ltd

O

The Oleander Press

Language and literature; travel; games & pastimes; reference; biography; Cambridge town, gown & county; Arabia past and present. Before sending a synopsis or idea (with SAE), read our manual The Small Publisher, with account of how The Oleander Press grew yet stayed small, and the sequel, The Oleander Press: 37 Years As A Small Publisher in The National Small Press Centre Handbook (1997), pp. 75-78. Latest titles are Contemporary Designer Bookbinders: A Worldwide Illustrated Directory (£30), Dennis Baron's De Vere Is Shakespeare: Evidence From The Biography And Wordplay (£9.95), and a reworking of The Oresteia by William Whallon to incorporate a version of the lost satyr play (£9.95).

Address: 17 Stansgate Avenue, Cambridge CB2 2QZ
Unsolicited Manuscripts: No

Ollav Healer Publications

Self-publishing company with the following publications: A Path Directed (Life of James Cassidy, WW1 veteran and Belfast City missionary 1892-1970); Cousins (local history booklet); Clarendon, Belfast (locally set historical fiction); Circumstantial Evidence (evidence supporting biblical facts).

Editor(s): D Cassidy
Address: 9 Brunswick Park, Bangor, Co Down BT20 3DR
Telephone: 01247 473362
Unsolicited Manuscripts: No

Omnibus Press

Books about music (mostly pop) for the general reader.

Editor(s): Chris Charlesworth, Robert Dimery
Address: 8-9 Frith Street, London W1V 5TZ
Telephone: 0171 434 0066
Fax: 0171 734 2246
Website: www.omnibuspress.com
Imprints: Omnibus, Bobcat, Gramophone, RED, BBC Music Guides, Independent Music Press, Rogan House, Showcase, Firefly, Parker Mead, OZone
Parent Company: Music Sales
Unsolicited Manuscripts: To Robert Dimery

On Stream Publications

Mainly non-fiction practical books especially food, wine, health, academic. Now considering fiction. Company histories, commissioned books with strong editoral support, souvenir books, books of photography. No children's books or poetry.

Editor(s): Roz Crowley
Address: Cloghroe, Blarney, Co Cork, Ireland
Telephone: 35321 385798
Fax: As phone
Email: onstream@indigo.ie
Website: http//indigo.ie/~onstream
Payment Details: Royalites twice-yearly
Unsolicited Manuscripts: No - summaries only

O

Oneworld Publications

An independent publishing house specialising in books on world religions, comparative religion, mysticism, psychology and inspirational writing. Large enough to benefit from worldwide distribution by Penguin Books, we are also small enough to ensure that we publish only quality titles by authors who are leaders in their field. Consistently producing cutting-edge texts by leading academics, Oneworld is frequently acclaimed for its work in increasing interfaith understanding and religious tolerance, while our inspirational and self-help books continue to attract favourable reviews.

Editor(s): Helen Coward
Address: 185 Banbury Road, Oxford OX2 7AR
Telephone: 01865 310597
Fax: 01865 310598
Email: oneworld@cix.co.uk
Website: www.oneworld-publications.com
Unsolicited Manuscripts: Yes

Onlywomen Press Ltd

The radical edge of feminist, lesbian literature: fiction, political theory, poetry, literary criticism, lesbian romance and crime novels.

Editor(s): Apply first to company as a whole
Address: 40 St Lawrence Terrace, London W10 5ST
Telephone: 0181 960 7122
Fax: 0181 960 2817
Email: onlywomen_press@compuserve.com
Imprints: Zest (lesbian romance), Onlywomencrime (lesbian crim novels), Liaison (feminist theory & research)
Payment Details: By publishing contract
Unsolicited Manuscripts: Yes

Open Books Publishing Ltd

Packagers of gardening books and general publishers.

Editor(s): Patrick Taylor
Address: Willow Cottage, Cudworth, Nr Ilminster, Somerset TA19 0PS
Telephone: 01460 52565
Fax: As phone
Email: patrickta@aol.com
Imprints: Somerset House
Unsolicited Manuscripts: Always write first

Open Gate Press

Founded in 1988 by a group of psycholanalysts, social psychiatrists and artists to provide a forum for psycholanalytic social studies - a branch of psychoanalysis which Freud hoped would be a major contribution to the 'liberation of humanity from the pathology of civilisations'. Despite some attempts since Freud's time to apply psychoanalysis to social problems, his hopes have not been fulfilled, and the raison d'etre of Open Gate Press is to remedy this. The company publishes a series Psychoanalysis And Society as well as writings by experts in various fields of the social sciences, with the objective of arousing the interest of a wide public. The aim of the publishers is also to bring life to the increasingly moribund state of philosophy. Finally, the publishers are keen to promote debate on a wide variety of environmental issues.

Address: 51 Achilles Road, London NW6 1DZ
Email: books@opengate.demon.co.uk
Website: www.opengate.demon.co.uk
Imprints: Open Gate Press, Centaur Press, Linden Press
Parent Company: Open Gate Press
Payment Details: Royalties twice-yearly
Unsolicited Manuscripts: Synopses & ideas for books welcome

O

Open University Press

Subjects published in the areas of health & social welfare, counselling & psychotherapy, psychology, women's studies, sociology, politics, criminology, education and higher education.

Editor(s): Jacinta Evans
Address: Celtic Court, 22 Ballmoor, Buckingham MK18 1XW
Telephone: 01280 823388
Fax: 01280 823233
Email: enquiries@openup.co.uk
Website: www.openup.co.uk
Imprints: Open University Press
Unsolicited Manuscripts: No

Orchard Books

Children's fiction : board books, picture books. Gift books. Young and older fiction.

Editor(s): Francesca Dow
Address: 96 Leonard Street, London EC2A 4RH
Parent Company: Watts Publishing Group
Payment Details: By negotiation
Unsolicited Manuscripts: Yes

Ordnance Survey

National map makers of Great Britain.

Address: Romsey Road, Maybush, Southampton SO16 4GU
Telephone: 08456 050505
Fax: 01703 792452
Email: custinfo@ordsvy.gov.uk
Website: www.ordsvy.gov.uk

O

Oriel Stringer

Publishers of ornithological books covering the breeding biology of wild birds and their nesting sites.

Editor(s): M J Dawson
Address: 66 Tivoli Crescent, Brighton BN1 5ND
Telephone: 01273 723413

Orion Children's Books

Fiction, age range 0-14+.

Editor(s): Managing Dir & Publisher: Judith Elliott
Address: Orion House, 5 Upper St Martin's Lane, London WC2H 9EA
Imprints: Orion Children's Books, Dolphin Paperbacks
Parent Company: Orion Publishing Group
Unsolicited Manuscripts: No

Osborne Books Ltd

Publishers of business education and accounting texts for secondary and tertiary sectors under the Osborne Books imprint. Also publishers of local history and general historical books under the Osborne Heritage imprint.

Editor(s): Michael Fardon
Address: Unit 1b, Everoak Estate, Bromyard Road, St Johns, Worcester WR2 5HN
Telephone: 01905 748071
Fax: 01905 748952
Email: books@osborne.u net.com
Website: www.osbornebooks.co.uk
Imprints: Osborne Books, Osborne Heritage
Payment Details: By negotiation
Unsolicited Manuscripts: To Editor

O

Otter Publications

Specialising in layperson's texts on motoring, law and business. Published book on a particular form of sports massage called soft tissue release, and this is an area we would like to explore and develop.

Editor(s): Jonathan Hutchings
Address: 9 Roman Way, Fishbourne, Chichester PO19 2QN
Telephone: 01243 539106
Fax: 01243 839669
Imprints: Otter Publications
Payment Details: 10% roylaty on net receipts
Unsolicited Manuscripts: Yes

Peter Owen

Literary (non-genre) adult fiction list, including work in translation. Biographies and memoirs of writers, artists, celebrities, etc. Only very rarely do we publish memoirs of lesser-known people. We also publish general non-fiction including history, literary criticism, arts subjects (not highly illustrated), social science, current affairs, philosophy, psychology and entertainment. Note that all manuscripts or, preferably, synopses and sample chapters, should be accompanied by return postage. No poetry.

Editor(s): Antonia Owen
Address: 73 Kenway Road, London SW5 0RE
Telephone: 0171 373 5628
Fax: 0171 373 6760
Email: admin@peterowen.u-net.com
Unsolicited Manuscripts: Only with prior request & SAE

Oxfam Publishing

Publishes and distributes books and other resource materials for development practitioners, policy makers, academics, schools, children and young people, as part of its programme of advocacy, education and information.

Editor(s): Catherine Robinson, Anke Lueddecke
Address: 274 Banbury Road, Oxford OX2 7DZ
Telephone: 01865 313774
Fax: 01865 313790
Email: dlogan@oxfam.org.uk
Website: www.oxfam.org.uk
Parent Company: Oxfam GB
Payment Details: Varied
Unsolicited Manuscripts: No

Oxford University Press

A department of the University of Oxford. Furthers the University's objective of excellence in research, scholarship and education by publishing worldwide. It is the world's largest university press, publishing more than 4,000 titles a year. It has a presence in more than 50 countries, employing some 3,500 staff. Turnover in 1997/998 was £282 million.

Address: Great Clarendon Street, Oxford OX2 6DP
Telephone: 01865 556767
Fax: 01865 556646
Email: enquiry@oup.co.uk
Website: www.oup.com
Parent Company: University of Oxford

P
Pallas Athene

Travel and art history.

Address: 59 Linden Gardens, London W2 4HJ
Unsolicited Manuscripts: Yes

Parkway Publishing

Books on Middle East, mainly Egypt. Non-fiction: facsimile editions of famous travel books. Examples: 100 Miles Up The Nile by Amelia Edwards; Letters From Egypt by Florence Nightingale.

Address: 4-5 Academy Building, Fanshaw Street, London N1 6LQ
Telephone: 0171 613 5533
Fax: 0171 613 4433

Parthian Books

New Welsh fiction and drama in English. Previous titles include Work, Sex & Rugby; Streetlife; The Mayor Of Aln.

Address: 53 Colum Road, Cardiff CF10 3EF
Telephone: 01222 341314
Fax: As phone
Payment Details: 10% net sales
Unsolicited Manuscripts: No. Synopsis with sample chapters

PASS Publications (Private Academic & Scientific Studies Ltd)

Publish a series of 10 books for GCE A level in pure mathematics, comprehensively covering the syllabus of most examination boards. They uniquely include (in Part 2) complete solutions to all exercises at the end of each chapter. Can be purchased separately or as a set (set price £95). Publish detailed solutions for the Edexel exams (1994 and continuing) in pure mathematics, mechanics and statistics; produced every year in April and September for the January and June exams respectively. Also available for technicians are Electrical And Electronic Principles 1 & 2 (£12.95, £14.95) and Engineering Maths (2 books, £9.95 for both).

Editor(s): Anthony Nicolaides
Address: 11 Baring Road, London SE12 0JP
Telephone: 0181 857 4752
Fax: 0181 857 9427

Pastest

Revision books relating to post-graduate and undergraduate medical exams.

Editor(s): Sue Harrison
Address: Egerton Court, Parkgate Estate, Knutsford, Cheshire WA16 8DX
Telephone: 01565 752000
Fax: 01565 650264
Email: sue@pastest.co.uk
Website: www.pastest.co.uk
Payment Details: Negotiable
Unsolicited Manuscripts: Yes

Paternoster Publishing

Paternoster publishes books to advance the Christian faith and encourage a bibical world view and lifestyle.

Editor(s): Mark Finnie
Address: PO Box 300, Kingstown, Carlisle CA3 0QS
Imprints: Paternoster, Solway
Parent Company: Send the Light
Payment Details: Royalty 10-14% net receipts
Unsolicited Manuscripts: Yes

Paupers' Press

Publish booklets containing 10,000-15,000-word essays, mostly on literary criticism. Occasionally produce full-length books - but only to accommodate an exceptional manuscript. Publish up to 6 new titles a year, which are distributed in the US by Borgo Press. Also operate as a centre for Colin Wilson studies, publishing his work and essays on it by well-known Wilson scholars. Examples of titles: Sex And The Intelligent Teenager by Colin Wilson; Witchcraft And Misogyny by Samantha Giles; Woody Allen's Trilogy Of Terror by Christina Byrnes. We also distribute selected titles for the US publishers Borgo Press and Robert Briggs Associates.

Editor(s): Colin Stanley
Address: 27 Melbourne Road, West Bridgeford, Nottingham NG2 5DJ
Telephone: 0115 9815063
Fax: As phone
Email: stan2727uk@aol.com
Website: http://members.aol.com/stan2727uk/pauper.htm
Imprints: Paupers' Press
Unsolicited Manuscripts: No. Write in first instance outlining content of essay

PBN Publications

Publish transcripts of local (Sussex) archives which are of particular interest to family and local historians. Publications are either in book form or on microfilm.

Address: 22 Abbey Road, Eastbourne BN20 8TE
Telephone: 01323 731206

Pearson Education

Educational publisher - all levels, preschool through postgraduate; all subjects.

Address: Edinburgh Gate, Harlow, Essex CM20 2JE
Telephone: 01279 623623
Fax: 01279 431059
Email: pearsoned-ema.com
Website: www.pearsoned.com
Imprints: Longman, Addison-Wesley, Prentice Hall, Financial Times Management, Macmillan, Scott Foresman
Parent Company: Pearson Plc
Unsolicited Manuscripts: Yes

P
Pearson Publishing

Educational resources for primary and secondary schools. All subjects including school management and policy titles. Resources include photocopiable resources, student handbooks, revision guides, software, IT training materials. Titles can be ordered via website. Sample sheets can also be downloaded.

Editor(s): Maura Rutter, Donna Bones
Address: Chesterton Mill, French's Road, Cambridge CB4 3NP
Telephone: 01223 350555
Fax: 01223 356484
Email: infor@pearson.co.uk
Website: www.pearson.co.uk
Payment Details: Royalties on publisher's net receipts, sometimes royalty advances paid
Unsolicited Manuscripts: To George Pearson

J M Pearson & Son (Publishers) Ltd

Founded 1981; specialise in canal and railway related materials; all titles produced in-house.

Address: Tatenhill Common, Burton-on-Trent DE13 9RS
Telephone: 01283 713674
Fax: As phone
Email: jpearson@netcomuk.
Website: www.page-net.co.uk/pearsons
Unsolicited Manuscripts: No

Peartree Publications

Christian musicals and educational piano music.

Editor(s): Roger M Stepney
Address: 61 Peartree Lane, Little Common, Bexhill-On-Sea, East Sussex TN39 4PE
Unsolicited Manuscripts: No

Peepal Tree Press

Began publishing in 1986. Peepal Tree focuses on the Caribbean and its Diaspora, and also publishes writing from the South Asian Diaspora and Africa. Its books seek to express the popular resources of transplanted and transforming cultures. Has now published over 100 quality literary paperback titles, with fiction, poetry and literary, cultural and historical studies. We publish around 15 English language titles a year, with writers from Guyana, Jamaica, Trinidad, Nigeria, Bangladesh, Montserrat, St Lucia, America, Canada, the UK, India and Barbados.

Editor(s): Jeremy Poynting
Address: 17 Kings Avenue, Leeds LS6 1QS
Telephone: 0113 2451703
Fax: As phone
Email: hannah@peepal.demon.co.uk
Payment Details: Generally 10% net
Unsolicited Manuscripts: Telephone first for submission guidelines

Pegasus Publications Ltd

Illustrated non-fiction books: homeopathy, mythology, health, nature, military, art and crafts. We also publish children's information books and fantasy-related subjects. Send sae for return of manuscripts.

Editor(s): Ray Bonds
Address: 7 St Georges Square, London SW1V 1RX
Telephone: 0171 976 4300

Pen & Sword Books Ltd

Military history especially WW1, WW2, Falklands and Napoleonic. Local history, highly illustrated focusing on nostalgia. Battlefield guides containing then and now pictures. Regimental histories all regiments and squadrons considered, even if disbanded.

Editor(s): Tom Hartman, Brian Elliott,Nigel Cave, Henry Wilson
Address: 47 Church Street, Barnsley S70 2AS
Telephone: 01226 734 222
Fax: 01226 734 438
Email: charles@pen-and-sword.demon.co.uk
Website: www.yorkshire-web.co.uk/ps
Imprints: Wharncliffe, Leo Cooper
Parent Company: Barnsley Chronicle Holdings Ltd
Payment Details: Royalties are paid twice a year
Unsolicited Manuscripts: Yes. Please send a synopsis

Pentathol Publishing

No new material needed at present.

Editor(s): A E Cowen
Address: PO Box 92, 40 Gibson Street, Wrexham LL13 7NS
Unsolicited Manuscripts: No

Peridot Press Ltd

Peridot Press publishes easy-to-read, regularly updated reference books including The Gap Year Guidebook and The Internet Guidebook. Main readers are sixth-formers, their parents, schools and small business. We do not usually take unsolicited manuscripts but we occasionally employ people for short-term research and database work.

Address: 2 Blenheim Crescent, London W11 1NN
Telephone: 0171 221 7404
Website: www.peridot.co.uk
Imprints: Peridot

Permanent Publications

Publishers of Permaculture Magazine and specialist books on environmental issues, sustainable design and permaculture.

Editor(s): Madeleine Harland, A M Glanville-Hearson
Address: The Sustainability Centre, East Meon, Hants GU32 1HR
Telephone: 01730 823311
Fax: 01730 823322
Email: hello@permaculture.co.uk
Website: www.permaculture.co.uk
Imprints: Permanent Publications
Parent Company: Hyden House Ltd
Unsolicited Manuscripts: No

Perpetuity Press

Specialist books and journals in the field of risk, security, crime prevention, policing and community safety. Journals include the Security Journal, Risk Management: An International Journal and Crime Prevention And Community Safety: An International Journal. Books include Crime At Work; Learning From Disasters: a management approach; Crime and Security: managing the risk to safe shopping; and Zero Tolerance Policing. Subjects covered by our publications include the following: CCTV; fraud; civil recovery; staff dishonesty; retail crime; abuse and violence within the workplace; risk management; business continuity planning; repeat victimisation; computer security; product contamination; robbery; crises and disaster management; financial risk; contingency planning; human error and vulnerability; environmental threats; crime against businesses. All our publications are jargon free and will help you to identify and develop successful strategies for managing security, risk and crime prevention by evaluating existing measures and assessing new policies and initiatives.

Editor(s): Karen Gill
Address: PO Box 376, Leicester LE2 3ZZ
Telephone: 0116 270 4186
Fax: 0116 270 7742
Email: info@perpetuitypress.co.uk
Website: www.perpetuitypress.co.uk/securitybooks/
Unsolicited Manuscripts: Yes

Perseus Books Group

Social sciences and humanities, especially politics, international relations, area studies, sociology, religion, history, philosophy and cultural studies.

Editor(s): Sue Miller
Address: 12 Hid's Copse Road, Cumnor Hill, Oxford OX2 9JJ
Imprints: Basic Books, Counterpoint, Civitas, Public Affairs, Westview Press, Perseus Books
Unsolicited Manuscripts: Yes

Petroc Press

Educational books and other media for doctors, GPs, junior doctors in training as well as qualified professionals.

Editor(s): P L Clarke
Address: 36 Thames Court, High Street, Goring-on-Thames, Reading RG8 9AQ
Telephone: 01491 875252
Fax: 01491 875200
Email: petroc@librapharm.co.uk
Website: www.librapharm.co.uk
Imprints: Petroc Press
Parent Company: Librapharm Ltd
Payment Details: Royalties paid annually
Unsolicited Manuscripts: Yes

P
Phaidon Press Ltd

Publishes books on art, architecture, design, photography, decorative arts, fashion and music.

Editor(s): Deputy Publisher: Amanda Renshaw
Address: Regent's Wharf, All Saints Street, London N1 9PA
Telephone: 0171 843 1000
Fax: 0171 843 1010
Email: tspruyt@phaidon.com
Unsolicited Manuscripts: No

Pharmaceutical Press

Publishes information on all aspects of medicine for an international audience of pharmacists, GPs, nurses and other health professionals.

Address: 1 Lambeth High Street, London SE1 7JN (Orders to: PO Box 151, Wallingford, Oxon OX10 8QU)
Telephone: 01491 829 272
Fax: 01491 829 292
Email: rpsgb@cabi.org
Website: www.pharmpress.com

Phillimore & Co Ltd

British local and family history, genealogy, heraldry and institutional history.

Editor(s): Noel Osborne, Simon Thraves
Address: Shopwyke Manor Barn, Chichester, West Sussex PO20 6BG
Telephone: 01243 787636
Fax: 01243 787639
Email: bookshop@phillimore.co.uk
Website: www.phillimore.co.uk
Payment Details: Royalties by negotiation
Unsolicited Manuscripts: Yes with return postage

Picador

International fiction and non-fiction, in hardback and paperback.

Editor(s): Publisher: Peter Straus; Senior Editorial Director: Ursula Doyle; Editorial Director: Maria Rejt; Senior Editor: Richard Milner; Editor: Mary Mount
Address: 25 Eccleston Place, London SW1W 9NF
Parent Company: Macmillan
Unsolicited Manuscripts: Yes

Piccadilly Press

Children's picture books, very simple character-based storybooks (very limited range). Teenage books (10-15 years old) fiction and non-fiction, fast paced and humorous. Parenting Books a series on 'how to help your child'.

Editor(s): Judith Evans
Address: 5 Castle Road, London NW1 8PR
Payment Details: Depending on the manuscript
Unsolicited Manuscripts: Yes, but not the whole manuscript, letter and chapter will be OK

Pisces Angling Publication

Books on fishing. Recent titles include My Way With The Pole by Tom Pickering & Colin Dyson (£12.95 hardback; £9.95 softback) and Fantastic Feeder Fishing by Archie Braddock (£9.95).

Address: 8 Stumperlowe Close, Sheffield S10 3PP
Telephone: 0114 2304038

Pitkin Unichrome Ltd

Highly illustrated souvenir guides for the tourist industry, specialising in cathedrals, churches, historic cities, great events and famous people.

Editor(s): Managing Ed: Shelley Grimwood; Ed: Jenni Davis
Address: Healey House, Dene Road, Andover SP10 2AA
Telephone: 01264 334303
Fax: 01264 334110
Email: guides@pitkin.u-net.com
Website: www.britguides.com
Parent Company: Johnsons Newspaper Group
Unsolicited Manuscripts: No

The Playwrights Publishing Co

Full length and one act plays; serious and light for professional and amateur performance, full age range catered for plus all-female and monologues; scripts circulated to UK libraries; listings to USA and Europe; reading fee charges (details on request).

Editor(s): Tony Breeze, Liz Breeze
Address: 70 Nottingham Road, Burton Joyce, Nottinghamshire NG14 5AL
Telephone: 01159 313356
Imprints: Playwrights Publishing, Ventus Books
Unsolicited Manuscripts: Yes, with SAE & reading fee

Plenum Publishers

Plenum Publishing is now part of Kluwer Academic Publishers. The UK company, based in London, provides an editorial base for new journals and books at postgraduate, research and professional levels in life sciences, physical sciences and social sciences.

Editor(s): Ken Derham, Joanna Lawrence
Address: New Loom House, 101 Back Church Lane, London E1 lLU
Telephone: 0171 264 1910
Fax: 0171 264 1919
Email: mail@plenum.co.uk
Website: www.plenum.co.uk
Imprints: Plenum Press, Kluwer Academic-Plenum Publishers
Parent Company: Kluwer Academic-Plenum Publishers, New York
Payment Details: Royalty on sales negotiable according to type of book
Unsolicited Manuscripts: Yes

Plexus Publishing Limited

Publishers of high quality illustrated books with an emphasis on the following subjects: biography, popular music, rock 'n' roll, popular culture, art, photography and cinema.

Editor(s): Sandra Wake
Address: 55A Clapham Common Southside, Clapham, London SW4 9BX
Telephone: 0171 622 2440
Fax: 0171 622 2441
Email: plexus@plexusuk.demon.co.uk
Unsolicited Manuscripts: Yes

Plunkett Foundation

The Foundation is an independent charitable trust which supports the development of co-operatives and rural enterprises, both in the UK and overseas. Founded in 1919, the Foundation supports itself through membership fees, donations, and fees earned from work carried out. This includes project development and management, training, information provision and publications. Produce two annual publications, The World Of Co-operative Enterprise and Directory Of Agricultural Co-operatives, and a limited range of other co-operative titles.

Editor(s): Publications Manager: Wendy Hurp
Address: 23 Hanborough Business Park, Long Hanborough, Oxford OX8 8LH
Telephone: 01993 883636
Fax: 01993 883576
Email: info@plunkett.co.uk
Payment Details: No payment
Unsolicited Manuscripts: Considered only for World Of Co-operative Enterprise - must be on related topics and no more than 3000 words

Pluto Publishing Ltd

Britain's leading independent publisher of works by and for the broad left community. We advocate no specific political alignment. We publish 50-60 books a year in the fields of anthropology, sociology, politics, history, development and cultural studies.

Editor(s): Roger van Zwanenberg, Anne Beech
Address: 345 Archway Road, London N6 5AA
Telephone: 0181 348 2724
Fax: 0181 348 9133
Email: pluto@plutobks. demon.co.uk
Website: www.plutobooks.com
Unsolicited Manuscripts: Accepted if within publishing scope. Please submit prospectus and CV first.

The Poetry Business

A small independent literary publisher of contemporary poetry and fiction. List includes Michael Schmidt, Dorothy Nimmo and Michael Laskey. Run an annual book and pamphlet competition - apply for details. Also publish The North magazine: new poetry, reviews and articles.

Editor(s): Peter Sansom, Janet Fisher
Address: The Studio, Byram Arcade, Westgate, Huddersfield HD1 1ND
Telephone: 01484 434840
Fax: 01484 426566
Email: poetbus@pop3.poptel.org.uk
Imprints: Smith/Doorstop Books
Payment Details: Royalties
Unsolicited Manuscripts: Sample 12 poems only please

℘
Poetry Now

Publishes anthologies of more modern verse, likes to deal with topical, provocative issues but will also consider poetry on any subject. New poets always welcome, there are no entry fees and we publish a wide range of poetry. Poetry Now also publishes a quarterly magazine featuring workshops, competition news, profiles and articles of interest. In each issue there is also poetry published on five different subjects, changing each issue. We are always looking for guest editors (must have had poetry published), article writers, etc. If you contact us by email, please include postal address.

Editor(s): Heather Killingray
Address: Remus House, Coltsfoot Drive, Woodston, Peterborough PE2 9JX
Telephone: 01733 898101
Fax: 01733 313524
Email: suzy@forwardpress.co.uk
Imprints: Strongwords (18-25yr olds), Women's Words (Female poets only)
Parent Company: Forward Press Ltd
Payment Details: Small payments which vary depending on publication - call for details
Unsolicited Manuscripts: Single poems only

Poetry Now Young Writers

Poetry written by young people aged between 8 & 18 yrs inclusive. Two series of books published per year: April-September 8-11 yr olds, October-March 11-18 yr olds. Poems usually submitted through schools, but individual entries are accepted. Poems can be written on any subject and in any style, but must not exceed 30 lines in length. If you choose to contact us by email, please include postal address.

Editor(s): Managing Eds: Sarah Andrew, Kerrie Pateman; Senior Ed: Carl Golder; Eds: Simon Harwin, David Thomas, Michelle Warrington, Allison Dowse
Address: Remus House, Colstfoot Drive, Woodston, Peterborough PE2 9JX
Telephone: 01733 890066
Fax: 01733 313524
Email: suzy@forwardpress.co.uk
Parent Company: Forward Press Ltd
Payment Details: Prizes:- Per Series: 1 x £1000 5 x £250 10 x £100 awarded to schools. Per Book: 1 x £20 4 x £5 Book Tokens awarded to the writers of the five best poems.
Unsolicited Manuscripts: Yes

Polar Publishing

Design, print and produce quality sports publications (football, cricket). Catalogue available.

Editor(s): Julian Baskcomb
Address: 2 Uxbridge Road, Leicester LE4 7ST
Telephone: 0116 261 0800
Fax: 0116 261 0559
Imprints: Polar Publishing
Parent Company: Polar Print Group
Payment Details: Individual agreements
Unsolicited Manuscripts: Yes

℘
The Policy Press

Welfare and poverty; community care - general, housing, mental health; ageing and later life; disability issues; governance; health; domestic violence. Housing and planning; construction; urban and regional policy; labour markets and training; management, business and organisational change. Policy & Politics journal (quarterly).

Editor(s): Dawn Louise Pudney
Address: 34 Tyndall's Park Road, Bristol BS8 1PY
Telephone: 0117 973 8797
Fax: 0117 973 7308
Email: tpp@bristol.ac.uk
Website: www.bristol.ac.uk/publications.tpp
Unsolicited Manuscripts: Would prefer proposals first

Polygon

New fiction, Scottish culture, general interest, poetry, travel, Gaelic, guides, oral history and folklore.

Editor(s): Editorial Dir: Jackie Jones; Ed Asst: Alison Bowden
Address: 22 George Square, Edinburgh EH8 9LF
Parent Company: Edinburgh University Press
Unsolicited Manuscripts: No

Polygram Outloud

PolyGram are one of the oldest players in the spoken word industry, dating back to the 1950s with classic recordings including the entire Shakespeare collection (currently being re-released), poetry and many pieces of classic literature. In recent years PolyGram has worked closely with its video lables VVL and PVL to acquire some of the best comedians in the UK. Establishing links with the comedians at an early stage of their career has given us a great working relationship and a strong link with the comedy circuit. Since 1st September PolyGram Spoken Word has relaunched as PolyGram Outloud to reflect the changing image of our catalogue. By adding the Cult Listening label to our stable we are giving a clear message of where the industry has its future.

Editor(s): Product Manager: Alex Mitchison
Address: 1 Sussex Place, Hammersmith, London W6 9XS
Telephone: 0181 910 5028
Fax: 0181 910 5400
Email: mitchiso@uk.polygram.com
Imprints: Funny Business, Cult Listening, Argo, Speaking Volumes
Parent Company: Polygram Filmed Entertainment

Populace Press

Small independent publisher specialising in children's titles. We serve as a springboard for career authors, and also encourage one-off writers of all ages. Publications are not restricted to book format only; as a new publisher we look to the Internet as an excellent medium for future development of storytelling.

Editor(s): Mary Cooke
Address: 31 Malmesbury Road, Chippenham, Wilts SN15 1PS
Telephone: 01249 461131
Fax: As phone
Email: populacepress@mailhost.net
Website: www.mailhost.net/~populacepress
Payment Details: No advances. Quarterly for 1st eighteen months, then annual royalties
Unsolicited Manuscripts: Yes

David Porteous Editions

Non-fiction publishers of high quality colour illustrated books on hobbies and leisure pursuits for the UK and international markets. Subjects include watercolour painting, papercrafts, cross stitch, salt dough, papier mache and other crafts.

Address: PO Box 5, Chudleigh, Newton Abbot, Devon TQ13 0YZ
Telephone: 01626 853310
Fax: 01626 853663
Payment Details: Royalties
Unsolicited Manuscripts: No - letter/synopsis first

Portland Press Ltd

Scientific, technical and medical books in the fields of biochemistry, molecular biology, metabolism, physiology, neurobiology, etc. From school textbooks to research level monographs and proceedings.

Editor(s): Rhonda Oliver
Address: 59 Portland Place, London W1N 3AJ
Telephone: 0171 580 5530
Fax: 0171 323 1136
Email: edit@portlandpress.co.uk
Website: www.portlandpress.co.uk
Parent Company: The Biochemical Society
Unsolicited Manuscripts: No

Power Publications

Sample titles: Pub Walks In Somerset; Pub Walks In Dorset; Ancient Stones Of Dorset; Penstemons; A Century Of Cinema In Dorset; Mountain Bike Guide To Hants & New Forest; Ferndown A Look Back.

Address: 1 Clayford Avenue, Ferndown, Dorset BH22 9PQ
Telephone: 01202 875223
Fax: As phone
Imprints: Pub Walk Series, Mountain Bike Guides, Local History
Unsolicited Manuscripts: Yes

T & A D Poyser

Ornithology and natural history for the academic and advanced amateur audience. Includes treatment of individual species and subjects of an ecological and behavioural nature; field guides and species-finding guides.

Editor(s): Andrew Richford
Address: 24-28 Oval Road, London NW1 7DX
Parent Company: Academic Press
Payment Details: Royalty on net receipts
Unsolicited Manuscripts: Yes, but outlines sufficient for preliminary appraisal/not full ms

P
Praxis Books

An independent small press with an eclectic mix of titles - reissues, personal experiences, travel. Whatever takes our fancy. Most relevant title: The Poet's Kit by Katherine Knight (£5).

Editor(s): Rebecca Smith
Address: Sheridan, Broomers Hill Lane, Pulborough, West Sussex RH20 2DU
Email: 100543.3270@compuserve.com
Website: www.beckysmith.demon.co.uk
Imprints: Praxis Books
Payment Details: Shared costs, shared proceeds
Unsolicited Manuscripts: Yes, with return postage

PRC Publishing Ltd

Promotional publishing, hardback non-fiction covering most areas - lifestyle, history, military, art, architecture, wildlife etc.

Editor(s): Simon Forty, Martin Howard
Address: Kiln House, 210 New Kings Road London SW6 4NZ
Telephone: 0171 736 5666
Fax: 0171 736 5777
Email: martin@prcpub.com
Website: www.prcpub.com
Imprints: PRC, Parkgate
Parent Company: Collins & Brown
Payment Details: Negotiable
Unsolicited Manuscripts: Yes

Prentice Hall

Publishes books and CD-ROMS for teaching and learning English as a foreign language at all levels. Particular strengths are business English, English for specific purposes and English for academic purposes.

Address: Campus 400, Maylands Avenue, Hemel Hempstead HP2 7EZ
Telephone: 01442 881891
Fax: 01442 882288
Email: orders@prenhall.co.uk
Website: www.pheurope.co.uk

Prestel UK

Leading publisher in art, architecture and photography. In 1999 celebrates 75 years of publishing and 15 years of its English language list. Particularly successful English titles include The Pegasus Library - Passions That Drive The Masters; The Children's Series - Adventures In Art; and the Prestel African and Asian art list.

Editor(s): Philippa Hurd
Address: 4 Bloomsbury Place, London WC1A 2QA
Telephone: 0171 323 5004
Fax: 0171 636 8004

P
Mathew Price Ltd

Education through delight. Co-edition specialists for fiction and non-fiction for 1 to 10-year-olds. Board books, novelties, nursery rhymes, fairy tales, horror stories, picture books and natural history.

Address: The Old Glove Factory, Bristol Road, Sherborne, Dorset DT9 4HP
Telephone: 01935 816010
Fax: 01935 816310
Email: mathewp@mathew-price.com
Unsolicited Manuscripts: To Sue Davies

Prim-Ed Publishing Ltd

Specialises in producing an extensive range of high quality, photocopiable classroom resources, including hundreds of titles/activities especially suitable for the Literacy Hour. Authored by teachers, our titles provide tried and tested classroom activities which are designed to cut preparation time whilst maintaining a high level of content quality and task value. Clear instructions, page layouts and relevant graphics are features of our titles which help to stimulate increased motivation, interest and concentration. Prim-Ed have also launched a range of double-sided, laminated wall maps and a wide selection of CDs suitable for nursery, primary, secondary school age and home use to complement the well-established and successful copymasters.

Address: 5a Kelsey Close, Attleborough Fields Industrial Estate, Nuneaton CV11 6RS
Telephone: 01203 322260
Fax: 01203 322861
Email: sales@prim-ed.com
Website: www.prim-ed.com/

Princeton University Press

Art, politics, international studies, music, mathematics, economics, psychology, life science, religion, Far East and Middle Eastern studies, physics, astrophysics, gender studies, anthropology and law.

Address: 1 Oldlands Way, Bognor Regis, West Sussex PO22 9SA
Unsolicited Manuscripts: No

Prion Books Ltd

Publish books on food & drink, humour, beauty, health, psychology, military, martial arts, popular culture, film & cinema. Also reprint biographical fiction and historical titles.

Editor(s): Andrew Goodfellow
Address: Imperial Works, Perren Street, London NW5 3ED
Telephone: 0171 482 4248
Fax: 0171 482 4203
Email: books@prion.co.uk
Imprints: Prion
Unsolicited Manuscripts: Yes, with return postage

Prism Press Book Publishers Ltd

Mind, body, spirit; psychology; personal growth; ecology; alternative medicine.

Editor(s): Diana King
Address: The Thatched Cottage, Partway Lane, Hazelbury Bryan, Sturminster Newton, Dorset DT10 2DP
Telephone: 01258 817164
Fax: 01258 817635
Payment Details: Royalties twice a year
Unsolicited Manuscripts: No, but synopsis and biographical details yes

P

Pritam Books

Books on teaching Pujabi, Urdu, English for Punjabi-speakers. Graded series. Also Punjabi & Urdu bilingual dictionaries. List available.

Address: 102 Sandwell Road, Handsworth, Birmingham B21 8PS

Psychology Press

This imprint was created specifically to serve the needs of researchers, professionals and students concerned with the science of human and animal behaviour. It publishes at all levels, including primary research journals, monographs, professional books, student texts and credible scientifically valid popular books. Psychology Press intends to publish psychology in its broadest sense, encompassing work of psychological significance by people in related areas, such as biology, neuroscience, linguistics, sociology, artificial intelligence, as well as the work of mainstream psychologists. Its publications will be of interest to any discipline which is concerned in any way with the science of human and animal behaviour.

Address: 27 Church Road, Hove, E Sussex BN3 3FA
Telephone: 01273 207 411
Fax: 01273 205 612
Email: information@psypress.co.uk
Website: www.tandf.co.uk/homepages/pphome.htm
Parent Company: Taylor & Francis Ltd

The Psychotherapy Centre

An established therapy, training, referral and publishing centre, helping people to understand themselves, live their lives more effectively, and resolve their emotional problems, relationship behaviour and psychogenic conditions. Some of its numerous publications, such as Emotional Problems: Different Ways Of Dealing With Them; Enjoy Parenthood and Selecting A Therapist are written in-house by the practitioners. For some others, such as Group Therapy: We Tried It, or Two Therapies And After, well-written, accurate, informative and interesting write-ups of personal experiences are welcome - though there is unlikely to be any payment unless the publication takes off and becomes a best-seller.

Address: 1 Wythburn Place, London W1H 5WL
Telephone: 0171 723 6173
Payment Details: No payment apart from free copies
Unsolicited Manuscripts: Quality accounts of personal experiences of problems & therapies are considered

Public Record Office

The Public Record Office is the national archives of the United Kingdom. Publishes a wide range of historical titles; specialities are family history, primary source material and academic titles.

Editor(s): Sheila Knight, Melvyn Stainton
Address: Ruskin Avenue, Kew, Surrey TW9 4DU
Telephone: 0181 392 5266
Fax: As phone
Email: bookshop@pro.gov.uk
Website: www.pro.gov.uk/
Imprints: Public Record Office, PRO Publications
Unsolicited Manuscripts: To Sheila Knight

P
Publishing House

Publishes fiction and non-fiction books by Vernon Coleman, and handles serial and foreign rights sales. Around 40 books in print. Buys around £500,000 worth of advertising a year for promotion. Also publishes Dr Vernon Coleman's Health Letter (subscribers in 17 countries). Foreign rights sold in 22 languages and books sold in over 50 countries.

Editor(s): Sue Ward
Address: Trinity Place, Barnstaple, Devon EX32 9HJ
Telephone: 01271 328768
Fax: As phone
Email: sue@vernoncoleman.com
Website: www.vernoncoleman.com
Imprints: European Medical Journal, Chilton Designs, Blue Books
Unsolicited Manuscripts: No

The Publishing Training Centre At Book House

Publish training materials, and offer a mail order service (Book Publishing Books) for training materials and books about publishing. Also offer a wide range of courses on all aspects of the publishing industry. Most are available in London and Oxford although some can be studied via distance learning. Courses cover the following broad subject areas: editorial; computing; electronic publishing; journals publishing; management; marketing; production; rights & contracts. Basic Proofreading, Basic Editing and Effective Copywriting are all available by distance learning. Course guide or mail order catalogue available on application.

Address: 45 East Hill, Wandsworth, London SW1P 2QZ
Telephone: 0181 874 2718
Fax: 0181 870 8985
Email: publishingtraining@bookhouse.co.uk
Website: www.train4publishing.co.uk

Quadrille

Founded in 1994 with the objective of creating a small list of innovative books with serious front list potential while simultaneously establishing a core backlist. Publishes high-quality illustrated non-fiction in the chosen fields of cookery, gardening, interiors, crafts, magic and health.

Address: 5th floor, Alhambra House, 27-31 Charing Cross Road, London WC2H 0LJ
Telephone: 0171 839 7117
Fax: 0171 839 7118
Email: enquiries@quadrille.co.uk
Unsolicited Manuscripts: Non-fiction synopses & ideas welcome

Quadrillion Publishing Ltd

Publisher of mass-market illustrated non-fiction titles. Subject areas: cookery, crafts, popular history, gardening, pop culture, transport, gift. Some 100 new titles published each year. Own list and distribution in US (with sales and marketing) based in New York. Published in US under CLB imprint. Also publish an extensive children's list under the Zig-Zag imprint; subjects: reference and early-learning series for ages 2-12. Pepperpot is a gift and stationery range distributed under the Pepperpot Island brand in the UK and US.

Address: Godalming Business Centre, Woolsack Way, Godalming, Surrey GU7 1XW
Telephone: 01483 426277
Fax: 01483 426947
Email: wss@quad-pub.co.uk
Imprints: CLB, Zig-Zag, Pepperpot
Payment Details: Outright purchase of copyright; flat fee: additional payment for foreign rights sales
Unsolicited Manuscripts: Synopsis & covering letter only

ℚ

Quartet Books Ltd

Literary fiction, literature in translation, popular non-fiction, literary and music biography, music - popular, rock and jazz.

Editor(s): Jeremy Beale, Stella Kane
Address: 27 Goodge Street, London W1P 2LD
Telephone: 0171 636 3992
Fax: 0171 637 1866
Email: quartetbooks@easynet.co.uk
Imprints: Robin Clarke
Parent Company: Namara Group
Payment Details: Royalties paid twice yearly
Unsolicited Manuscripts: Yes

Quartz Editions

Primarily, highly illustrated children's fiction and non-fiction. We also publish some adult non-fiction, again highly illustrated.

Editor(s): Susan Pinkus
Address: Premier House, 112 Station Road, Edgware HA8 7AQ
Imprints: Quartz
Payment Details: Royalty basis, sometimes outright fee
Unsolicited Manuscripts: Yes

Queen Anne Press

Sporting yearbooks, official coaching manuals and sponsored sports titles.

Editor(s): Adrian Stephenson
Address: Windmill Cottage, Mackerye End, Harpenden, Herts AL5 5DR
Telephone: 01582 715866
Fax: 01582 715121
Email: orders@lenqap.demon.co.uk
Parent Company: Lennard Associates Ltd
Payment Details: By negotiation
Unsolicited Manuscripts: No

Questa Publishing

Publishes small guidebooks of Walks With Children.

Editor(s): Terry Marsh
Address: 27 Camwood, Bamber Bridge, Preston PR5 8LA
Telephone: 01772 321243
Fax: As phone
Unsolicited Manuscripts: No

Quiller Press Ltd

Sponsored Books - ie non-fiction which can be sponsored by companies and organisations, yet merit sales through the book trade.

Editor(s): J J Greenwood
Address: 46 Lillie Road, London SW6 1TN
Telephone: 0171 499 6529
Fax: 0171 381 8941
Email: orders@combook.co.uk
Imprints: Quiller Press
Payment Details: Royalties
Unsolicited Manuscripts: No

Quintet Publishing

International co-edition publisher of non-fiction and reference titles. We publish in all major categories.

Editor(s): Anna Southgate, Diana Steedman, Oliver Salzmann
Address: 188-194 York Way, London N7 9QR
Telephone: 0171 700 2001
Fax: 0171 700 5785
Email: annas@quarto.com
Imprints: The Apple Press, New Burlington Books, Max Books
Parent Company: Quarto Group Inc

Radcliffe Medical Press Ltd

Publishers of high quality management and clinical books and electronic media for primary and secondary care. Radcliffe has an unrivalled list of practical books for general practitioners, dealing with the many management and organisational issues they face in the rapidly changing National Health Service. In addition, we publish titles on specific clinical areas, and thoughtful works on varied topics such as patients' rights, euthanasia, public health and child welfare.

Editor(s): Gillian Nineham, Jamie Etherington, Heidi Allen
Address: 18 Marcham Road, Abingdon, Oxon OX14 1AA
Telephone: 01235 528820
Fax: 01235 528830
Email: medical@radpress.win-uk.net
Website: www.radcliffe-Oxford.com
Unsolicited Manuscripts: Yes

Ragged Bears Ltd

Quality children's publishing company.

Editor(s): Henrietta Stickland
Address: Milborne Wick, Sherborne, Dorset DT9 4PW
Telephone: 01963 251600
Fax: 01963 250889
Email: raggedbears.co.uk
Unsolicited Manuscripts: Yes we do receive them - do send SAEs

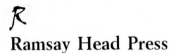

Ramsay Head Press

Books of Scottish interest, autobiographies, biographies, fiction, poetry, academic, art, architecture, language books and literary criticism.

Editor(s): Conrad Wilson
Address: 15 Gloucester Place, Edinburgh EH3 6EE
Telephone: 0131 225 5646
Fax: As phone

Ransome Publishing

Award-winning multimedia CD-ROM publisher. List of titles includes educational curriculum-based subjects such as maths, English, science and geography for primary and secondary education. Ransom is known especially for two award-winning CD-ROMs titled The History Of The Universe and The History Of Life. Two science titles for ages 10 upwards, for use in the school and at home. List also includes leisure titles for the home market for natural history lovers and reference users; ranges from dogs, birds, whales & dolphins and bears & pandas in our animal encyclopedia, to a children's adventure game called Mia - The Search For Grandma's Remedy, using state-of-the-art graphics for 4-9 year olds. Ransom Publishing is preparing for a busy 1999 with more new and exciting releases for school and home use; contact for catalogue to find out more.

Editor(s): Jenny Ertle
Address: Ransom House, 2 High Street, Watlington OX9 5PS
Telephone: 01491 613711
Fax: 01491 613733
Email: ransom@ransompublishing.co.uk
Website: www.ransom.co.uk

Ravenswood Publications Ltd

Niche publisher for the academic and practitioner markets in public service finance, management and law. Current area of specialist interest is local authority leisure & recreation management. Authors required to contribute to the marketing database for their publication. At present publishing in hard copy only, but open to offers on electronic output. PLS is mandated for collection of photocopy fees, and will be mandated for digitisation of printed materials in 1999.

Address: 35 Windsor Road, London N7 6JG
Telephone: 0171 272 5032
Fax: As phone
Email: denise.naylor@virgin.net
Unsolicited Manuscripts: Contact first to check subject, or send CV only

Reader's Digest Children's Publishing Ltd

Early learning, information and reference (0-12 years). Very strong emphasis on novelty formats and unusual editorial approaches. Innovative production techniques and book-plus-toy formats are features. No picture storybooks.

Editor(s): Cathy Jones
Address: King's Court, Parsonnage Lane, Bath BA1 1ER
Imprints: Reader's Digest Children's Books
Parent Company: Reader's Digest
Unsolicited Manuscripts: Yes

Reading And Language Information Centre

The Reading and Language Information Centre specialises in short, practical publications on matters of topical interest to teachers.

Editor(s): Viv Edwards
Address: The University of Reading, Bulmershe Court, Reading, Berks RG6 1HY
Telephone: 0118 931 8820
Fax: 0118 931 6801
Email: reading-centre@reading.ac.uk
Website: www.rdg.ac.uk/AcaDepts/eh/ReadLang/home.html
Payment Details: 7½% royalties.
Unsolicited Manuscripts: Yes

Reaktion Books Ltd

Founded in Edinburgh in 1985 and moved to its London location in 1988. Reaktion Books publishes art history, design, architecture, history, cultural studies, Asian studies, politics, geography and photography. 14 new titles in 1998, including Why Wars Happen by Jeremy Black, Terminal Architecture by Martin Pawley, Grand Hotels by Elaine Denby and Landscape And Englishness by David Matless.

Editor(s): Michael R Leaman
Address: 11 Rathbone Place, London W1P 1DE
Telephone: 0171 580 9928
Fax: 0171 580 9935
Email: reaktionbooks@compuserve.com
Website: www.reaktionbooks.co.uk
Payment Details: Royalties paid twice-yearly
Unsolicited Manuscripts: No, synopses and ideas welcome

Reardon Publishing (The Cotswold Publisher)

A family-run publishing house founded in 1976, producing publications related to the Cotswold area. Reardon Publishing also acts as a distributor for other publishers and so we are able to offer a wide range of Costwold books, maps, walking cards, videos and postcards in our specialised subjects of walking, driving, cycling, folklore and tourism in both the Cotswolds and associated counties. Titles include, for example, The Cotswold Way Guide, Video And Map, Cotswold Rideabout, The Haunted Cotswolds, Cotswold Driveabout. Send £1 for illustrated booklist and mail order details.

Editor(s): Nicholas Reardon, Peter T Reardon
Address: 56 Upper Norwood Street, Leckhampton, Cheltenham GL53 0DU
Telephone: 01242 231800
Website: www.reardon.co.uk
Imprints: Walkabout series, Driveabout series and Rideabout series of guide books and walkcards
Payment Details: Royalties paid twice-yearly
Unsolicited Manuscripts: Yes, with return postage

Redstone Press

Small, independent publisher, publishing Redstone Diary annually, plus one or two books on art-related subjects.

Address: 7A St Lawrence Terrace, London W10 5SU
Telephone: 0171 352 1594
Fax: 0171 352 8749
Email: redstone.press@virgin.net
Unsolicited Manuscripts: No

Reflections Of A Bygone Age

Books using old picture postcards as illustrations highlighting localities and themes including local history, transport, sport, politics plus Picture Postcard Annual and Postcard Collecting: a beginner's guide to picture postcard collecting. Also Collect Modern Postcard catalogues (3 editions).

Editor(s): B G Lund
Address: 15 Debdale Lane, Keyworth, Notts NG12 5HT
Telephone: 0115 937 4079
Fax: 0115 937 6197

Regency House Publishing Ltd

Publishers and packagers of mass market non-fiction titles suitable for international co-editions, specialising in art, craft, cookery, transport.

Editor(s): Nicolette Trodd
Address: 3 Mill Lane, Broxbourne, Herts EN10 7AZ
Telephone: 01992 479988
Fax: 01992 479966
Imprints: Regency House, Troddy Books
Payment Details: To be arranged
Unsolicited Manuscripts: No

Research Studies Press Ltd

An independent publisher of academic and professional books in growing areas of science. Publish principally in the fields of engineering (particularly electronic, electrical, mechanical and materials engineering), computing, botany and forestry. Usually publish in series, each under the control of an editor eminent in the field. Accept books on the recommendation of the Series Editor, though ideas from other sources are welcomed.

Editor(s): Guy Robinson
Address: 15-16 Coach House Cloisters, 10 Hitchin Street, Baldock, Herts SG7 6AE
Telephone: 01462 895060
Fax: 01462 892546
Email: vaw@rspltd.demon.co.uk
Website: www.research-studies-press.co.uk
Payment Details: % Royalties
Unsolicited Manuscripts: No, sample material only

Rex Natura Ltd

Commercial arm of the Rex Foundation Wildlife Trust, with a brief to publish books, both fiction and non-fiction, and related artwork, resulting from the wildlife research of the Rex Foundation. The research is predominantly undertaken in the field in Africa and Asia, the Foundation's mission being the protection of the cheetah and leopard and their prey-bases, and the dissemination to the public of 'good news' natural history.

Editor(s): L Godsall Bottriell, P Bottriell
Address: PO Box 141, Aylesbury, Bucks HP17 0YD
Telephone: 01442 826678
Fax: 01296 625299
Parent Company: The Rex Foundation
Unsolicited Manuscripts: No

ℛ
RIBA Publications

Architecture, design and biographies.

Address: Construction House, 56-64 Leonard Street, London EC2A 4LT
Telephone: 0171 251 0791
Fax: 0171 608 2375
Email: riba.publications@ribabooks.com
Website: www.ribabookshop.com
Parent Company: RIBA Companies
Unsolicited Manuscripts: No

RICS Books

RICS Books has been the official bookseller and publisher for The Royal Institution of Chartered Surveyors since 1981 and is the leading supplier of published material to the surveying, construction, property and related professions. As official publisher to the Institution, RICS Books produces a wide range of material for all surveying professionals. The emphasis is on provision of essential information prepared in close collaboration with the RICS which helps members keep abreast of changing legislation, policy and practice.

Address: Surveyor Court, Westwood Business Park, Coventry CV4 8JE
Telephone: 0171 222 7000
Fax: 0171 334 3851
Email: covbooks@rics.org.uk
Website: www.rics.org.uk
Parent Company: RICS Business Services
Unsolicited Manuscripts: Yes - to Publishing Manager

Rivelin Grapheme Press

A discreet poetry house. No manuscripts please. First approach by letter with bibliography/biography. No agents.

Address: Merlin House, Church Street, Hungerford, Berkshire RG17 0JG
Telephone: 01488 684645
Fax: 01488 683018
Unsolicited Manuscripts: No. First approach by letter.

Roadmaster Publishing

Transport histories especially road and some aspects of Kent local history.

Editor(s): Malcolm Wright
Address: PO Box 176, Chatham, Kent ME5 9AQ
Imprints: Roadmaster
Payment Details: Author Royalty usually 10% of selling price
Unsolicited Manuscripts: Yes

Robinson Publishing

Fantasy anthologies; SF anthologies; horror anthologies; horror fiction; crime anthologies; crime fiction; true crime; mind,body,spirit; health; general non-fiction.

Editor(s): Krystyna Green
Address: 7 Kensington Church Court, London W8 4SP
Telephone: 0171 938 3830
Fax: 0171 938 4214
Email: enquiries@robinsonpublishing.com
Imprints: Robinson, Magpie
Payment Details: Royalties paid half-yearly
Unsolicited Manuscripts: No - freelance editors complete the anthologies. Do not submit short stories or poetry

ℛ
Robson Books Ltd

General non-fiction: humour, sport, autobiographies, history, cinema, biographies, music, gardening, cookery, natural history and travel.

Editor(s): Jeremy Robson, Kate Mills
Address: 10 Blenheim Court, Brewery Road, London N7 9NT
Telephone: 0171 700 7444
Fax: 0171 700 4552
Imprints: Chrysalis
Payment Details: 2 royalty payments a year
Unsolicited Manuscripts: Call first and then with SAE if asked to submit

Barry Rose Law Publishers

Independent company specialising in law, legal biography and history, local government law.

Editor(s): Barry Rose
Address: Little London, Chichester, West Sussex PO19 1PG
Telephone: 01243 783637
Fax: 01243 779278
Email: books@barry-rose-law.co.uk
Imprints: Countrywise Press
Unsolicited Manuscripts: No

Rough Guides Ltd

Publishers of travel guides, phrasebooks and reference books.

Editor(s): Editorial Dir: Martin Dunford
Address: 62-70 Shorts Gardens, London WC2H 9AB
Telephone: 0171 556 5000
Fax: 0171 556 5050
Email: mail@roughguides.co.uk
Website: www.roughguides.com

Rowman & Littlefield

Humanities and social sciences especially the classics; philosophy, political theory, sociology and history.

Editor(s): Sue Miller
Address: 12 Hid's Copse Road, Cumnor Hill, Oxford OX2 9JJ
Imprints: Ivan R Dee, Lexington Books
Unsolicited Manuscripts: Yes

Rowton Press

Leading publisher for horse-racing titles - also publishes sports books.

Editor(s): D Thomas
Address: PO Box 10, Oswestry Salop SY11 1RB
Telephone: 01691 679111
Fax: 01691 679114
Email: odds.on@btinternet.com
Payment Details: By arrangement
Unsolicited Manuscripts: Yes

Royal College Of General Practitioners

The Royal College of General Practitioners (RCGP) is the academic organisation in the UK for general practitioners. Its aim is to encourage and maintain the highest standards of general medical practice and act as the voice of general practitioners on education, training and standard issues. For many, RCGP publications represent the external face of the College. Under its Royal Charter the College is entitled to 'diffuse information on all matters affecting general medical practice' and as a consequence has developed a long and prestigious list of publications. The College is justifiably proud of its varied titles, which range from the latest research and ideas in contemporary medicine to practical guidelines for dealing with specific medical conditions. By identifying new and topical areas of interest, the College has remained at the forefront of medical publishing.

Editor(s): Denis Pereira Gray
Address: 14 Princes Gate, Hyde Park, London SW7 1PU
Telephone: 0171 581 3232
Fax: 0171 225 3047
Email: info@rcgp.org.uk
Website: www.rcgp.org.uk

Royal College Of Psychiatrists

In addition to three prestigious psychiatric journals, the College publishes a variety of books and reports related to psychiatry. In keeping with the College's aims, the emphasis is on publications which advance the science and practice of psychiatry, promote study and research in psychiatry and related subjects, and promote public knowledge of mental health issues.

Editor(s): Greg Wilkinson
Address: 17 Belgrave Square, London SW1X 8PG
Telephone: 0171 235 2351
Fax: 0171 245 1231
Email: djago@rcpsych.ac.uk
Website: www.rcpsych.ac.uk
Imprints: Gaskell, Royal College Of Psychiatrists
Payment Details: On application
Unsolicited Manuscripts: Yes

Royal Institute Of International Affairs

International affairs, including economics, politics, public policy, and security issues. Also publish two journals, The World Today (monthly) and International Affairs (quarterly).

Editor(s): Margaret May; Journals eds: Graham Walker (The World Today), Caroline Soper (International Affairs)
Address: Chatham House, 10 St James's Square, London SW1Y 4LE
Telephone: 0171 957 5700
Fax: 0171 957 5710
Email: contact@riia.org
Website: ww.riia.org
Imprints: Chatham House Papers, RIIA Discussion Papers, RIIA Briefing Papers
Unsolicited Manuscripts: No, except for journal articles

ℛ
The Rubicon Press

Ancient history (Egypt, Turkey and Greece); history (kings and queens of Britain), nineteenth century travel, biography and literature. All written by academics for the general reader.

Editor(s): Juanita Homan, Anthea Page
Address: 57 Cornwall Gardens, London SW7 4BE
Telephone: 0171 937 6813
Fax: As phone
Unsolicited Manuscripts: Yes

Russell House Publishing Ltd

RHP's books and training manuals are designed to help anyone studying or working in these areas to develop their thinking and practice: social policy, social care, helping children & families, work with young people, activities for training & work with young people, combating social exclusion, striving for safer communities, working with offenders. Although principally focussed on policy and practice in the UK, we also publish the journal Social Work In Europe, and other comparative works.

Address: 4 St George's House, Uplyme Road Business Park, Lyme Regis DT7 3LS
Telephone: 01297 443948
Fax: 01297 442722
Payment Details: Royalties
Unsolicited Manuscripts: Yes if relevant to our areas of publication

The Rutland Press

Publishers of the RIAS Illustrated Architectural Guides To Scotland series; monographs; technical; Scottish urban design. Aim to publish fully-illustrated guides for all regions of Scotlland by 2001.

Address: 15 Rutland Square, Edinburgh EN1 2BE
Telephone: 0131 229 7545
Fax: 0131 228 2188
Email: rutland@rias.org.uk
Website: www.rias.org.uk
Parent Company: Royal Incorporation of Architects in Scotland
Unsolicited Manuscripts: No

The Salariya Book Company

Children's non-fiction; mainly history, science and natural history.

Address: 25 Marlborough Place, Brighton BN1 1UB
Telephone: 01273 603306
Fax: 01273 693857
Email: salariya@fastnet.co.uk
Unsolicited Manuscripts: No

$\mathcal{S}$
Saltire Society

Scottish history, poetry and literary studies.

Editor(s): Saltire Society Publications Committee
Address: 9 Fountain Close, 22 High Street, Edinburgh EH1 1TF
Telephone: 0131 556 1836
Fax: 0131 557 1675
Email: saltire@saltire.org.uk
Payment Details: 7½% Royalties
Unsolicited Manuscripts: Yes

Sandhill Press Ltd

Specialise in publishing books of local interest to Northumberland.

Editor(s): Beryl Sanderson
Address: 17 Castle Street, Warkworth, Morpeth, Northumberland NE65 0UW
Telephone: 01665 712483
Fax: 01665 713004
Unsolicited Manuscripts: No

Sangam Books Ltd

History & culture, biography & memoirs, women's studies, politics, economics, literary criticism, fiction, cookery, science & technology, city guides, poetry, medical, law & legislation.

Editor(s): A De Souza
Address: 57 London Fruit Exchange, Brushfield Street, London E1 6EP
Telephone: 0171 377 6399
Fax: 0171 375 1230
Email: goatony@aol.com
Parent Company: Orient Longman Ltd, India
Unsolicited Manuscripts: No

Saqi Books

Since 1983 Saqi Books has been publishing books on Middle Eastern culture & history and related areas. List includes titles in the following subject areas: Islamic art & architecture; fiction & poetry; history & religion; political studies; women's studies & writing; literary studies & languages; anthropology; illustrated books.

Editor(s): Mai Ghoussoub
Address: 26 Westbourne Grove, London W2 5RH
Telephone: 0171 229 8542
Fax: 0171 229 7492
Email: saqibooks@dial.pipex.com
Imprints: Saqi Books, Echoes, Dar Al Saqi
Parent Company: Arab Books Ltd
Unsolicited Manuscripts: Yes

S

Savannah Publications

Specialist works of reference: orders, medals, decorations, navy, army, air force, military biography and military genealogy.

Editor(s): Diana Birch
Address: 90 Dartmouth Road, Forest Hill, London SE23 3HZ
Telephone: 0181 244 4350
Fax: 0181 244 2448
Email: savpub@dircon.co.uk
Imprints: Savannah Publications, JB Hayward & Son
Parent Company: Savannah Publications
Payment Details: By arrangement
Unsolicited Manuscripts: Yes

Save The Children

Save the Children publishes a wide range of materials for professionals, academics and practitioners working with children in the UK and overseas. Free catalogues available.

Address: 17 Grove Lane, London SE5 8RD
Telephone: 0171 703 5400
Fax: 0171 708 2508
Email: publications@scfuk.org.uk
Website: www.savethechildren.org.uk
Imprints: Save the Children
Unsolicited Manuscripts: No

SAWD Books

Local interest books, also cookery, gardening and general non-fiction.

Editor(s): Allison Wainman, David Wainman
Address: Plackett's Hole, Bicknor, Sittingbourne, Kent ME9 8BA
Telephone: 01795 472262
Fax: 01795 422633
Email: wainman@sawd.demon.co.uk
Parent Company: Sawd Publications
Payment Details: Royalties bi-annually
Unsolicited Manuscripts: Synopses considered

Alastair Sawday Publishing

Small independent publishers who specialise in accommodation guides. Countries covered: Britain, France,Spain, Portugal and Ireland. Also Paris Hotels.

Address: 44 Ambra Vale East, Bristol BS8 4RE
Telephone: 0117 929 9921
Fax: 0117 925 4712
Email: asbristol@aol.com

S

SB Publications

Local history, pictorial local history books, travel guides (GB only) - walking & touring, pictorial transport history, (especially railway and maritime), mythology, unknown, unusual, ghosts & legends. All books should be based on events in the UK.

Editor(s): Stephen Benz, Brigid Chapman, Judy Moore
Address: 19 Grove Road, Seaford, East Sussex BN25 1TP
Telephone: 01323 893498
Fax: 01323 893860
Payment Details: Royalties, 10% of selling price; paid annually no advances
Unsolicited Manuscripts: Yes with SAE

Scandinavia Connection

English-edition Scandinavian books about Scandinavian countries - Norway, Finland, Denmark, Sweden, Iceland.

Address: 26 Woodsford Square, London W14 8DP
Telephone: 0171 602 0657
Fax: 0171 602 8556
Email: books@scandinavia-connection.co.uk
Website: www.scandinavia-connection.co.uk
Parent Company: Max Morgan-Witts Productions Ltd
Unsolicited Manuscripts: No

Scarthin Books

Local studies with a wider scholarly appeal; specialised monographs written for the educated layman.

Editor(s): David Mitchell
Address: The Promenade, Scarthin, Cromford, Derbyshire DE4 3QF
Telephone: 01629 823272
Imprints: Family Walks
Payment Details: Royalties quarterly
Unsolicited Manuscripts: Unsolicited synopses considered

Scholastic Children's Books

Children's books publisher. High quality fiction and original individual titles; best-selling non-fiction; picture books; pre-school and licensed titles.

Address: Commonwealth House, 1-19 New Oxford Street, London WC1A 1NU
Telephone: 0171 421 9000
Fax: 0171 421 9001
Website: www.scholastic.co.uk
Imprints: Point, Hippo, Little Hippo, Scholastic Press
Parent Company: Scholastic USA
Unsolicited Manuscripts: Admin for fiction/non-fiction/pre-school dept

S
SCI - Society Of Chemical Industry

An association with members in 65 countries which exists to improve understanding and the exchange of information between researchers, industrialists, financiers and educators. Learned and non-partisan, SCI provides access to the latest independent and informed expertise on the application of science for the public benefit. Publishing is a significant part of SCI's range of international activities. As well as commissioned volumes, the society occasionally publishes conference proceedings from its programme of specialist meetings. SCI produces four learned journals: Journal Of Chemical Technology & Biotechnology, Journal Of The Science Of Food And Agriculture, Pesticide Science and Polymer International. All four welcome submissions from those working in interdisciplinary science. SCI also presents original and sound research in its Lecture Paper Series, accessible via the SCI website. The internationally renowned magazine Chemistry And Industry, respected as a source of news and independent comment on science and industry, is produced twice-monthly by SCI.

Editor(s): Jennifer Bolgar, Maria Burke (Chemistry & Industry)
Address: International Headquarters, 14-15 Belgrave Square, London SW1X 8PS
Telephone: 0171 598 1572
Fax: 0171 245 1279
Email: secretariat@chemind.demon.co.uk
Website: http://sci.mond.org
Imprints: Lecture Papers Series
Payment Details: Please telephone for guidance
Unsolicited Manuscripts: For journals and Chemistry & Industry, yes

Science Museum Publications

History of science and technology, public understanding of science, museology, railway history, photographic history, reference and museum guide books.

Editor(s): Ela Ginalska
Address: Exhibition Road, London SW7 2DD
Fax: 0171 938 8169
Email: publicat@nmsi.ac.uk
Website: www.nmsi.ac.uk
Imprints: Science Museum
Parent Company: National Museum of Science & Industry
Payment Details: Fee arranged with author
Unsolicited Manuscripts: Yes

SCM Press

Publishers of theological books with special emphasis on biblical, philosophical and modern theology. Books on sociology of religion and religious aspects of current issues. A division of SCM-Canterbury Press Ltd.

Editor(s): JohnBowden, Margaret Lydamore
Address: 9-17 St Albans Place, London N1 0NX
Parent Company: Hymns Ancient and Modern Ltd
Payment Details: Standard royalty
Unsolicited Manuscripts: Yes with return postage - but better to send outline first

S

Scottish Braille Press

Printers and publishers of braille, producers of audio/large print and tactile diagrams and material on disc.

Address: Craigmillar Park, Edinburgh EH16 5NB
Telephone: 0131 662 4445
Fax: 0131 662 1968
Email: scot.braille@dial.pipex.com
Website: www.scottish-braille-press.org
Imprints: Thistle Books
Parent Company: The Royal Blind Asylum and School
Unsolicited Manuscripts: No

Scottish Council For Voluntary Organisations (SCVO)

SCVO is the umbrella body for voluntary organisations in Scotland. Through our members, elected representatives, paid staff and volunteers, SCVO seeks to promote the interests of voluntary organisations and improve their effectiveness.

Address: 18-19 Claremont Crescent, Edinburgh EH7 4QD
Telephone: 0131 556 3882
Fax: 0131 556 0279
Email: enquiries@scvo.org.uk
Website: www.sol.co.uk/s/scvo
Unsolicited Manuscripts: No

Scripture Union

Publisher of Bible reading notes, Sunday school resources, general Christian adult books and children's fiction and picture books.

Editor(s): Tim Carr (church resources), Andrew Clark (Bible resources)
Address: Queensway Union, 207-209 Queensway, Bletchley, Milton Keynes MK2 2EB
Telephone: 01908 856000
Fax: 01908 856111
Email: info@scriptureunion.org
Website: www.scripture.org.uk/
Unsolicited Manuscripts: Syonpsis and sample chapter to Chris Kembrey

Seafarer Books

Books on traditional sailing, mainly narrative; also travel literature. Send letter or synopsis only please.

Editor(s): P Eve
Address: 2 Rendlesham Mews, Rendlesham, Woodbridge, Suffolk IP12 2SZ
Telephone: 01394 460313
Fax: 01394 461314
Email: merlinpres@aol.com
Parent Company: Merlin Press Ltd
Payment Details: Royalties on copies sold
Unsolicited Manuscripts: No

S
Martin Secker & Warburg

Literary fiction and general non-fiction.

Editor(s): Geoff Mulligan, David Miller
Address: Random House, 20 Vauxhall Bridge Road, London SW1V 2SA
Parent Company: Random House
Unsolicited Manuscripts: No

Seren Books

General literary publisher specialising in writing in the English language from Wales. Publishing around 30 new titles a year, the list includes poetry, fiction, biography, drama, criticism and art. Most books have a direct connection to Wales through author (birth or residence) or subject matter, though Seren also publishes Border Lines, a series of introductory biographies of writers, artists and composers who lived, worked and found inspiration on both sides of the English-Welsh border. Seren is the imprint of Poetry Wales, a quarterly magazine publishing the best in poetry from Wales and the world.

Editor(s): Amy Wack (poetry/drama), Mick Felton (fiction/biography/criticism/art), John Powell Ward (Border Lines)
Address: First Floor, 2 Wyndham Street, Bridgend CF31 1EF
Parent Company: Poetry Wales Press Ltd
Payment Details: By negotiation
Unsolicited Manuscripts: With SAE for return

Serif

Quality cookery, history, Irish and African studies. No fiction.

Editor(s): Stephen Hayward
Address: 47 Strahan Road, London E3 5DA
Website: www.serif.demon.co.uk
Payment Details: Standard royalty rates
Unsolicited Manuscripts: No

Serpent's Tail Ltd

Inspired by Continental paperback original publishing houses and founded in 1986 to give a voice to writers outside the mainstream. During its first year Serpent's Tail published 12 books, 6 of which were translations. Now publishing 40 books a year, including original British and American fiction, music and popular culture books, crime fiction, tranlations and short story anthologies.

Address: 4 Blackstock Mews, London N4 2BT
Telephone: 0171 354 1949
Fax: 0171 704 6467
Payment Details: No payment involved re manuscripts
Unsolicited Manuscripts: After query

S

Settle Press

Travel guides.

Editor(s): David Settle
Address: 10 Boyne Terrace Mews, London W11 3LR
Payment Details: Royalty
Unsolicited Manuscripts: No

Severn House Publishers Ltd

Hardcover fiction by well-known authors primarily for library publication.

Editor(s): Sara Short
Address: 9-15 High Street, Sutton, Surrey SM1 1DF
Telephone: 0181 770 3930
Fax: 0181 770 3850
Email: editorial@severnhouse.com
Website: www.severnhouse.com
Payment Details: Standard royalty terms
Unsolicited Manuscripts: No, via agents only please

Shaw & Sons Ltd

Law and local government.

Editor(s): Crispin Williams
Address: Shaway House, 21 Bourne Park, Bourne Road, Crayford, Kent DA1 4BZ
Imprints: Shaw & Son
Payment Details: Royalties only
Unsolicited Manuscripts: Yes

S

Sheaf Publishing Ltd

Local interest books, non-fiction only.

Address: 191 Upper Allen Street, Sheffield S3 7GW
Telephone: 0114 273 9067
Unsolicited Manuscripts: No, make prior arrangement

Sheffield Academic Press Ltd

Founded in 1976. Originally known as JSOT Press. Now the leading academic publisher of biblical titles. Recently expanded its list to include archaeology, European studies, literary studies, history & culture, languages, scientific, professional and reference.

Address: Mansion House, 19 Kingfield Road, Sheffield S11 9AS
Telephone: 0114 2554433
Fax: 0114 2554626
Email: admin@sheffac.demon.co.uk
Website: www.shef-ac-press.co.uk
Imprints: Sheffield Academic Press, JSOT Press, Almond Press
Unsolicited Manuscripts: Manuscripts, synopses, ideas & proposals welcome. No fiction

⑤
Sheffield Hallam University Press

In-house publishing company of Sheffield Hallam University, with many years' experience in publishing books, computer software, videos, CDs and games. Authors are drawn from educational and business institutions, nationally and internationally.

Editor(s): Monica Moseley
Address: Learning Centre, City Campus, Pond Street, Sheffield S1 1WB
Telephone: 0114 225 4702
Fax: 0114 225 4478
Email: shupress@shu.ac.uk
Imprints: SHU Press
Parent Company: Sheffield Hallam University

Sheldon Press

Publishers of health and self-help books for the popular market. Our health books are written for non-experts, and include titles such as Birth Over 35, The Candida Diet Book and Curing Arthritis The Drug-free Way. Our self-help books are written for a similar readership, and include Crunch Points For Couples, How To Improve Your Confidence and The Good Stress Guide. Our new series of books on natural remedies such as cider vinegar, garlic and antioxidants sets out the real benefits of these products. All our books are reliable, no-nonsense reference books for the general reader.

Editor(s): Joanna Moriarty
Address: Holy Trinity Church, Marylebone Road, London NW1 4DU
Telephone: 0171 387 5282
Fax: 0171 388 2352
Email: jmoriarty@spck.org.uk
Payment Details: By negotiation
Unsolicited Manuscripts: Please send a synopsis and sample chapter

Sheldrake Press

Publishers of highly illustrated non-fiction. Subjects include travel, history, railways, architecture & interior design, cookery, music, gift stationery, art and reference. Titles include The Wild Traveller's Guide, The Victorian Hours Book, The Kate Greenaway Baby Book, European Museum Guide and The Coasts Of Europe.

Editor(s): J S Riggs
Address: 188 Cavendish Road, London SW12 0DA
Telephone: 0181 675 1767
Fax: 0181 675 7736
Email: mail@sheldrakepress.demon.co.uk
Imprints: Museum Media Publishers
Parent Company: Sheldrake Holdings Ltd
Payment Details: Subject to negotiation
Unsolicited Manuscripts: Check first by telephone

Shepheard-Walwyn (Publishers) Ltd

We publish in three broad areas - all non-fiction: books originated in calligraphy; history, political economy & philosophy, not in a narrow academic sense, but to help us understand where we are and how, by understanding better, things might be improved; books of Scottish interest.

Editor(s): Anthony Werner
Address: Suite 34, 26 Charing Cross Road, London WC2H 0DH
Payment Details: Royalties are paid six-monthly or yearly depending on market potential of book
Unsolicited Manuscripts: Yes, but with return postage - synopsis preferred.

S

Shetland Times Publishing

Publish books on local interest subjects.

Address: Prince Alfred Street, Lerwick, Shetland ZE1 0EP
Telephone: 01595 693622
Fax: 01595 694637
Email: publishing@shetland-times.co.uk
Website: www.shetland-books.co.uk
Imprints: The Shetland Times Ltd
Parent Company: The Shetland Times Ltd

The Short Publishing Co Ltd

The company's imprint is Short Books, which publishes The Guide To English Language Teaching In Schools And Colleges In Britain. Next planned book is Music Europe, a guide to the leading classical music festivals in Europe.

Editor(s): Richard Mendelsohn, Katharine Mendelsohn
Address: 18 Quarry Road, Winchester, Hants SO23 0JG
Telephone: 01962 855068
Fax: As phone
Email: shortbooks@easynet.co.uk
Imprints: Short Books
Unsolicited Manuscripts: No

Shropshire Books

Publish books and leaflets about Shropshire to help residents and visitors explore and understand the county. Main subject areas covered so far are walking, cycling, history, archaeology, transport, folklore, wildlife, architecture, agriculture, gardens, literature and many more. Complete booklist available.

Editor(s): Helen Sample
Address: Column House, 7 London Road, Shrewsbury SY2 6NW
Telephone: 01743 255043
Fax: 01743 255050
Email: susan.white@shropshire-cc.gov.uk
Website: www.virtual-shropshire.co.uk/
Parent Company: Shropshire County Council
Unsolicited Manuscripts: Send to Editor

Sigma Press

Walking, cycling, outdoor leisure, local history, sport, dance, travel guides and folklore.

Editor(s): Graham Beech
Address: 1 South Oak Lane, Wilmslow, Cheshire SK9 6AR
Telephone: 01625 531035
Email: sigma.press@zetret.co.uk
Website: www.sigmapress.co.uk
Imprints: Sigma Leisure
Payment Details: By royalty
Unsolicited Manuscripts: Synopsis (& SAE) preferred

S

Simon & Schuster Ltd

General trade publishing, fiction and non-fiction, hardback and paperback. The children's books publishing launches in 1999.

Editor(s): M Fletcher, C Ledingham, H Gummer
Address: Africa House, 64-78 Kingsway, Holborn, London WC2B 6AH
Telephone: 0171 316 1900
Fax: 0171 316 0331
Imprints: Pocket Books, Scribner, Earthlight, S&S Children's Books, Star Trek
Parent Company: Simon & Schuster Inc, New York
Payment Details: By contract
Unsolicited Manuscripts: No

Singular Publishing Group Inc

Speech therapy, audiology, otolaryngology, special education, occupational and physical therapy.

Editor(s): Noel McPherson
Address: 19 Compton Terrace, London N1 2UN
Parent Company: Singular Publishing Group Inc, San Diego
Payment Details: Negotiable
Unsolicited Manuscripts: Yes

Charles Skilton Ltd

General book publishers including reference, fine art, architecture and fiction.

Editor(s): James Hughes
Address: 2 Caversham Street, London SW3 4AH
Telephone: 0171 351 4995
Fax: As phone
Imprints: Luxor Press, Albyn Press, Fortune Press
Parent Company: Skilton
Payment Details: By negotiation
Unsolicited Manuscripts: Introductory letter required first

Skoob Books Ltd

Esoterica and occult, Far Eastern literature in English and well known poetry. We will not be taking in any new material for the foreseeable future.

Editor(s): Mark Lovell
Address: 76A Oldfield Road, Stoke Newington, London N16 0RS
Imprints: Skoob Seriph, Skoob Esoterica, Skoob Pacifica
Unsolicited Manuscripts: No

S

SLG Press

Short pamphlets and books about the spiritual life, prayer, and things which help towards a greater understanding of Christian tradition.

Address: Convent of The Incarnation, Fairacres, Oxford OX4 1TB
Telephone: 01865 721301
Fax: 01865 790860
Imprints: Fairacres Publications
Payment Details: A portion of the print run in lieu of royalties
Unsolicited Manuscripts: Yes but no poetry please

Slow Dancer Press

Established in 1997 as a poetry press, in 1998 Slow Dancer enlarged its list to include some fiction. It now publishes four fiction and four poetry titles each year. We do not accept unsolicited manuscripts, nor approaches from agents - we find our own work.

Editor(s): John Harvey
Address: 91 Yerbury Road, London N14 4RW
Telephone: 0171 561 9979
Fax: As phone
Email: slowdancer@mellotone.co.uk
Website: www.mellotone.co.uk
Imprints: Slow Dancer Poetry, Slow Dancer Fiction
Unsolicited Manuscripts: No

S

Smith Settle Ltd

Local and regional history (Yorkshire & North of England); general interest; fine and limited editions; customs and folklore; outdoor and leisure.

Editor(s): Ken Smith, Mark Whitley
Address: Ilkley Road, Otley, West Yorkshire LS21 3JP
Telephone: 01943 467958
Fax: 01943 850057
Email: sales@smith-settle.co.uk
Payment Details: By negotiation
Unsolicited Manuscripts: Yes but send synopsis in first instance

Smith-Gordon & Co Ltd

Independent science, technology, medicine publisher established 1988. Works internationally, mainly at the postdoctoral level in life sciences: books, journals, newsletters.

Editor(s): E Smith-Gordon
Address: 13 Shalcombe Street, London SW10 0HZ
Telephone: 0171 351 7042
Fax: 0171 351 1250
Email: publisher@smithgordon.com
Unsolicited Manuscripts: Life sciences only, and at author's risk

S
Colin Smythe Ltd

Primarily publishers of Irish literature and criticism as well as acting as agent for authors and/or their literary estates.

Editor(s): Colin Smythe
Address: PO Box 6, Gerrards Cross, Bucks SL9 8XA
Telephone: 01753 886000
Fax: 01753 886469
Imprints: Van Duren, Dolmen Press
Payment Details: Royalties
Unsolicited Manuscripts: No

Snapshot Press

Specialises in haiku and related poetry, publishing individual collections, anthologies and two journals, Snapshots (haiku) and Tangled Hair (tanka). Spring 1999 sees the publication of The New Haiku (edited by John Barlow & Martin Lucas) - the first anthology of its kind, featuring arguably the best English-language haiku and senryu published in specialist haiku magazines in the UK and Ireland during 1998. Snapshot Press also publishes the winning entry of the Snapshots Haiku Collection Competition - an annual competition for unpublished collections of haiku, senryu and/or tanka. (Send sae for details, closing date 31 July.)

Editor(s): John Barlow
Address: PO Box 35, Sefton Park, Liverpool LI7 3EG
Email: snapshotpress@hotmail.com
Website: www.mccoy.co.uk/snapshots
Payment Details: Royalties
Unsolicited Manuscripts: Yes, for journals & comp. Other material solicited

Social Affairs Unit

The SAU is an independent research and educational trust committed to the promotion of lively and wide-ranging debate on social affairs. Its authors - over 200 - have analysed the factors which make for a free and orderly society in which enterprise can flourish. It is committed to international co-operation in ideas - eg The Loss Of Virtue and This Will Hurt published as National Review Books; Gentility Recalled published in co-operation with the Acton Institute and joint Anglo-European projects on food and alcohol policy. Current areas of work include consumer affairs, the critical appraisal of welfare and public spending and problems of freedom and personal responsibility.

Editor(s): Digby Anderson
Address: Suite 5/6 Morley House, 314-322 Regent Street, London W1R 5AB
Telephone: 0171 637 4356
Fax: 0171 436 8530
Email: sausales@compuserve.com

Social Work Monographs

Publish up to 10 new titles each year. A complete checklist containing over 100 titles is available on subjects such as family & child care, child abuse, care of the elderly, mental health, people with disabilities, theory & research & social work with offenders.

Editor(s): A McDonald
Address: School of Social Work, Elizabeth Fry Building, University of East Anglia, Norwich NR4 7TJ
Telephone: 01603 592087
Fax: 01603 593552
Email: j.hancock@uea

𝒮
Society For General Microbiology

Publisher of three learned scientific jounals - Microbiology (monthly), Journal Of General Virology (monthly) and International Journal Of Systematic Bacteriology (quarterly). Also publishes the magazine Microbiology Today, and with Cambridge University Press, the SGM Symposium Series of books on current topics in microbiology. SGM is a limited company and registered charity.

Address: Marllborough House, Basingstoke Road, Spencers Wood, Reading RG7 1AE
Telephone: 0118 988 1800
Fax: 0118 988 5656
Website: www.socgenmicrobiol.org.uk
Payment Details: No payments are made
Unsolicited Manuscripts: Scientific research papers are subject to peer review

The Society For Promoting Christian Knowledge (SPCK)

Publishes for the Christian book market. There are books covering all the following areas: prayer and meditaion; biography and letters; personal growth and relationships; counselling; healing and pastoral care; church, mission and ministry; social and ethical issues; theology and religious studies; science and religion; biblical studies; church history; liturgical studies and worship resources. SPCK aims to cover a broad spectrum of religious viewpoints, and fulfils its mission through helping people to understand and develop their personal faith. Founded in 1698, it comprises a chain of bookshops and a Worldwide branch, which supports the work of churches around the globe.

Editor(s): Simon Kingston (SPCK), Joanna Moriarty (Sheldon Press), Alison Barr (Triangle & Azure)
Address: SPCK, Holy Trinity Church, Marylebone Road, London NW1 4DU
Telephone: 0171 387 5282
Fax: 0171 388 2352
Email: spck@spck.org.uk
Website: www.spck.org.uk
Imprints: SPCK, Triangle, Lynx Communications, Azure, Sheldon Press
Parent Company: SPCK
Payment Details: Individual agreement
Unsolicited Manuscripts: To imprint editor

S

Society For The Promotion Of Roman Studies

Leading organisation in the UK for those interested in the study of Rome and the Roman Empire. Its scope is wide, covering Roman history, archaeology, literature and art down to about AD700. It has a broadly-based membership, drawn from over forty countries and from all ages and walks of life. The Society publishes two journals, the Journal Of Roman Studies, which contains articles and book reviews dealing with the Roman world in general, and Britannia, which has articles and reviews specifically on Roman Britain; also two monograph series - the JRS and Britannia monographs.

Editor(s): S R F Price (JRS), M G Fulford (Britannia)
Address: Senate House, Malet Street, London WC1E 7HU
Telephone: 0171 862 8727
Fax: 0171 862 8728
Email: romansoc@sas.ac.uk
Imprints: Society for the Promotion of Roman Studies

Society For The Study Of Medieval Languages & Literature

Publishes the journal Medium Aevum on subjects in the language and literature of medieval European countries, including English. Also publishes an occasional series under the title Medium Aevum Monographs in the same areas. Manuscripts (normal length between 50,000 and 70,000 words, are refereed,and a contribution to publication costs (in the region of £500 to £700) is normally required.

Editor(s): H Cooper (English), University College Oxford; N Palmer (Germanic), St Edmund Hall, Oxford; E Kennedy (Romance), The White Cottage, Byles Green, Upper Bucklebury, Reading RS7 6SG
Address: Hon Treasurer, SSMLL, Magdalen College, Oxford OX1 4AU
Telephone: 01865 276087
Fax: As phone
Email: david.pattison@magd.ox.ac.uk
Website: http://units.ox.ac.uk/departments/modlang/ssmll/
Unsolicited Manuscripts: To editors as appropriate

Society For Underwater Technology

Multi-disciplinary international learned society dedicated to the active promotion of the development, dissemination and exchange of ideas, information and technology arising from or related to the underwater environment. Publishes a quarterly learned journal, newsletters and conference proceedings.

Editor(s): D Brown, P C Collar
Address: 76 Mark Lane, London EC3R 7JN
Telephone: 0171 481 0750
Fax: 0171 481 4001
Email: kirsty@sutpubs.demon.co.uk
Website: www.sut.org.uk

Society Of Dyers & Colourists

Professional organisation specialising in all aspects of the science and technology of colour and coloration. It publishes a series of books dealing with dyes and pigments, and with the coloration of various substrates, especially textiles.

Address: PO Box 244, Perkin House, 82 Grattan Road, Bradford BD1 2JB
Website: www.sdc.org.uk

$\mathcal{S}$
Society Of Genealogists

Educational charity. Publishes books related to genealogy and family history. Prospective authors should first contact the Society with a proposal.

Address: 14 Charterhouse Buildings, Goswell Road, London EC1M 7BA
Telephone: 0171 251 8799
Fax: 0171 250 1800
Email: sales@sog.org.uk
Website: www.sog.org.uk
Payment Details: Half-yearly royalties by cheque
Unsolicited Manuscripts: No

The Society Of Metaphysicians Ltd

Neometaphysics: new fundamental science and its applications. Includes paraphysics, parapsychology, psychic science, psychic, estoeric and mystical studies. Evaluation of consciousness: in terms of empathy. Neometaphysics (fundamental laws) and politics . . . and religion . . . and the physical sciences. World unity and environmental matters. Journal The NeoMetaphysical Digest invites short articles.

Editor(s): John J Williamson, Alana J Mayne, Eleanor Swift
Address: Archers Court, Stonestile Lane, The Ridge, Hastings, East Sussex TN35 4PG
Telephone: 01424 751577
Fax: 01424 722387
Email: newmeta@btinternet.com
Imprints: MRG (Metaphysical Research Group)
Payment Details: By mutual agreement
Unsolicited Manuscripts: Yes

Southgate Publishers

Educational publisher. Books for primary teachers especially in the curriculum areas of environmental education, mathematics, personal & social education, music & dance, and assembly books. Publishes with the Campaign for Learning - books related to lifelong learning, including workforce training materials.

Address: 15 Barnfield Avenue, Exmouth, Devon EX8 2QE
Telephone: 01395 223801
Fax: 01395 223818
Email: kav96@dial.pipex.com
Imprints: Mosaic Educational Publications
Parent Company: Southgate Publishers Ltd
Unsolicited Manuscripts: No - write first with synopsis, or telephone

Souvenir Press

Independent publishers, now in their 48th year with a wide-ranging largely non-fiction list including Human Horizons on disability (Condor trade paperbacks). Recently published the standard Solutions For Writers by Sol Stein. Best-selling authors include Arthur Hailey, Erich Von Daniken, Charles Berlitz, Herman Wouk, Knut Hamsun, Carl Rogers, Wilhelm Reich and Ronald Searle. 55 books a year including reprints.

Editor(s): Editor in Chief: Tessa Harrow
Address: 43 Great Russell Street, London WC1B 3PA
Telephone: 0171 580 9307
Fax: 0171 580 5064
Imprints: Souvenir Press, Condor, Condor Independent Voices, Human Horizons
Parent Company: Souvenir Press Ltd
Payment Details: Royalties twice-yearly
Unsolicited Manuscripts: Enquiry first summarising subject & author's CV

S

SPA Books Ltd

History - military and Scottish; art and crafts; biographies.

Editor(s): Steven Apps
Address: PO Box 47, Stevenage, Herts SG2 8UH
Imprints: Strong Oak Press
Unsolicited Manuscripts: No - synopsis please in first instance

Spellmount Limited

Publishers of high-quality history and military history books. All historical periods are covered but with particular emphasis on the Napoleonic period, World War 1 and World War 2. Autobiographies are not considered.

Editor(s): Jamie Wilson
Address: The Old Rectory, Staplehurst, Kent TN12 0AZ
Telephone: 01580 893730
Fax: 01580 893731
Email: spellmount.demon.co.uk
Imprints: Spellmount
Payment Details: By negotiation
Unsolicited Manuscripts: Synopsis with return postage please

E & F N Spon

Architecture, building, civil engineering construction, planning, landscape . . . all building environment subjects, at university student or professional level (ie not DIY). Sports science, leisure and recreation management, again at student or professional level (not players or fans).

Editor(s): Michael Doggwiler (environmental & geotechnical engineering); Marie-Louise Logan (civil engineering); Caroline Mallinder (architecture); Tim Robinson (construction law & management, environmental health); Sally Wride (sports science & leisure management)
Address: 11 New Fetter Lane, London EC4P 4EE
Telephone: 0171 583 9855
Fax: 0171 824 2303
Email: (editor's name)@routledge.co.uk
Website: www.efnspon.com
Imprints: Spon
Parent Company: Routledge
Payment Details: Royalties, paid once a year
Unsolicited Manuscripts: Yes, in relevant subjects

Square One Publications

Personal publishing house handling memoirs, mainly military, and books of local interest.

Editor(s): Mary Wilkinson
Address: The Tudor House, 16 Church Street, Upton-on-Severn, Worcs WR8 0HT
Telephone: 01684 594522
Fax: 01684 594640
Email: marywilk@aol.com
Payment Details: Depends on individual manuscripts
Unsolicited Manuscripts: Yes

S

ST Publishing

Independent publisher specialising in youth culture, music and football. ST Publishing focuses on youth cults and music, Low Life is dedicated to pulp fiction related to youth cults, and Terrace Banter is a football imprint dedicated to the fans.

Editor(s): George Marshall
Address: PO Box 12, Lockerbie DG11 3BW
Email: stpbooks@aol.com
Imprints: ST Publishing, Low Life, Terrace Banter
Parent Company: ST Publishing
Payment Details: Advance plus royalties twice-yearly
Unsolicited Manuscripts: Synopsis & sample chapter preferred

Stagecoach: The First Educational Course For Under-Fives

Teachers/parent self-teaching or minimal guidance for the under-fives. 29 workbooks, loose sheet, black/white print photocopiable. Includes mathematics, cognitive, art & craft, letters, word-building, reading. For different age-groups can be used in conjunction with any other teaching materials. Four stages: Stage One 3 years+ - letters a-z; Stage Two 3½+ - letters/words a-z; Stage Three 4 years+ - letters/words/reading; Stage Four 4½+ - reading/writing. Project packs: body; christmas; music; earth, air, fire & four seasons.

Editor(s): R L Day
Address: Carriers Crossing, Woodford Road, Stratford-sub-Castle, Salisbury SP4 6AE
Telephone: 01722 782369

The Steel Construction Institute

Develops and promotes the effective use of steel in construction. It is an independent, membership-based organisation. SCI's research and development activities cover many aspects of steel construction including multi-storey construction, industrial buildings, light gauge steel framing systems, development of design guidance on the use of stainless steel, fire engineering, bridge and civil engineering, offshore engineering, environmental studies, and development of structural analysis systems and information technology.

Address: Silwood Park, Ascot, Berks SL5 7QN
Telephone: 01344 623345
Fax: 01344 622944
Email: library@steel-sci.com
Website: www.steel-sci.org

Rudolf Steiner Press

The works of Rudolf Steiner translated into English, and other authors whose work is related to Steiner's ideas. Books which contain new research and ideas of a spiritual and scientific nature. No fiction, poetry or children's books.

Editor(s): S Gulbekian
Address: 51 Queen Caroline Street, London W6 9QL
Telephone: 0181 748 0571
Imprints: Sophia Books
Parent Company: Temple Lodge Publishing
Unsolicited Manuscripts: No

S

Stenlake Publishing

Photographic local history books; transport history books; maritime history books and industrial history books.

Editor(s): Oliver Van Helden
Address: Ochiltree Sawmill, The Lade, Ochiltree, Ayrshire KA18 2NX
Telephone: 01290 423114
Payment Details: By Negotiation
Unsolicited Manuscripts: No

Henry Stewart Publications

International publisher of business journals. Range includes journals of the following: brand management; database marketing; communication management; targeting measurement & analysis for marketing; nonprofit & voluntary sector marketing; corporate reputation review; financial services marketing; corporate real estate; financial crime; financial regulation & compliance; money laundering control; small business & enterprise development.

Editor(s): International editorial boards
Address: Russell House, 28-30 Little Russell Street, London WC1A 1JT
Telephone: 0171 404 3040
Fax: 0171 404 2081
Email: ed@hspublications.co.uk
Website: www.henrystewart.co.uk

Stobart Davies Ltd

Wood and wood related crafts.

Editor(s): Brian Davies
Address: Priory House, 2 Priory Street, Hertford SG14 1RN
Unsolicited Manuscripts: Yes

Arthur H Stockwell Ltd

Book publishers - all types of work considered.

Editor(s): B Nott
Address: Elms Court, Torrs Park, Ilfracombe EX34 8BA
Telephone: 01271 882557
Fax: 01271 862988

Stokesby House

School textbooks and learning. Support materials - biology, human biology and environmental studies.

Address: Stokesby, Norfolk NR29 3ET
Telephone: 01493 750645
Fax: 01493 750146
Email: stokesbyhouse@btinternet.com
Unsolicited Manuscripts: No

S

STRI - Sports Turf Research Institute

We write and publish a range of specialist titles relating to the maintenance management and construction of natural turf playing surfaces including golf courses, sports pitches, bowling greens, lawn tennis courts, racecourses etc. We also publish a quarterly 36-page full colour magazine International Turfgrass Bulletin; a scientific Journal Of Turfgrass; and an annual trade directory, STRI-Green Pages. We also sell our titles, plus a growing list of other publishers' related titles, via mail order.

Address: St Ives Estate, Bingley, West Yorks BD16 1AU
Telephone: 01274 565131
Fax: 01274 561891
Email: info@stri.co.uk
Website: www.stri.co.uk
Unsolicited Manuscripts: Only publish titles written inhouse by specialists

Stride

We expect the work to show an engagement with the knowledge of contemporary poetics: we are not interested in rhyming doggerel, light verse or the merely confessional. We are interested in linguistically innovative work, and work in more traditional [whether formal or free] genres that reinvent the way we see the world. We publish a small amount of experimental literary fiction titles [either short stories, prose-poem collections or novels]. We do not publish anything in the following genres: romance; historical; war; memoirs; rhymes for children; haiku; action; adventure; spy; sci-fi and fantasy. Fiction submissions should be sent in traditional manuscript form; but we will expect the work to be available to us on computer disc if the book is accepted. We are also interested in books of interviews for our Stride Conversation Pieces series; and documents [theses; essays; unedited interviews] for our Research Documents series. These should be in the field of arts, music [particularly jazz and 'out-rock'] or literature.

Editor(s): Rupert Loydell
Address: 11 Sylvan Road, Exeter, Devon EX4 6EW
Email: rml@madbear.demon.co.uk
Website: www.madbear.demon.co.uk
Imprints: Stride Research Documents, Stride Conversation Pieces, Apparition Press, Stride
Parent Company: Stride Publication
Payment Details: Free copies
Unsolicited Manuscripts: Yes with SAE

S

Summersdale Publishers

Non-fiction publishing house, specialising in travel, humour, gift, self-help and guide books. 40 titles in 1998.

Editor(s): Liz Kershaw
Address: 46 West Street, Chichester, West Sussex PO19 1RP
Telephone: 01243 771107
Fax: 01243 786300
Email: summersdale@summersdale.com
Website: www.summersdale.com
Payment Details: No advances, annual royalties
Unsolicited Manuscripts: No, send letter & synopsis in first instance

Sunflower Books

Travel guidebooks - the Landscapes series of countryside guides, (walks, car tours and picnics in popular overseas holiday destinations). Mss must be to the precise format of the series, and location must be agreed in advance. Note: The company name seems to attract many proposals for children's books and poetry. Sunflower Books does not publish in these categories.
Address: 12 Kendrick Mews, London SW7 3HG
Telephone: 0171 589 1862
Fax: As phone
Email: mail@sunflowerbooks.co.uk
Website: www.sunflowerbooks.co.uk
Parent Company: P A Underwood Ltd
Payment Details: By standard authors' royalty contract
Unsolicited Manuscripts: No

S

Supportive Learning Publications

Educational publishers specialising in the following: work books for children; photocopiable worksheet packs for schools; English as a second language for children and adults. Subjects covered include English, maths, science, history, geography, technology, art, craft, music, early learning etc. We also publish material specifically written for reluctant readers, produced as short plays or sketches with, usually, a comedy/adventure theme. The reading age of these plays is approximately 9 years but with an interest level of 7 to 14 years.

Editor(s): Phil Roberts
Address: 23 West View, Chirk, Wrexham LL14 5HL
Telephone: 01691 774778
Fax: 01691 774849
Email: slpuk.demon.co.uk
Website: www.slpuk.demon.co.uk
Payment Details: Negotiable
Unsolicited Manuscripts: Yes

Sussex Publications

Audio-visual materials only. No interest in books unless they are texts to accompany audiotapes, videotapes, slide sets, tape slide sets, computer programs, CD-ROMs and microfilms. All subjects covered.

Address: 23 North Wharf Road, London W2 1LA
Telephone: 0171 266 2202
Fax: 0171 266 2314
Email: microworld@ndirect.co.uk
Website: www.ndirect.co.uk/~microworld
Imprints: Sussex Tapes, Sussex Video. Associates: Audio-Forum, The Language Source, World Microfilms, Pidgeon Audio-Visual
Unsolicited Manuscripts: N/A

S

Sutton Publishing Ltd

History, archaeology, military, aviation, naval history, transport (railway, motor & canal), biographies, anthologies, old photograph books, classic reprints, art and architectural history.

Editor(s): Jane Crompton, Jonathan Falconer, Simon Fletcher, Jaqueline Mitchel
Address: Phoenix Mill, Thrupp, Stroud, Gloucestershire GL5 2BU
Imprints: Pocket Classics, Budding Books, Alan Sutton
Parent Company: The Guernsey Press
Unsolicited Manuscripts: Yes Synopses only with SAE

Ta Ha Publishers Ltd

Books on Islam & Muslim world, and children's books.

Editor(s): A Clarke
Address: 1 Wynne Road, London SW9 0BB
Telephone: 0171 737 7266
Fax: 0171 737 7267
Email: sale@taha.co.uk

Taigh Na Teud Music Publishers

Publish Scottish traditional music and song with a specialisation in Highland and Gaelic material. Also some Gaelic non-music items.

Editor(s): Christine Martin (music), Alasdair Martin (Gaelic)
Address: 13 Breacais, Ard, Isle of Skye IV42 8PY
Telephone: 01470 822 528
Fax: 01471 822 811
Email: taighnateud@martin.abel.co.uk
Website: www.abel.net.uk/~martin
Imprints: Taigh Na Teud
Payment Details: Royalties paid 6-monthly in arrears - 10% retail
Unsolicited Manuscripts: Contemporary tunes in the Highland idiom

Take That Ltd

Financial markets, personal finance, computing, Internet, gambling.
Editor(s): C Brown
Address: PO Box 200, Harrogate HG1 2YR
Fax: 01423 526035
Email: sales@takethat.co.uk
Website: www.takethat.co.uk
Imprints: Take That Books, NET Works, Cardoza, TTL
Parent Company: Take That Ltd
Payment Details: 10%, no advances
Unsolicited Manuscripts: Yes

T

Tarquin Publications

Mathematics, paper engineering, patterns, things involving paper cutting, folding or models. Fundamental science treated in a three-dimensional way.

Editor(s): Gerald Jenkins
Address: Stradbroke, Diss, Norfolk IP21 5JP
Website: www.tarquin-books.demon.co.uk
Imprints: Tarquin
Payment Details: Royalties and advance paid
Unsolicited Manuscripts: No - send a brief description in a letter

Tate Gallery Publishing Ltd

Publishers of art books, exhibition catalogues and gallery guides of modern art from 1900 and British art since 1550 to the present day.

Address: Millbank, London SW1P 4RG
Telephone: 0171 887 8869
Fax: 0171 887 8878
Email: tqpl@tate.org.uk
Website: www.tate.org.uk
Imprints: Tate Gallery Publishing
Unsolicited Manuscripts: No

Taylor Graham Publishing

Publishers of academic books and journals, in areas of information technology, information management, librarianship, and education themes in general.

Address: 500 Chesham House, 150 Regent Street, London W1R 5FA

The Templar Company plc

Children's picture books and novelties. Children's trade non-fiction; particularly natural history, history, geography, science and early learning first concepts.

Editor(s): Amanda Wood
Address: Pippbrook Mill, London Road, Dorking, Surrey RH4 1JE
Imprints: Templar Publishing
Payment Details: Advances and royalties for author ideas taken up
Unsolicited Manuscripts: Yes

Tempus Publishing Ltd

History publishers with special interests in local and regional history. Large series of regional books containing old photographs (the Archive Photographs series), including books on town history, transport, sport and other regional history including oral history. Also some early history and archaeology books.

Editor(s): David Buxton (topographical, regional & oral history), Campbell McCutcheon (transport & industrial history), Peter Kemmis-Betty (early history & archaeology)
Address: The Mill, Brimscombe Port, Brimscombe, Stroud GL5 2QG
Telephone: 01453 883300
Fax: 01453 883233
Email: tempusuk@tempus-publishing
Parent Company: Tempus Publishing Group
Payment Details: Royalty in most cases
Unsolicited Manuscripts: To to relevant listed editor

𝒯
Textile & Art Publications Ltd

Textile & Art Publications brings together a specialist group of individuals with many years' experience in the art world and in the production, publishing, distribution and marketing of international art books, often linked to exhibitions. We have unique access to many major private collections and a reputation for producing generously-illustrated books to the highest academic, design and production standards, concentrating on a limited number of major titles each year. The company is building a varied list of books, covering Oriental, Islamic, Pre-Colombian and Medieval art; and has also produced international language co-editions of its titles for other publishers.

Editor(s): Michael Franses
Address: 12 Queen Street, Mayfair, London W1X 7PL
Telephone: 0171 499 7979
Fax: 0171 409 2596
Email: post@textile-art.com
Website: www.textile-art.com
Imprints: Textile & Art Publications

Thames & Hudson Ltd

Thames & Hudson, which celebrates its 50th anniversary in 1999, is one of the world's best-known publishers of illustrated books. Concentrating on books of high textual and visual quality for an international audience, its programme of more than 150 titles per year focuses on the arts of all kinds, archaeology, architecture & design, graphics, history, mythology, photography, popular culture and travel & topography.

Editor(s): Editorial Head: Jamie Camplin
Address: 181a High Holborn, London WC1V 7QX
Telephone: 0171 845 5000
Fax: 0171 845 5050
Email: editorial@thbooks.demon.co.uk
Website: www.thameshudson.co.uk
Imprints: Thames & Hudson
Payment Details: Royalties paid twice-yearly
Unsolicited Manuscripts: Send preliminary letter & outline before manuscripts

Thames Publishing

Thames: books about English classical music and musicians, particularly of earlier part of 20th century. Autolycus: booklist only of poetry (no new publications).

Editor(s): John Bishop
Address: 14 Barlby Road, London W10 6AR
Telephone: 0181 969 3579
Imprints: Thames, Autolycus
Unsolicited Manuscripts: No

Third Age Press

An independent publishing company which recognises that the period of life after full-time employment and family responsibility can be a time of fulfillment and continuing development. The books encourage older people to make the best of the rest of their lives, but are also relevant to those working with older people or teaching students of gerontology or geriatrics. To date topics covered have included the following: writing and recording life stories, memory, health, alternative therapies, changes and challenges in later life, walking through Europe and the history of the old-age pension. Through its Perspectives series, Third Age Press also produces self-published memoirs.

Editor(s): Dianne Norton
Address: 6 Parkside Gardens, London SW19 5EY
Telephone: 0181 947 0401
Fax: 0181 944 9316
Email: dnort@thirdagepress.co.uk
Website: www.thirdagepress.co.uk
Imprints: Third Age Press
Unsolicited Manuscripts: Yes if within areas detailed

T
Thistle Press

Scottish regional travel guides; local history; archaeology & geology with Scottish content; general Scottish interest; academic books on the environmental sciences. Member Scottish Publishers Association.

Editor(s): Keith Nicholson, Angela Nicholson
Address: West Bank, Western Road, Insch, Aberdeenshire AB52 6JR
Telephone: 01464 821 053
Fax: As phone
Email: info@thistlepress.co.uk
Website: www.thistlepress.co.uk
Payment Details: Annual royalties as per contract
Unsolicited Manuscripts: Yes

Thomas Cook Publishing

Produce a wide range of travel-related books, maps and timetables. Three new ranges in 1999: The Classic series published in conjunction with Classic FM - first book in the series is Classic Short Breaks, covering over 100 European cities. Signpost Guides - a 10-book series for self-drive holidaymakers, featuring destinations such as California, New Zealand and regional France. Independent Traveller's Guides - a 4-book series aimed at budget travellers covering Europe, USA, Australia and New Zealand. Other publications in the Thomas Cook Publishing portfolio include: European & Overseas Timetables - updated monthly; International Air Travel Handbook; Travellers Guides (54-book series); Touring Handbooks (13-book series); European & South Asian phrasebooks; World Atlas Of Travel; Golden Age Of Travel; Greek Island Hopping 1999; Your Passport To Safer Travel; Rail maps of Great Britain & Ireland and Europe; Where To Ski And Snowboard; Hot Spots Guides (25-book series).

Editor(s): Stephen York
Address: PO Box 227 Thorpe Wood, Peterborough PE3 6PU
Telephone: 01733 503571/2
Fax: 01733 503596
Website: www.thomascook.co.uk
Parent Company: Thomas Cook Group
Unsolicited Manuscripts: Yes

Thorntons Of Oxford

Oxford's oldest bookshop.

Address: 11 Broad Street, Oxford OX1 3AR
Telephone: 01865 242939
Fax: 01865 204021
Website: www.demon.co.uk/thorntons
Imprints: W A Meeuws
Unsolicited Manuscripts: No

Thoth Publications

Publishers of metaphysical, western mystery tradition, and esoteric works, with each manuscript given care and attention by those with the knowledge within the particular field.

Editor(s): Tom Clarke
Address: 64 Leopold Street, Loughborough LE11 5DN
Telephone: 01509 210626
Fax: 01592 238034
Email: thothpub@ad.com

T

Tiger Books International Plc

We do not publish original works - we buy finished books from publishers and packagers.

Address: 26a York Street, Twickenham TW1 3LJ
Telephone: 0181 892 5577
Fax: 0181 891 6550
Email: enquiries@tigerbooks.co.uk
Imprints: Sheridan Book Co, Senate Books
Unsolicited Manuscripts: No

Timber Press Inc

Leading publisher of books on gardening, horticulture and botany. Specialises in authoritative treatments of particular plant groups written by internationally renowned authors. Whether you are a keen gardener or a professional grower, Timber Press can help to inform you about the different genera, propagation and cultivation of many plants, trees and shrubs.

Address: 10 Market Street, Swavesey, Cambridge CB4 5QG.
Telephone: 01954 232959
Fax: 01954 206040
Email: timberpressuk@btinnternet.com
Website: www.timberpress.com
Parent Company: Timber Press, Portland, Oregon

Topaz Publications

Publishers of legal texts in relation to Irish law only.

Editor(s): Davida Murdoch
Address: 10 Haddington Lawn, Glenageary, Co Dublin, Ireland
Telephone: 00353 1 2800460
Unsolicited Manuscripts: No

TQMI Media & Publications

TQMI provide books and CD-ROMs that enable organisations to: communicate the practices and principles of continuous improvement, clearly and effectively, to staff at all levels; educate and train staff in how to implement improvements; reinforce senior management's commitment to continuous improvement; motivate and encourage staff to become involved in improvement. We also help organisations customise these publications with their own logo etc, or write bespoke titles to meet customers' specific needs.

Address: The Stables, Tarvin Road, Frodsham, Hants WA6 6XN
Telephone: 01590 624646
Fax: 01590 624647
Email: publications@tqmi.co.uk
Website: www.tqmi.co.uk
Imprints: TQM International Ltd

Training Publications Ltd

Main areas: basic engineering manufacture, including NVQ-related material, science and technology. Subsidiary areas: small but expanding archaeological and ancient history list, also biology and natural history.

Address: 3 Finway Court, Whippendell Road, Watford WD1 7EN
Telephone: 01923 243730
Fax: 01923 213144
Email: trainingpubs@btinternet.com
Imprints: Entra, EMTA, EIT, EITB
Parent Company: Engineering & Marine Training Authority
Payment Details: Negotiable
Unsolicited Manuscripts: Yes

T
Transedition Limited

Transedition has three operations - packaging, rights acquisition and translation. Packages illustrated reference books for the international marketplace. Acquires English-language rights from European publishers and European rights from American publishers, which are translated, repackaged and sold as co-editions. Offers its translation services to other publishers through its subsidiary Translate-A-Book. Transedition buys or packages and translates and sells illustrated reference and coffee table books and series. Subject areas of interest are art and antiques, children's non-fiction, cinema, gardening, history, religion, sport, transport.

Address: 43 Henley Avenue, Oxford OX4 4DJ
Telephone: 01865 770 549
Fax: 01865 712 500
Email: all@transed.co.uk
Unsolicited Manuscripts: No

Transport Bookman Publication Ltd

Specialise in publishing motoring books, particularly on the subject of motor racing, biographies and historical.

Address: 8 South Street, Isleworth, Middlesex TW7 7BG
Telephone: 0181 560 2666
Fax: 0181 569 8273

Trematon Press

Specialises in equestrian subjects, mostly side-saddle riding.

Editor(s): C E Turner
Address: Trematon Hall, Saltash, Cornwall PL12 4RU
Telephone: 01752 842351
Fax: 01752 848920

Trentham Books Ltd

Books for professional use by teachers and lecturers and other practitioners in education, social work and law. Not books for classroom use; not children's books, biography, fiction or poetry. No packs or other non-book material.

Editor(s): Gillian Klein
Address: Westview House, 734 London Road, Oakhill, Stoke on Trent ST4 5NP
Telephone: 01782 745567/844699
Fax: 01782 745553
Email: th@trentham-books.co.uk
Website: www.trentham-books.co.uk
Imprints: Trentham
Payment Details: Annual royalty calculated 31st August and payable within six weeks thereafter
Unsolicited Manuscripts: Yes

Triangle Books

Publishers of Christian books, particularly in the areas of prayer, spirituality and personal growth. We also publish books on mission and the church in the modern world, as well as stories of faith in action. Triangle books are aimed at a popular Christian readership.

Editor(s): Alison Barr
Address: Holy Trinity Church, Marylebone Road, London NW1 4DU
Telephone: 0171 387 5282
Fax: 0171 388 2352
Email: abarr@spck.org.uk
Website: www.spck.org.uk
Parent Company: SPCK
Payment Details: By negotiation
Unsolicited Manuscripts: Send synopsis & sample chapter

𝒯
Trinitarian Bible Society

Publishers of accurate and reliable protestant versions of the Bible, or part thereof, in several languages. Translations are drawn from the Hebrew Masoretic text and from the Greek Textus Receptus.

Editor(s): G W Anderson
Address: Tyndale House, Dorset Road, London SW19 3NN
Telephone: 0181 543 7857
Fax: 0181 543 6370

Triumph House

Triumph House publishes Christian poetry books on various themes. It also produces a quarterly magazine, Triumph Herald, featuring items such as personal testimonies, Bible stories, prayers and general Christian arts news. Includes a section for young Christians to share their poetry along with a few crossword puzzles and word searches. A year's subscription to the magazine (four issues) is £12 in the UK and £18 for overseas. The Spotlight Poets imprint also publishes books of poetry containing twelve authors with each one having ten pages of the book dedicated to them and their work. The poems can be on a variety of subjects and themes. Please write or telephone for an information pack on any of the above. You can also contact us by email, but please be sure to include your postal address.

Editor(s): Managing Ed: Steve Twelvetree; Ed: Kelly Deacon
Address: Remus House, Coltsfoot Drive, Woodston, Peterborough PE2 9JX
Telephone: 01733 898102
Fax: 01733 313524
Email: suzy@forwardpress.co.uk
Imprints: Spotlight Poets
Parent Company: Forward Press Ltd
Unsolicited Manuscripts: Send covering letter with sample poems only

Trog Associates Ltd

Standards into management systems. Engineering DIY workbooks - ISO 9001 Design Consultancy; Design & Manufacturing; 9002 Service Organisation; 14001 Environmental; 2000 Health & Safety; 9000 Corporate Communications. Software DIY workbooks - ISO 9001: Tickit; RAD; SSADM; Prince - Project Management; Service Delivery/Operations Management.

Editor(s): Author/Publisher/Trainer: Eric Sutherland
Address: PO Box 243, UK - South Croydon, Croydon, Surrey CR1 6TP
Telephone: 0181 7867094
Fax: 0181 6863580
Email: trog@dial.pipex.com
Website: www.nvo.com/management-systems-author
Unsolicited Manuscripts: No

Trotman & Co Ltd

Careers education - includes guides to further and higher education, guides on specific careers and classroom resources at secondary level.

Editor(s): Morfydd Jones
Address: 2 The Green, Richmond, Surrey TW9 1PL
Website: www.trotmanpublishing.co.uk
Payment Details: Royalty or fee
Unsolicited Manuscripts: Yes but prefer an outline synopsis in the first instance

T

Trust For Wessex Archaeology Ltd

Publishes specialist and academic monographs on archaeological sites and surveys in the Wessex region.

Editor(s): Julie Gardiner
Address: Portway House, Old Sarum Park, Salisbury SP4 6EB
Telephone: 01722 326867
Fax: 01722 337562
Email: wessexarch@dial.pipex.com
Unsolicited Manuscripts: No

TSR

Publisher of the world-renowned adventure game Dungeons & Dragons. Celebrating its 25th anniversary this year, the game further generated a wide variety of best-selling fantasy novels including the book series Dragonlance. The aquisition of TSR by Wizards of the Coast enabled the company to reach further into the fantasy market with major additions to its novel lines including the exciting new science fiction series Alternity. With established book lines including Forgotten Realms, Greyhawk and Planescape, plus award-winning authors Margaret Weis, Tracey Hickman, R A Salvatore and Diane Duane (of Star Trek fame), TSR is a well-respected name in fantasy fiction. Its silver anniversary is celebrated all year long with special products, classic best-sellers updated for the current market, and a few surprises designed to make 1999 a year to remember.

Address: Nicholsons House, Nicholsons Walk, Maidenhead, Berks SL6 6LD
Telephone: 01628 780801
Fax: 01628 780602
Email: lee-crocker@uk.wizards.be
Website: www.wizards.com
Parent Company: Wizards of the Coast

Tufton Books

Religion, theology and religious education.

Editor(s): Liz Marsh
Address: Faith House, 7 Tufton Street, Westminster, London SW1P 3QN
Telephone: 0171 222 6958
Fax: 0171 976 7180
Email: tuftonbook@aol.com
Parent Company: The Church Union
Unsolicited Manuscripts: Yes

Twelveheads Press

Has been publishing books about industrial transport and maritime history since 1978. Specialises in the geographical area of the west of England, Cornwall in particular, but extends to other areas if appropriate to interests. Only publish books on subjects that the editors know well or are interested in, thus ensuring the highest standards.

Editor(s): Michael Messenger, Alan Kittridge, John Stengelhofen
Address: Chy Mengleth, Twelveheads, Truro, Cornwall TR4 8SN
Telephone: 01209 820978
Email: admin@twelveheads.demon.co.uk
Website: www.twelveheads.demon.co.uk
Imprints: Twelveheads Press
Payment Details: Royalties half-yearly
Unsolicited Manuscripts: No - send synopsis & details

T
Two Heads Publishing

Sport: football and cricket.

Editor(s): Charles Frewin
Address: 9 Whitehall Park, London N19 3TS
Unsolicited Manuscripts: No

UCL Press

Social sciences, politics & international relations, media & culture studies, geography, archaeology, history and criminology.

Editor(s): Caroline Wintersgill, Luciana O'Flaherty, Kate Brewin
Address: 1 Gunpowder Square, London EC4A 3DE
Parent Company: Taylor & Francis Group
Unsolicited Manuscripts: No

UKCHR - United Kingdom Council For Human Rights

Monitor human rights in the United Kingdom, where there has been a radical restructuring of society. This process continues under New Labour. Publish leaflets and booklets on human rights issues, and a reference book on race, poverty and health: Of Germs, Genes & Genocide.

Address: Flat No 7, Sunley House, 10 Gunthorpe Street, London E1 7RW
Telephone: 0171 377 2932
Fax: 0870 055 3979
Email: ukchr@ukcouncilhumanrights.co.uk
Website: www.ukcouncilhumanrights.co.uk

𝓊

University of Birmingham Press

Social sciences, humanities, linguistics and literature.

Editor(s): Vicki Whittaker
Address: Information Services, Main Library, University of Birmingham, Edgbaston, Birmingham B15 2TT
Parent Company: University of Birmingham
Unsolicited Manuscripts: No

University Of Exeter Press

An established scholarly publisher. Around 25 titles a year in the arts and humanities, including European studies, medieval studies, history, classical studies, film history, theatre studies, linguistics, landscape studies.

Editor(s): Simon Baker
Address: Reed Hall, Streatham Drive, Exeter EX4 4QR
Telephone: 01392 263066
Fax: 01392 263064
Email: uep@ex.ac.uk
Website: www.ex.ac.uk/uep/
Unsolicited Manuscripts: No

U
University Of Hertfordshire Press

Best known as a publisher of books on gypsies and travellers (history, sociology, literature etc) including the English language editions of the international publishing programme known as the Interface Collection. Also publishes serious academic books on parapsychology including the highly respected Guidelines series (volumes to date include psychic testing and ESP), regional and local history, astronomy (in the series Building Blocks Of Modern Astronomy) and document management (on behalf of Cimtech Ltd) including the Document Management Directory, now in its tenth edition. The Press has recently appointed distributors in the UK and North America, is expanding its publishing programme, and welcomes approaches from potential authors in the areas within which it specialises.

Editor(s): W A Forster
Address: Learning Information Services, University of Hertfordshire, College Lane, Hatfield AL10 9AD
Telephone: 01707 284681
Fax: 01707 284666
Email: uhpress@herts.ac.uk
Website: www.herts.ac.uk/uhpress
Imprints: University of Hertfordshire Press, Cimtech
Parent Company: University of Hertfordshire
Unsolicited Manuscripts: To the Editor

University of Wales Press

History, religion and philosophy; European studies including literature and politics and Celtic studies including Welsh studies.

Editor(s): Susan Jenkins
Address: 6 Gwennyth Street, Cathays, Cardiff CF2 4YD
Telephone: 01222 231919
Fax: 01222 230908
Email: press@press.wales.ac.uk
Website: www.wales.ac.uk/press
Imprints: GPC Books, Gwasg Prifysgol Cymru
Parent Company: University of Wales
Payment Details: Royalty rates by negotiation
Unsolicited Manuscripts: No

Usborne Publishing

Children's books. Usborne books are accessible, fun, visually exciting and inviting and start at a point which naturally engages a child's interest. As a result, Usborne books have been chosen by teachers, parents and carers for over twenty years to help children develop a love of reading and thirst for knowledge.

Editor(s): Peter Usborne, Jenny Tyler
Address: 83-85 Saffron Hill, London EC1N 8RT
Telephone: 0171 430 2800
Fax: 0171 430 1562
Email: mail@usborne.co.uk
Website: www.usborne.com
Unsolicited Manuscripts: No, all titles created in-house

Vacher Dod Publishing Ltd

Political reference book publisher, covering Westminster, Whitehall and Europe.

Editor(s): Michael Bedford (House of Lords); Lesley Gunn (House of Commons); Rohan Dale (Europe)
Address: PO Box 3700, Westminster, London SW1E 5NP
Telephone: 0171 828 7256
Fax: 0171 858 7269
Email: politics@vacherdod.co.uk
Imprints: Dod's Parliamentry Companion, Vacher's Parliamentary Companion, Vacher's European Companion
Payment Details: By negotiation
Unsolicited Manuscripts: No

$\mathcal{V}$
The Vegetarian Society

Articles to do with vegetarian lifestyle, health, nutrition, environment, travel products and vegetarian celebrities etc; all content must be directly related to vegetarianism.

Editor(s): John Schofield
Address: Parkdale, Dunham Road, Altrincham, Cheshire WA14 4QG
Telephone: 0161 928 0793
Fax: 0161 926 9182
Email: johns@vegsoc.demon.co.uk
Website: www.vegsoc.org
Imprints: The Vegetarian
Payment Details: I haggle
Unsolicited Manuscripts: Yes

Veloce Publishing PLC

Automotive (car and motorcycle) histories, full-colour automotive books, practical & technical automotive manuals and books.

Editor(s): Rod Grainger
Address: 33 Trinity Street, Dorchester, Dorset DT1 1TT
Telephone: 01305 260068
Fax: 01305 268864
Email: veloce@veloce.co.uk
Website: www.veloce.co.uk
Imprints: Veloce
Payment Details: Royalty basis
Unsolicited Manuscripts: Yes

Vennel Press

Small press specialising in contemporary Scottish poetry, and, in its Au Quai imprint, poetry in translation. Authors include W N Herbert, David Kinloch, Donny O'Rourke, Gael Turnbull, Hamish Whyte and Peter McCarey.

Editor(s): Richard Price, Leona Medlin
Address: 8 Richmond Road, Staines, Middx TW18 2AB
Imprints: Au Quai
Parent Company: Vennel Press
Payment Details: Negotiable
Unsolicited Manuscripts: No

Veritas Foundation Publication Centre

Poland, Eastern Europe, religion, Catholicism and Christianity, prayer books, memoirs and history.

Editor(s): Thomas Wachowiak
Address: 63 Jeddo Road, London W12 9EE
Telephone: 0181 7494957
Fax: 0181 7494965
Email: thomas@veritas.knsc.co.uk
Payment Details: Author to cover all costs
Unsolicited Manuscripts: No

Verso Ltd

Political science, history, cultural studies, media studies, philosophy and women's studies. We are the largest of our kind in the world.

Editor(s): Jane Hindle, Robin Blackburn
Address: 6 Meard Street, London W1V 3HR
Imprints: New Left Books
Unsolicited Manuscripts: Yes

VERTIC (Verification Research, Training & Information Centre)

Publishes briefing notes, research reports and a verification yearbook on issues relating to the verification and monitoring of international agreements, especially in the areas of arms control and disarmament, the environment and peace accords.

Editor(s): Trevor Findlay
Address: Carrara House, 20 Embankment Place, London WC2N 6NN
Telephone: 0171 9250867
Fax: 0171 9250861
Email: info@vertic.org
Website: www.fhit.org/vertic

Verulam Publishing Ltd

Publish local history and language education titles.

Editor(s): David Collins
Address: 152a Park Street Lane, Park Street, St Albans AL2 2AU
Telephone: 01727 872770
Fax: 01727 873866
Imprints: Verulam, Impact Books
Unsolicited Manuscripts: No

Virgin Publishing Ltd

Publish a wide range of books for the general consumer market, but do not publish any poetry, children's books or general fiction. Specialise in non-fiction books about popular culture, especially music, tv, sport, and in certain genres of fiction published strictly within imprint guidelines.

Virgin Publishing Non-fiction (All published under Virgin imprint)

Non-fiction books for the general reader, specialising in popular culture, especially music, TV and sport. Unsolicited manuscripts are not accepted. Unsolicited submissions of a synopsis and some sample text are accepted, but only within the subject areas indicated. Authors are advised to request and read the company's house style sheet before submitting proposals.

Senior Ed: Rod Green (film, tv & radio tie-ins, celeb humour, pop culture); Eds: Lorna Russell (film, tv & radio tie-ins, biography, true crime, paranormal); David Gould (popular reference); Jonathan Taylor (sport). Editorial Dir: Carolyn Thorne (lifestyle, health, music, media, pop culture (illustrated only); Eds: Ian Gittens, Stuart Slater (pop music - reference, bios, criticism, illus only). Publisher: Peter Darvill-Evans; Ed: Simon Winstone (cult tv, other fan-based pop culture). Sen Ed: Kerri Sharp; Eds: James Marriot, Kathleen Bryson (sexuality, fetishism).

Virgin Publishing Fiction (Virgin imprint unless otherwise stated)

Unsolicited manuscripts not accepted. Unsolicited submissions of a synopsis and some sample text are accepted, but only for the imprints and series listed. Virgin do not publish one-off stand-alone novels. Authors' guidelines available for each imprint; submissions accepted only from authors who have read and followed the relevant guidelines. There are sometimes new series in development - authors should watch the press for announcements.

Publisher as editor: Peter Darvill-Evans (science fiction - Virgin Worlds; tv tie-ins & all following subjects); Sen Ed: Kerri Sharp (erotic fiction by women - Black Lace); Eds: Simon Winstone (science fiction - New Adventures); James Marriot (erotic fiction - Nexus); Kathleen Bryson (gay & lesbian erotica - Idol & Sapphire imprints)

Address: Thames Wharf Studios, Rainville Road, London W6 9HT
Telephone: 0171 368 3300
Fax: As phone
Email: <name>@virgin-pub.co.uk
Imprints: Virgin
Payment Details: Usually by royalties on sales, but we'll consider other arrangements.
Unsolicited Manuscripts: No

ν
Virtue Books Ltd

Publishers and distributors of cookery books and books on food and wine to the catering trade, to gourmet food shops and delicatessens. We carry all the quality cookbooks available today.

Address: Edward House, Tenter Street, Rotherham S60 1LB
Telephone: 01709 65005
Fax: 01709 829982
Email: mgv@virtue.co.uk
Website: www.virtue.co.uk
Parent Company: E Russum & Sons Ltd
Payment Details: By arrangement
Unsolicited Manuscripts: No

Volcano Press Ltd

Islam in Britain, Europe and the USA. Women's studies, preferably Muslim women and human rights issues.

Editor(s): A Hussain
Address: PO Box 139, Leicester LE2 2YH
Telephone: 0116 2706714
Fax: As phone
Email: asaf@volcano.u-net.com
Payment Details: Yearly 5-10% royalties
Unsolicited Manuscripts: No

Walden Publishing Ltd/World Of Information

W

Publisher of country business and economic information. Five annual reviews: Middle East, Africa, Asia & Pacific, Americas, Europe. Regional development series: The OAU Report (35 years in the service of Africa); The ASEAN Report (Embracing the challenge); The ADB Report (Sustaining Africa's growth); The OAS Report (50 years of the OAS).

Editor(s): Bernie Campbell
Address: 2 Market Street, Saffron Waldon, Essex CB10 1HZ
Telephone: 01799 521150
Fax: 01799 524805
Email: waldenpub@easynet.co.uk
Website: www//worldinformation.com
Unsolicited Manuscripts: No

Wales Tourist Board

The Wales Tourist Board produces annually its A View of Wales magazine which features articles written by well known personalities and travel correspondents on their holiday experiences in Wales. The publication is primarily aimed at changing prospective visitors' perceptions of Wales, and encouraging new high-profile visitors to Wales. This is being done under the premise of 'Wales - two hours and a million miles away'.

Editor(s): D Rhys Jones
Address: Production Services Department, Brunel House, 2 Fitzalan Road, Cardiff CF24 0YH
Telephone: 01222 475214
Imprints: A View of Wales Magazine
Payment Details: By negotiation
Unsolicited Manuscripts: No, but prospective contributors welcome to contact the Editor

W
Walkways/Quercus

Walkways publishes books of walks, especially long-distance footpaths, with the emphasis on the western Midlands. Quercus publishes general interest books about the western Midlands region, including history, mysteries, landscape & geography, biographies and natural history.

Editor(s): John Roberts
Address: 67 Cliffe Way, Warwick CV34 5JG
Telephone: 01926 776363
Fax: As phone
Imprints: Walkways, Quercus
Payment Details: 10% royalty on retail price
Unsolicited Manuscripts: No, approach first

Warner Chappell Plays Ltd

Contemporary drama playscripts.

Editor(s): Michael Callahan
Address: Griffin House, 161 Hammersmith Road, London W6 8BS
Telephone: 0181 563 58888
Fax: 0181 563 5801
Imprints: Warner/Chappell Plays, Warner/Chappell Classics
Parent Company: Warner/Chappell Music Ltd
Unsolicited Manuscripts: No

Waterside Press

Law publisher with leading edge in criminal justice, youth justice, prisons, policing, family matters, mediation, conflict resolution, restorative justice, relationships, women's legal rights, domestic violence, victims, community programmes, justice and the arts. Independently owned and managed.

Editor(s): Bryan Gibson
Address: Domum Road, Winchester SO23 9NN
Telephone: 01256 882250
Fax: 01962 855567
Email: 106025.1020@compuserve.com
Imprints: Waterside Press
Payment Details: Royalty basis; occasionally advances, but not usually
Unsolicited Manuscripts: Please approach us first before submitting ms

Paul Watkins

Small, enthusiastic press run by Shaun Tyas from a book-ridden Victorian terrace house in the centre of Stamford. Specialities include local and medieval history, maritime and literary criticism. No creative writing.

Editor(s): Shaun Tyas
Address: 18 Adelaide Street, Stamford, Lincs PE9 2EN
Telephone: 01780 756793
Email: apwatkins@msn.com
Imprints: Paul Watkins, Shaun Tyas
Unsolicited Manuscripts: Prefer synopsis

W

Owen Wells Publisher

Books on law and practice for the probation service and related professions in the criminal justice system. Probably the smallest serious academic/professional publisher anywhere.

Editor(s): Owen Wells
Address: 23 Eaton Road, Ilkley, W Yorks LS29 9PU
Telephone: 01943 602270
Fax: 01943 816732
Email: ow@owpub.demon.co.uk
Imprints: Owen Wells Publisher

White Cockade Publishing

Social & cultural history, oral history, architectural & design history, decorative arts; mainly nineteenth and twentieth century, and particular Scottish interest. Books to satisfy both the specialist and general reader.

Editor(s): Perilla Kinchin
Address: White Cockade Publishing, 71 Lonsdale Road, Oxford OX2 7ES
Telephone: 01865 510411
Fax: 01865 514034
Email: pk@whitecockade.demon.co.uk
Unsolicited Manuscripts: Letter first

W

White Eagle Publishing Trust

All books are produced within the organisation. No manuscripts accepted from external sources or commissioned.

Address: New Lands, Brewells Lane, Liss, Hants GU33 7HY
Parent Company: The White Eagle Lodge
Payment Details: None
Unsolicited Manuscripts: No

White Row Press

Publisher of Irish interest non-fiction, and (sometimes) prose. Good, well thought out ideas welcome.

Editor(s): Peter Carr
Address: 135 Cumberland Road, Dundonald, Belfast BT16 2BB
Telephone: 01232 482586
Unsolicited Manuscripts: Yes if Irish interest non-fiction

Whiting & Birch

Social work, human sciences, psychology and sexual medicine.

Editor(s): David Whiting
Address: PO Box 872, London SE23 3HL
Payment Details: By arrangement
Unsolicited Manuscripts: Yes

W

Whittet Books

Natural history: pets, animals and the countryside.

Editor(s): A Whittet
Address: Hill Farm, Stonham Road, Cotton Stowmarket, Suffolk IP14 4RQ
Telephone: 01449 781877
Fax: 01449 781898
Parent Company: A Whittet & Co
Unsolicited Manuscripts: Yes

Whittles Publishing

Our expanding publishing programme covers two main areas: engineering and science (mainly civil engineering and construction, surveying and photogrammetry, imaging and applied photography, chemical engineering and materials); nautical/maritime and Scottish (lighthouse, lightships and things maritime, Scottish interest and Scottish reference).

Editor(s): Keith Whittles
Address: Roseleigh House, Harbour Road, Latheronwheel, Caithness KW5 6DW
Telephone: 01593 741240
Fax: 01593 741360
Email: whittl@globalnet.co.uk
Website: www.users.globalnet.co.uk/~whittl
Payment Details: Royalty payment will vary according to the project
Unsolicited Manuscripts: Yes

Whurr Publishers Ltd

W

Speech and language therapy, audiology, dyslexia, nursing, occupational therapy, physiotherapy, psychology, psychiatry, psychotherapy, counselling, business (especially European business), management, economics and special education.

Editor(s): Commissioning Editors: Jim McCarthy, Colin Whurr
Address: 19B Compton Terrace, London N1 2UN
Unsolicited Manuscripts: Yes

WI Books Ltd

WI Books is the publishing division of the National Federation of Women's Institutes. It publishes books for WI members on a range of subjects including cookery, crafts and gardening, often written by WI members who are already experts in their field.

Editor(s): Claire Bagnall
Address: 104 New King's Road, London SW6 4LY
Telephone: 0171 371 9300
Fax: 0171 736 3652
Parent Company: WI Enterprises, National Federation of Women's Institutes
Unsolicited Manuscripts: Yes

ᴡ
Wild Goose Publications

Religious books, tapes and songbooks. We also publish books on sociology and politics.

Editor(s): Managing Editor: Sarelle Reid
Address: Unit 15, 6 Harmony Row, Glasgow G51 3BA
Telephone: 0141 440 0985
Fax: 0141 440 2338
Email: admin@wgp.iona.org.uk
Website: www.iona.org.uk
Parent Company: The Iona Community
Payment Details: Royalties every 6 months
Unsolicited Manuscripts: Yes

Neil Wilson Publishing Ltd

Food and drink, hillwalking and climbing, whisky, humour, biography, travel, leisure, true crime, Scottish and Irish interest are the main subject areas. Whisky and whisky-related topics are especially strong, and the authors include four former Glenfiddich Award Winners, with sales in excess of 250,00 copies.

Editor(s): Neil Wilson
Address: 303a The Pentagon Centre, 36 Washington Street, Glasgow G3 8AZ
Telephone: 0141 221 1117
Fax: 0141 221 5363
Email: nwp@eqm.co.uk
Website: www.nwp.co.uk
Payment Details: Royalties twice-annually
Unsolicited Manuscripts: Yes

![W]

Windhorse Publications

Buddhism, meditation and related subjects.

Address: 11 Park Road, Moseley, Birmingham B13 8AB
Telephone: 0121 449 9696
Fax: 0121 449 9191
Unsolicited Manuscripts: Yes

Windrow & Greene

Military history, emphasis on highly illustrated treatment of uniforms, weapons, equipment, etc. Automotive marques, directories, some aviation and modelling techniques.

Editor(s): Simon Forty
Address: 5 Gerrard Street, London W1V 7LJ
Payment Details: By negotiation
Unsolicited Manuscripts: No, but sample chapters and synopses welcome

The Windrush Press

Independent publisher, established 1987. Military history, general history, 'ancient mysteries', Traveller's History series, humour, non-fiction. Not fiction, travel writing or poetry.

Editor(s): Victoria Huxley
Address: Little Window, High Street, Moreton in Marsh, Gloucestershire GL56 0LL
Telephone: 01608 652012/652025
Fax: 01608 652125
Email: windrush@netcomuk.co.uk
Unsolicited Manuscripts: Yes, letter synopsis/sample only, SAE essential for return

Winslow Press Ltd

Speech therapy, occupational therapy, special needs education and care for the elderly.

Editor(s): Stephanie Martin
Address: Telford Road, Bicester, Oxon OX6 0TS
Telephone: 01869 244644
Fax: 01869 320040
Email: info@winslow-press.co.uk
Website: www.winslow-press.co.uk
Payment Details: Determined by contract
Unsolicited Manuscripts: Yes

WIT Press/Computational Mechanics Publications Ltd

A major publisher of engineering research. Produces books by leading researchers and scientists at the cutting edge of their specialties, thus enabling readers to remain at the forefront of scientific developments. List presently includes monographs, edited volumes, books on disk and software in areas such as acoustics, advanced computing, architecture and structures, biomedicine, boundary elements, earthquake engineering, environmental engineering, fluid mechanics, fracture mechanics, heat transfer, marine and offshore engineering, transport engineering.

Editor(s): Dir of Publishing: Lance Sucharov
Address: Ashurst Lodge, Ashurst, Southampton SO40 7AA
Telephone: 01703 293223
Fax: 01703 292853
Email: witpress@witpress.com
Website: www.witpress.com
Parent Company: C M Inc
Payment Details: By contract
Unsolicited Manuscripts: Yes

Witan Books & Publishing Services

Founded in 1980 and guided by ecological and humanitarian principles. Publishes books on general subjects, especially biography, education, the environment, geography, history, politics, popular music and sport. Witan Publishing Services was developed as an offshoot to help writers get their work into print; it offers a comprehensive service including proofreading, editing, design and guidance to publication. Sample titles: Principles Of Open Learning; The Last Poet: The Story Of Eric Burdon; The Valiants' Years: The Story Of Port Vale; The Man Who Sank The Titanic? The Life And Times Of Captain Edward J Smith; The Mercia Manifesto: A Blueprint For The Future Inspired By The Past; The Potteries Derbies.

Editor(s): Jeff Kent
Address: Cherry Tree House, 8 Nelson Crescent, Cotes Heath via Stafford ST21 6ST
Telephone: 01782 791673
Imprints: Witan Books
Parent Company: Witan Creations
Payment Details: Advances and royalties paid to authors
Unsolicited Manuscripts: Yes with SAE

Witherby & Co Ltd

Insurance publications: marine insurance, reinsurance, motor, liability, construction, offshore oil and gas, life assurance, captives, environmental, business interruption, aviation, insurance dictionaries, risk management. Shipping publications: surveying, safety, oil pollution, salvage, mooring, offshore engineering, the shipping of oil, gas and chemicals, marine survival and rescue, tanker structures, dictionaries.

Editor(s): Alan Witherby
Address: 32-36 Aylesbury Street, London EC1R 0ET
Telephone: 0171 251 5341
Fax: 0171 251 1296

W

The Women's Press

Literary fiction; crime fiction; health; women's studies; handbooks; literary criticism; psychology; therapy and self-help; the arts; politics; media; writing by black women and women of colour; disability issues and lesbian issues. All books must be women-centered and have a feminist message or theme.

Editor(s): Helen Windrath, Kirsty Dunseath, Charlotte Cole
Address: 34 Great Sutton Street, London EC1V 0LQ
Telephone: 0171 251 3007
Fax: 0171 608 1938
Imprints: Livewire Books
Payment Details: Advance and royalties
Unsolicited Manuscripts: Yes

Women's Sports Foundation

Only UK organisation solely committed to promoting women and girls' sport. Produces a range of publications highlighting issues relating to women and girls' sport.

Address: 305-315 Hither Green Lane, Lewisham, London SE13 6TJ
Telephone: 0181 697 5370
Fax: As phone
Email: info@wsf.u-net.com
Website: www.wsf.org.uk

W

The Woodfield Press

Publishers of Irish local history and biography. Established in 1996; six books published to date.

Editor(s): Freelance
Address: 17 Jamestown Square, Inchicore, Dublin 8, Ireland
Telephone: 01454 7991
Fax: 01492 0676
Email: terri.mcdonnell@itps.co.uk
Imprints: The Woodfield Press
Payment Details: Royalty - 10-12% of net invoice value

Woodstock Books

Facsimile reprints of literary texts in series: Revolution And Romanticism 1789-1834, ed by Jonathan Wordsworth; Hibernia, ed by John Kelly; Decadents, Symbolists, Anti-Decadents, ed by Ian Small & R K R Thornton.

Editor(s): James Price
Address: The School House, South Newington, Banbury OX15 4JJ
Telephone: 01295 720598
Fax: 01295 720717
Imprints: Woodstock Books
Unsolicited Manuscripts: No

W

Wordsworth Editions Ltd

Leading publisher of low-cost paperbacks. Series include Wordsworth Classics, Wordsworth Children's Library, Wordsworth Reference, Wordsworth Poetry Library, Wordsworth Classics Of World Literature, Wordsworth Military Library, Wordsworth Royal Paperbacks. Wordsworth are primarily reprint publishers, but occasionally commission books, especially in the reference area.

Editor(s): Editorial Director: Marcus Clapham
Address: 6 London Street, London W2 1HL
Telephone: 0171 706 8822
Fax: 0171 706 8833
Email: 100434.276@compuserve.com
Imprints: As described
Unsolicited Manuscripts: No

Wordwright Books

We are a packager gradually moving into publishing. We offer a full range of out-of-house services from concept to your warehouse: proofing, editing, writing to your specification,design, print-brokering, publicity and marketing. Subject matters include military, social and women's history. Also illustrated books on subjects like cookery, gardening, art, natural history; and juveniles.

Editor(s): Charles Perkins, Veronica Davis
Address: 25 Oakford Road, London NW5 1AJ
Telephone: 0171 284 0056
Fax: 0171 284 0041
Email: wordwright@clara.co.uk
Payment Details: Royalty or fee
Unsolicited Manuscripts: No best to submit an outline or query first

World Of Discovery/Oliver Books

Oliver Books, with 20 years' experience, publishes over 400 titles a year - calendars and ephemera in the rock, pop and film personality field. World Of Discovery, launched two years ago, markets a range of higher quality generic titles and fully licensed product. For the year 2000 there are more than 100 titles including 30+ licensed calendars. Endorsers include the BBC, Sky Television, The Tate Gallery, Harpers & Queen, and seven tourist authorities.

Address: Unit 9, Wimbledon Stadium Business Centre, Riverside Road, London SW17 0BA
Telephone: 0181 944 0944
Fax: 0181 944 1598
Email: matthew@oliverbooks.co.uk
Website: www.oliverbooks.co.uk
Imprints: World Of Discovery, Petprints
Parent Company: Oliver Books Ltd

World Scientific

International publisher of high-level books, textbooks, international proceedings and journals in physics, chemistry, mathematics, engineering, computer science, life science, medicine, economics and management science. World Scientific also publish the Nobel Lectures series written by Nobel laureates. Also of note is our sister company, Imperial College Press which was initiated in May 1995.

Editor(s): Sunil Nair
Address: 57 Shelton Street, London WC2H 9HE
Telephone: 0171 836 0888
Fax: 0171 836 2020
Email: sales@wspc2.demon.co.uk
Website: www.worldscientific.com
Imprints: Imperial College Press
Parent Company: World Scientific Publishing (PTE) Ltd, Singapore

Wrightson Biomedical Publishing Ltd

Publisher of books and journals in clinical medicine and biomedical science. Topics of particular interest: psychiatry, neuroscience, gastroenterology, dermatology, gerontology, cardiology. We are known for the high quality and speed of publication of our books.

Editor(s): Judy Wrightson
Address: Ash Barn House, Winchester Road, Stroud, Petersfield, Hants GU32 3PN
Telephone: 01730 265647
Fax: 01730 260368
Imprints: Wrightson Biomedical
Unsolicited Manuscripts: Yes

Writers And Readers Ltd

Philosophy, science, politics, religion, history, literature, music, psychiatry, women's studies, black studies, social science, biographies, autobiographies, novels, arts, media, theatre and US studies.

Address: 6 Cynthia Street, London N1 9JF
Telephone: 0171 226 3377
Fax: 0171 359 1406
Email: begin@writersandreaders.com
Website: www.writersandreaders.com
Imprints: For Beginners, Black Butterfly Children's Books, Harlem River Press, Writers and Readers Inc (USA)
Payment Details: Negotiable
Unsolicited Manuscripts: Yes

Writers' Bookshop

Publishers of writers' aids. Annual directories such as the Small Press Guide and self-help titles such as Successful Writing by Teresa McCuaig and Poetry: How To Get Published, How To Get Paid by Kenneth C Steven. Manuscript submissions and ideas in all areas of interest to writers are invited.

Editor(s): Anne Sandys
Address: Remus House, Coltsfoot Drive, Woodston, Peterborough PE2 JX
Telephone: 01733 898103
Fax: 01733 313524
Parent Company: Forward Press Ltd
Payment Details: 15% royalties
Unsolicited Manuscripts: Yes, please include postage for return

The X Press

Black interest popular novels, particularly reflecting contemporary ethnic experience: 20/20 - cult classic fiction; Nia - black literary fiction & non-fiction; Black Classics - reprints of American/African/British black classic novels.

Editor(s): Steve Pope, Doton Adebayo
Address: 6 Hoxton Square, London N1 6NU
Telephone: 0171 729 1199
Fax: 0171 729 1771
Imprints: 20/20, Nia, Black Classics
Parent Company: The X Press
Unsolicited Manuscripts: Yes

y Yale University Press

Art, architecture and the humanities.

Editor(s): John Nicoll, Robert Baldock, Gillian Malpass
Address: 23 Pond Street, London NW3 2PN
Telephone: 0171 431 4422
Fax: 0171 431 3755
Email: sales@yaleup.co.uk
Imprints: Yale Universtiy Press, Pelican History of Art, Yale English Monarchs
Parent Company: Yale University Press, New Haven USA
Unsolicited Manuscripts: Yes

Roy Yates Books

Books for children in dual-language (bilingual) editions. Co-editions of established books translated into other languages. No original publishing undertaken.

Editor(s): Roy Yates
Address: Smallfields Cottage, Cox Green, Rudgwick, Horsham RH12 3DE
Imprints: Roy Yates Books, Ingham Yates
Unsolicited Manuscripts: No

Yes! Publications

Community publishing house based in Derry/Londonderry Northern Ireland. Established 1986. Main publication is Fingerpost Community Magazine, the longest-surviving community magazine in Ireland. Promotes local writers and issues by celebrating and giving credence to local stories and histories. Also promotes mutual understanding and tolerance by exploring issues of cultural identity in articles, essays, stories and poems.

Editor(s): Various
Address: 10-12 Bishop Street, Londonderry, Co Derry BT48 6PW
Telephone: 01504 261941
Fax: 01504 263700
Email: yes.pubs@business.ntl.com

Yesteryear Books

Books on classic cars, mainly British. A4 perfect-bound books, average 96 pages. Either road test collections or advert collections, both reprinted from period magazines, or owners' & buyers' guides.

Editor(s): D Young
Address: 60 Woodville Road, London NW11 9TN
Telephone: 0181 455 6992

Yore Publications

Specialist football book publisher, generally of an historical nature, from small paperbacks to substantial cased books. Currently the leading publisher of Football League club histories (over 20 to date) substantially written, illustrative and statistical. Also club (players) Who's Who books. Yore Publications is led by Dave Twydell, a member of the Football Writers' Association.

Editor(s): Dave Twydell
Address: 12 The Furrows, Harefield, Middx UB9 6AT
Telephone: 01895 823404
Fax: As phone
Email: yore.demon.co.uk
Website: www.yore.demon.co.uk/index.html
Imprints: Yore Publications
Payment Details: Varies
Unsolicited Manuscripts: Yes

Yorkshire Art Circus

Yorkshire Art Circus - leading community publishers, specialises in self-styled community books, using many voices around a given theme. Recent publications: Static - Life On The Site; The Story Of A House (Raymond Williams Prize winner 1998); Ranger, The Eyes And Ears Of The Peak National Park. Also publish autobiography. Springboard Fiction - publishes novels and short story anthologies by new writers. Recent titles: Annie Potts Is Dead by M Y Allam, Dark Places by Margery Ramsden.

Editor(s): Ian Daley, Adrian Wilson, Mark Illis
Address: School Lane, Glasshoughton, Castleford, West Yorks WK10 4QN
Telephone: 01977 550401
Fax: 01977 512819
Email: books@artcircus.org.uk
Website: www.artcircus.org..uk
Imprints: Yorkshire Art Circus, Springboard Fiction
Payment Details: Fiction - 7.5% royalty & small advance
Unsolicited Manuscripts: Yes

Z

Zeno Publishers

Established 1944 and specialising in all matters relating to Greece and Cyprus in Greek and English. Recently moved into information technology publications.

Editor(s): L D Loizou
Address: 6 Denmark Street, London WC2H 8LP
Telephone: 0171 2401968
Fax: 0171 8362522
Email: info@thegreekbookshop.com
Website: www.thegreekbookshop.com
Imprints: Loizou Publications